PAST MISTAKES

MEL SHERRATT

TEN DAYS AGO

Shaun Green was the first person on Jamie Sanderson's list. Jamie had gone over routes, found blind spots, stood in shadows unnoticed while he watched his victim. At work, at play, at home.

It was a street like many others, where people didn't come out much after they'd settled down to watch TV for the evening.

It surprised him how much people didn't take note of what was happening around them. He'd had ample opportunities to take down one of the men he despised so much, but timing was of the essence. Once he'd done this, there was no turning back.

Jamie had made his plan many years ago and was committed to following through with it. This was his time to get justice.

He'd waited years, so that everyone would have forgotten about him. By now, he'd be nothing but a distant memory they recalled every now and then and got back on with their lives without a second thought.

But he remembered them all. Every day of every month of

every year. He would go down his list until there was one person remaining. And then he'd decide what to do about her. She'd left him in the lurch when he was younger. She of all people needed to get what was coming to her.

He stepped out of the shadows when a man walked towards him. It was late Thursday evening, and Jamie knew Shaun went to the local pub for a few pints with his mates. He was always home by eleven.

Home. Where he had a wife and two kids.

Shaun had made a life for himself once out of prison. Jamie was happy to take that from him.

He pulled down his baseball cap, so it would be hard for a camera or door cam to catch his face, and marched forwards, banging into Shaun deliberately.

'Hey, watch it,' the man cried out.

'Sorry, mate, didn't see you.'

'You could hardly miss me, except that you had your head down.'

'Yeah, like I said...' Jamie showed his face. Revelled in the fear that crossed it when he recognised him. 'Ayup, Shaun.'

Jamie knew he had to be quick, picking the perfect place so he could take him out of view. The mild October month helped, Shaun's jacket open and giving him access to his chest.

'I told you I wasn't going to meet...'

Shaun's words stopped abruptly, exchanged by a grunt as Jamie pushed a knife in him so hard it would have felt like a punch.

Shaun's eyes widened. Blood covered his white shirt, the patch getting bigger by the second while it dawned on him what had happened.

Jamie held him up when he went limp, taking him along the alley that would lead to the back of the houses.

Shaun groaned with every step, his breath raspy. He even

tried calling out several times, but his voice was too low to be heard.

There was no one in the vicinity bar the two of them. Around the back of the houses, Jamie settled Shaun on the muddy cobbles and sat down beside him, watching as he drifted in and out of consciousness.

'I said I'd come and look you up, remember?' he said.

'Not... to do... this,' Shaun managed to say.

'You made my life hell. Before I beat the shit out of you.'

His head slipped to one side.

Jamie reached for his chin, squeezing it hard. He wanted Shaun to see him, know he was the last person he would ever set eyes on.

Shaun winced, his face draining of blood as quickly as it oozed from his stomach. 'Help me.'

'Like you *helped* me? I'm tired of seeing you all in my dreams every night, out there free to live your lives with no remorse, no thought about what you did, nor what happened to me because of it.'

Shaun wasn't listening anymore. Jamie shook his shoulder but got no response.

He waited for ten minutes, to be sure, and then stood up, leaving the body of Shaun Green behind. Let someone find him in the morning. Jamie would be well gone by then.

But for now, he'd done what he'd set out to do.

On to number two on his list.

CHAPTER ONE

THURSDAY

Michelle Price winced as she turned over in bed. Even lying on a pillow, the right side of her face stung. One eye would barely open, a tear coming out of its own accord.

A punch would do that to you.

Her husband, Brian, had been in a foul mood last night. He'd finished a week of nights but had been called in early because someone was off sick. Before he'd left, they'd had a massive row, and that was the result of it.

Michelle knew she needed to get out of the relationship, but with no money, or nowhere to stay until she got settled somewhere else, things were tough for her. She and Brian had been together for five years, married for three, and even with a wedding certificate things hadn't changed. She'd believed the usual crap when he said it would never happen again after the first time.

But it did. Again, and again.

It had started out as derogatory put-downs. Then it was him pushing her every now and then when he got angry.

It had taken a while for him to lay a hand on her. Even now, she could recall it vividly. She'd had her hair done as they were going out that evening. Instead of complimenting her, Brian had gone up like a bottle of pop saying she wanted to make herself attractive to other men. Of course, she'd done no such thing, but he wouldn't believe her.

He'd accused her of eyeing up Anthony, his friend from work. Anthony was married, and Michelle liked his wife. She could never betray their friendship, but equally, she wouldn't ever have an affair.

But Brian went on and on, and in the end had slapped her so hard her ears had rung. Afterwards he'd been sorry, but the bruising appearing from the attack meant she couldn't go out. Brian went on his own, leaving her upset and crying about what had happened.

Over time, things got worse. Brian always seemed to be angry with her. It came to the stage where she dreaded coming home. Like the last time he'd hit her, she'd woken up this morning, planning to leave him. Encouraging herself to get help, that she didn't have to live this way. She couldn't go on like this. He was brutal at times, and she was concerned he would go too far. But there came a point where she'd had enough.

There was only her friend, Colette, who knew what was going on. Michelle confided in her, crying on her shoulder when it got too much. Several times Colette had said she should come and stay with her and her husband, but she wanted more in place than a duvet on someone's sofa for the night.

Yet she never got round to planning anything.

Eventually, she went downstairs to make a mug of tea. She filled the kettle with water, seeing her neighbour, Irene, in the garden next door, hanging out the washing. She wondered how much Irene heard through the walls. Although she never said, Irene and her husband looked out for Michelle. She'd often hear someone knocking when Brian was shouting and her screams intensified. It would always be Irene, but she wouldn't be complaining about anything. She would make up an excuse that she'd run out of milk or something as trivial. It would help to calm Brian down enough for him to stop. Most of the time he'd storm out of the house.

Michelle dared to glimpse in the mirror, gasping at what she saw. He'd done a proper job on her this time. No amount of makeup would cover that up, and her top lip was cut and swollen, too. She got her phone and made a call.

'Hey, Michelle. Are you okay?' Colette answered.

'Not really.' Tears welled in her eyes, and she tried desperately to stop them from falling. But it was too painful to squeeze them shut. At least Colette couldn't see her, but the fact she'd asked if she was all right was enough to let her know she was worried about her.

'What has he done this time?'

'The usual, but he's made a mess of my face. I've had to call in sick at work. I won't be able to go in for a few days.'

'Oh, Michelle, you have to leave him, or else he'll go too far.'

'I don't know how.'

'Let me help you. We can get you to somewhere safe if you don't want to stay with us.'

'What happens if he finds me and has another go at me?'

'He won't. But he has to be told he can't keep doing this.'

'I know.'

'Shall I come over? It's my day off, and I don't have anything planned. We could go for a walk, get you out of the house?'

Michelle, who was still standing in front of the mirror,

wondered if that was wise. If Colette saw the state of her, she would be livid. She'd kept so much hidden from her until now.

But she couldn't do this on her own anymore.

'Would you?' she said. 'I'm a bit of a state, though.'

'More reason for me to visit. I'll grab us some pastries and I'll be over about ten, if that isn't too early?'

'Ten is fine. I'll leave the side gate open for you.' Fresh tears fell, the relief that she didn't have to be alone.

She disconnected her phone and went into the kitchen to drink her tea. It would be good to have company the way she was feeling and maybe get some fresh air. She hadn't seen Colette in a while. They kept in touch through messaging each other regularly, but it wasn't the same as seeing someone face to face.

Half an hour later, she was freshly showered. She heard the side gate open and went downstairs. She hoped it was Colette. Brian wasn't due home for another hour, if he came back at all. Sometimes he needed time to cool down once he realised what he'd done.

But if it wasn't Collette, he'd probably be bringing her a gift to pacify her along with an apology. She braced herself for him to show his face.

CHAPTER TWO

DI Allie Shenton arrived early for work that morning due to the murder case that was on her desk. A local man, forty-two-year-old Shaun Green, had been fatally stabbed ten days ago, and they were struggling to get evidence, witnesses, or anything that might help them find a suspect.

She had come in early to go over the paperwork again, see if there was anything she'd missed, or if she could task her team with something because of results that had come in from forensics or the path lab. So far, she had nothing.

DS Perry Wright appeared in the doorway to her office. 'We're all braving the canteen for breakfast and wondered if you wanted to join us.'

'For my sins, I think I would.' She logged out of her computer and stood up, stretching her arms to the ceiling.

'Aching back?' he queried.

'More like I didn't get much sleep last night. Mark was snoring like an old train.' She rolled her eyes. 'Man flu – honestly. He's been laid low for a week already. But at least he hasn't passed it on to me or Poppy. Yet.'

Poppy was their twelve-year-old foster daughter.

'Well, keep it to yourself if you do.' He pointed to her desk. 'Anything new we should know?'

'No. I've been going over everything, but I can't see anything we've missed. I might send Frankie out to reinterview everyone, see if there have been any further developments.'

'Nothing coming up on the system?'

'Nope.'

They left the office and went upstairs to the canteen. DC Sam Markham and DC Frankie Higgins were already seated, Sam with a plate of toast and Frankie had braved a fry-up. Both had steaming mugs of tea. Allie and Perry joined them after collecting their food, sliding trays on the table across from them.

'If you can't take a joke, then don't dish them out.' Sam laughed as Frankie gave her the finger in reply. 'Lyla says he's starting to have his hair cut so short that he reminds her of Uncle Fester.'

'Rude.' Frankie ran a hand over his crew cut. 'I'll have you know it takes a while to get the razor so close. I can't just jump in the shower and be on my way.'

Allie glanced at Sam when she sat down across from her, trying not to chuckle.

'You have nothing to do but run,' Sam cried. 'You, too, Perry. And neither of you have to put on make-up.'

'Well, not on a shift day.' Frankie smirked.

'*You* don't have to wear makeup nowadays,' Perry came to their defence. 'Look how amazing Pamela Anderson is without it. Drew Barrymore, too. I saw that clip on the TV.'

'If I forget to put lipstick on, I'm like the living dead,' Allie admitted. 'I feel dead, too, especially after a restless sleep. Honestly, if Mark didn't snore so much, I might get more than an hour or two. I don't know what's worse, him or the bloody menopause.'

'Oh, no. Here we go again with the M word.' Perry pretended to yawn.

'All I can say is that if it happened to men, the world wouldn't survive,' Allie quipped. 'No one tells you when you're in your prime about how nasty it can be. Mind you, I'm not sure I'd want to know. You can't prepare yourself for it anyway.' Her phone rang. 'DI Shenton.' She listened intently while her team continued with their breakfast amid the banter. 'Okay, we're on our way.'

'Boss?' Perry queried once she'd disconnected the call.

'There's been a woman assaulted in her home. Neighbour found her. Her injuries are severe, and there's a threat to life.' Allie downed the remainder of her coffee and stood up. 'I think we can all go for now and see how things are once we arrive. Sam, can you take Frankie in a pool car, in case either of you need to come back?'

'Will do.'

Chairs scraped and tables cleared, their chatter was a little less while they made their way to the station car park. Once in her car, Allie started the engine and buckled up.

She paused for the briefest of moments. Any case of this magnitude had her thinking of her sister, Karen. Although Allie was jumping to conclusions, she hoped this wasn't another case of a man beating a woman to her death.

Their victim lived in Pepper Street in the south of the city. Allie drove along Chadwick Street past Gladstone Pottery Museum. She enjoyed *The Great Pottery Throw Down* on the TV and had met one of its presenters, Keith Brymer-Jones, on several occasions at one charity event or another. It was good to have positive press about the city and extra visitors because of it.

At the end of the road, she turned left and drove along Normacot Road, finally coming out onto a housing estate. Pepper Street was a cul-de-sac, and the house they were after was at the head of it. Crime scene tape had already been tied across the road, and there were several liveried vehicles and a crime scene van.

'The ambulance left twenty minutes ago,' Perry said as Allie parked the car wherever she could. He read more details from his phone. 'Michelle Price, forty-two, blunt force trauma to the head, defence wounds on her arms, bruising appearing around her neck. Married to Brian and living here for the past ten years. Next-door neighbour wants us to pop round to talk to her.'

'First port of call anyway, once I'm done in here.'

Sam, who had been following behind, went past to find a space further along. Allie and Perry got out, and Allie locked up the car while she waited for them to rejoin her.

At the crime scene itself, they gave their details to the first officer and then made their way along a pleasant row of houses. Even though the woman was still alive, it was imperative the scene should be documented and worked in case things escalated.

The Prices' property was a carbon copy of the six they had passed. A garage was attached to the left, and a block-paved drive that would fit one car. Allie noted the tyre print across the corner of the small lawn, where mud had been churned up as if a wheel had spun. There was a porch with a side door and a bay window.

Eyes and ears on alert, they dressed in forensic gear and went into the property.

CHAPTER THREE

JAMIE SANDERSON - AGED 16

Jamie Sanderson closed the front door quietly, trying not to wake his mum. She'd come home from work that evening absolutely shattered and, before he'd even finished making her a mug of tea, had fallen asleep on the settee. He'd covered her with a throw, switched on the lamp, and set off to meet Colette.

She was waiting for him at the end of the street, waving when she spotted him. Jamie's smile grew with every step towards her. She was petite in a cute way, with large brown eyes and wavy blonde hair. He still couldn't believe he was dating her. He'd had his eye on her for months but didn't think she fancied him. In the end, Colette had asked him out, hinting that she wanted to go and see *The Sixth Sense* at the pictures and did he want to go with her. Jamie had been so nervous, but it had turned out okay.

Colette stood on her tiptoes to greet him with a kiss. He

grinned afterwards, already missing the feel of her lips against his.

'Where shall we go?' Jamie reached for her hand, and they walked.

'I'm meeting Michelle at the bus stop on Hamill Road. You don't mind, do you?'

''Course not.' He did really because he wanted to spend time with her alone, but he knew how important it was to indulge a girl by including her best friend every now and then.

It was then he spotted the bag she was holding. He pointed to it, and she held it up like it was a prize.

'Lager.'

'How are you able to get that from the shop? I mean, because you're sixteen, not because you don't look like a grown-up.'

'It's from the pub.' Colette laughed. 'My dad's always in there, so I get served through the hole in the wall that doubles up as the offie. Have you never seen it?'

He shook his head.

'You're such a quiet thing,' Colette teased. 'I think I'm going to enjoy bringing you out of your shell.'

'*I* think you've managed to do that already.'

With little warning, she reached up and kissed him again. Jamie wasn't that experienced with girls, having had the odd fumble here and there, but he was keeping his hands to himself at the moment. He wanted Colette to respect him. He would never take advantage of her or push her to do something she wouldn't want to.

It took ten minutes to get to the bus stop. Jamie's heart sank when he saw who was with Michelle. Kevin Ryland and Nick Farrington. He knew them from school but wouldn't call them mates.

He was certain they talked about him behind his back. Jamie came from a broken family and lived on the Bennett

Estate, whereas Kevin and Nick lived in privately owned homes on posh estates, with two parents and their wages coming in. It seemed idyllic to him.

Money was tight at their house because his dad had left soon after he was born. Jamie's mum worked in a local pottery firm. She'd been there for years. So at sixteen, he became the man about the house. He worked, collecting glasses at the pub and had a paper round each morning, which he hated, but it helped his mum with the cost of bills.

But even so, Jamie still didn't have anything equivalent to what those two got dished out in pocket money each week for doing nothing, even though he'd begin working next month after finishing school. Mum had got him a job in the slip house.

Kevin and Nick had started hanging around with him about a month ago. He'd been surprised at first. Usually they were quite hostile, calling him names, slinging the odd punch in the middle of his back as they raced past him. But during one break at school, they'd come across to talk to him. They invited him to the rec that night, where some of the other kids hung around. He wasn't going to go at first, wondering if he was being set up. But Mum had been nagging at him, so he'd had to get out of the house.

In the end, it had turned out to be a great evening. There had been about ten of them in total, half of them girls. That was when Jamie got to know Colette better. They'd begun chatting, becoming friendly straightaway.

Since then, Kevin and Nick, and Michelle, became his friends, too, even though he was a little wary of Kevin, who had a reputation for winning every scrap he got into. Jamie hoped he'd never be on the wrong side of him to find out if that was true.

'Hey,' Kevin shouted when he spotted them a few metres

away. 'We've been waiting for you. We've been thinking about doing a job on the newsagent's.'

'A job?' Jamie queried. 'What do you mean?'

'Robbing the old bastard. He's barred me twice, and I'm not having that.'

'What did he bar you for?'

'Thieving.' Kevin laughed. 'Serves him right if he can't keep an eye on his stock. So, are you in or not?'

'Well, I...' Jamie had never been a troublemaker, always trying to keep his nose clean. His mum would worry if he was getting up to all sorts.

But Kevin noticed his reluctance to speak.

'You're not scared, are you?'

'Of course not.'

'Have you never thieved anything?' Nick asked.

'Nothing.'

'First time for everything, then.' Kevin threw an arm around his shoulders. 'Don't worry, we'll show you how it's done. You can be the lookout this time. Are you in?'

Jamie couldn't say no, worried it would show fear in front of Colette. He glanced at her, and she nodded encouragement. It gave him the push he needed.

'Okay, I'm in.'

Kevin patted him on the back. 'Good man, we'll do it when we next meet.' He sniggered. 'Let you get yourself mentally prepared first.'

CHAPTER FOUR

In Pepper Street, the team found themselves in a narrow hall, stairs leading off it. A mirror to Allie's right was skewwhiff. The contents of a side table beneath it had fallen to the carpet, rose petals from a bowl scattered like confetti at a wedding under their feet. It didn't prove anything. They could have easily been knocked by a police officer or a paramedic getting in quickly, as a suspect rushing to get away.

Perry pointed to a patch of blood on the banister. 'Our suspects?'

'Probably. I doubt that poor woman could get out of here unaided. At least if our suspect is on record, he will be easily identifiable. At the most, it's evidence to build our case on.'

While Frankie and Sam scooted upstairs to see what they could find, Allie went into the kitchen. She grimaced at the sight of more blood on the floor, a clear space in the middle where the victim had lain. Around it, paramedic gear had been strewn as she assumed they had fought to save the woman's life. Empty plastic bags that had been ripped open in haste. Several strips of gauze removed from them all now a pinkish colour. Blue paper towelling screwed up in balls. It was like a massacre scene from a horror movie.

'Jeez, what the hell happened in here?' Allie remarked to the two men working on either side of the room.

They turned to her. Dave Barnett was a senior crime scene investigator, Toby Denton, a forensic photographer who was new in post. Behind in the vestibule that led to the garden was a woman crouched down dusting a doorway frame for prints. All were wearing forensic suits.

'Ah, my favourite detective.' Dave smiled, then spotted Perry behind her. 'I meant team, of course.'

'Of course.' Perry smirked light-heartedly.

'How are you all?'

'Good, ta.' Allie scanned the room, seeing so much she would remember for a while to come. Blood spatter covered the row of kitchen units, some even reaching the window above the sink. A chair had been overturned; a plate and mug smashed in the corner as if slung at the wall. A saucepan on the floor, perhaps used as the victim tried to defend herself.

Her shoulders dropped and she prayed for a good outcome. There had been some battle going on in there.

'How about you?' she went on.

'Oh, I'm well, too. Just waiting on grandchild number four. The little bugger is a week late, the cheek of it.' Dave rolled his eyes in jest.

Allie beamed. She'd known Dave since his children were in their teens so loved to hear about his ever-extending family. 'Do let me know when he or she arrives.'

'It's a boy.'

'Aw, no wonder he's late then. Men can be so unreliable.' Joking over, she stooped on her haunches, careful not to topple over. 'Were you here before the ambulance took her away?'

'I was, and it was pretty nasty. I'm used to the aftermath, but it's worse when our victim is still alive.'

'Any more news on that?'

'They managed to stabilise her enough to transport her to the hospital, and the trauma team are with her. She had pretty severe head injuries as well as a couple of defence wounds that need sorting on her arms, but it didn't seem to be life-threatening. Although we know how quickly that can change.'

Perry, who had been searching in drawers to get a flavour of the couple, held up two letters. 'Story of a tricky relationship. A holiday booking for next month, and a letter from the council about anti-social behaviour. Noise, apparently.'

'I wonder if that's what the neighbour next door wants to talk about.' Allie took another glance around and then stood again, her knees creaking alarmingly.

Frankie appeared in the doorway, Sam behind him.

'Nothing out of the ordinary upstairs, boss,' Frankie said. 'It seems like the attack was concentrated in here. What a mess. Is our vic okay?'

'For now, fingers crossed. It's lucky we got to her when we did. The neighbour was brave to come inside, most probably saved her life.' Allie checked the time. 'I'll go and speak to her now, I think. She might have valuable information. Perry, can you check around and see what else you can find?' She glanced at Sam and Frankie. 'You two do a bit of door knocking and then you can go back to the station. It'll be cut and dried if it is her husband, and at least we'll have the evidence to charge him if so.'

'Yeah, what a bastard,' Sam said quietly, eyeing the mess on the floor. 'He really meant to hurt her, didn't he?'

'I think so.' Allie noted Toby nodding.

His facial expressions gave away how angry he was, but he was controlling his temper.

Allie liked Toby. He'd moved from Birmingham a few months ago, on his own, but now he had a partner, Joshua. Usually, Toby was a Positive Pete, trying to make light of situations without anyone thinking he wasn't being respectful. But this attack seemed to be affecting him more than usual.

Allie knew that some cases got to her like that too. It was a thin line to tread, but she made a mental note to check in with him later to see if he was okay. Perhaps it had brought back memories of a family trauma. That might be something she could help him with, either listening or referring him for help.

Allie glanced around the room. They were like one big family, the police and their wider colleagues. Neither could do their jobs without one another.

And the phrase that you can choose your friends, but you can't pick your family? This was one set of relatives she didn't mind at all.

CHAPTER FIVE

When she'd bagged up her forensic gear, Allie slipped around to the adjoining property. A woman in her late sixties stood in the window. She moved to the door when she spotted Allie coming towards her.

'Is there any news about Michelle?' she asked, once Allie had introduced herself.

'Nothing yet, I'm afraid, but we'll let you know as soon as we can. It's Mrs Timmis, isn't it? You called for the emergency services.'

'Yes, Irene.' She beckoned to Allie. 'Please, come through to the kitchen.'

Allie followed her, the house having an opposite layout to the one she'd come from. The kitchen was immaculate in this one, with a chequered black-and-white floor covering and bright-orange accessories on the worktops. The window over the sink showed a well-maintained autumnal garden. From here she could see part of next door's garden, a four-foot fence separating the two houses.

Irene pulled out a chair for her at the table and then filled the kettle. A calendar with a photo of a cocker spaniel was next to the fridge.

'Coffee?' she offered Allie.

'I would love one, thanks. Lovely home you have.'

Irene turned to her with a faint smile. 'We've been here since it was built thirty years ago. That's me and my husband, Sid. He's in hospital at the moment, for a minor op. I'm picking him up later this afternoon. He's going to be devastated when I tell him what's happened.'

Allie got out her notebook, smiling gratefully when a mug was put in front of her.

'Would you like a biscuit? I have chocolate digestives in the cupboard.'

'No, thank you. Coffee is good, though.' She took a tiny sip, liking her drinks hot. 'Are you okay to go through what happened this morning, please?'

Irene sat across from her. 'I've been complaining about the noise for quite some time now. They're always arguing, you see. We hear him, Brian, shouting at Michelle constantly.'

'Do you mean a couple of times a week, once a week, once a –'

'Most nights, for a week at a time. I try to watch out for her. He works shifts, so when he's on days, he's often in the pub and shouty when he gets home. Michelle works at the bank in Longton, nine-to-five, so she has a bit of peace when he's on noons, too. She comes for tea every now and then. When he's on noons, he's not in until after ten, so it's usually quiet then. When he's working nights, it's hit and miss. If he's been to the pub in the afternoon, he can get quite loud, but if not, he seems to be a different person.'

'The shouting, is it one-sided?'

Irene nodded, taking a mouthful of her coffee. 'It's mostly Brian. The only time we hear Michelle is when she's crying out. It's horrible living next door to it.'

'I can imagine,' Allie soothed. 'So yesterday, Brian was on nights, I presume, if he was here this morning. Was there any noise before he left?'

'I heard him raising his voice around half past eight. I went out to put the rubbish in the bin, and I could see him in the kitchen window. He was pointing at Michelle, his face incandescent with rage. I wanted him to see me, you see, because sometimes it stops him in his tracks. Gets rid of his red mist, I think. But he was so intent on screaming in her face that he didn't.' She got up suddenly and went over to the worktop. She drew a tissue from a box and wiped at her eyes, and then her nose.

'I'm sorry to upset you, Irene,' Allie said sincerely.

'Oh, don't mind that. If it gets to me, imagine what Michelle goes through.' Irene sat down again. 'I came back into the house and got ready for work. I have a part-time job in the market. It had gone quiet next door, but as I left, I was walking up the path when Brian came out. I said hello to him, but he ignored me, and by the time he got into his car, I was on the pavement. Well, he reversed that fast he almost knocked me over. And then he drove like a madman down and out of the street. I went all cold and rushed to see if Michelle was okay. There was no answer, so I went round to the back, and that's... that's when I saw her on the floor and I called for help.'

'You've been very brave to recall that.' Allie smiled with appreciation. 'It must have been horrible to see.'

'Yes, she's like a daughter to me.' Irene wiped at her eyes again. 'I hope she's all right and that we hear soon.'

Allie had got what she'd come for so made her way back to the Prices' property. She found Perry in the living room, sitting on the settee with a box of photos he was rummaging through.

'Find anything useful?' she asked.

'Nothing except that letter from the council. The house is clean and tidy in all the other rooms. Frankie got his registration and make of car from a neighbour's CCTV. He nearly wiped the old dear out next door in his haste to get away.'

'She's been telling me. Have you called it in?'

'Yeah. It pinged on ANPR on the A50 out towards Trentham. Maybe he won't go far, but we can track him down if he's on an open road.'

'Hmm, let's hope he doesn't go to ground.'

'Do you think he's worried that he's killed her?'

Allie, who was now in the doorway, glanced at the kitchen floor again. 'I reckon he probably does.'

CHAPTER SIX

JAMIE SANDERSON – AGED 16

It was only a week since Kevin had mentioned the job. Meanwhile, Jamie had seen Colette three times on his own.

Colette was one of the girls all the boys wanted to date. Everyone talked about her at school, the boys and the girls. She was gorgeous, and he was dating her!

Tonight was the night they were going to steal some stuff from the newsagent's. Jamie didn't want to do it really, but it seemed to be a test of his loyalty to be part of their gang. At least being the lookout might not get him into trouble. He could run pretty fast if necessary.

He met Colette on the way to the bus stop. She greeted him with a full-on kiss that gave him a feeling in his groin that he needed to keep to himself for now. Still, he wrapped his arms around her.

They'd had sex at the weekend, twice actually. It had been

the first time for Jamie, and Colette said it was her first time, too, so that took away his nerves.

Nevertheless, he walked funny for a couple of minutes until he was back to normal. Colette didn't notice, thankfully.

'I think you're really brave doing the job this evening,' she said. 'It'll be great, you'll see.'

'Yeah, it'll be boss.'

She turned her face towards him and laughed. 'What are you like? No one says boss anymore. It's not... boss.'

Jamie laughed, too, hoping it hid his nerves. He wanted to get this over and done with and then get on with the rest of the evening. His mum had gone to bed with a headache before he'd come out, so he might be able to sneak Colette into the front room for a bit of time on their own.

He thought of other things for fear of having to walk funny again.

At the bus stop, Kevin, Nick, and Michelle were waiting for them. Kevin seemed a little unsteady on his feet, his eyes wide, pupils dilated.

'Are you okay?' Jamie asked.

'Yeah, yeah, man, everything is grand. Let's go and get this motherfucker.'

Colette gave him a good luck kiss before going to sit with Michelle. 'Don't be too long. Then we can go for a walk on our own.'

'Come on, lover boy.' Kevin patted him on the back. 'Time to do your first job.'

Ten minutes later, they arrived at the newsagent's. The shop was empty, except for the man behind the counter. Jamie stood watch by the door, on the pavement outside, keeping it wedged open with his foot while they went in. There were bright lights in the shop, in contrast to the dark night. He glanced to the road and back.

As soon as the shopkeeper spotted Kevin, Jamie saw him stand up and point at them.

'You're barred,' he shouted. 'Get out of my shop.'

'Or what?' Kevin stood tall to make himself appear intimidating, but it didn't do the trick.

'Keep your hair on, granddad,' Nick taunted. 'We're only after a few freebies, Winston, me old man.'

'Why, you cheeky... Oi, leave that alone.' Winston spotted Kevin pocketing a few bars of chocolate. 'Put it all back.'

'I only want a bit of it,' Kevin teased. 'Unless you let us through to the back room. I'm sure you have more than shop supplies in there.'

'Never you mind.' Winston glanced towards the door.

Kevin and Nick did the same, only to realise it was a trick. When they turned back to Winston, he was holding a rounders bat high in the air.

'If you two don't leave right now, I'm going to call the police.'

'They won't come, you know that.'

'But I can tell them who you are.'

Kevin thought for a moment and then glanced at Nick. 'Let's do him in and he won't be able to grass on us then.'

Nick's grin faltered. 'I don't want any trouble, Kev. My old man will batter me.'

'Then piss off and leave me because I want the cash in the till.'

'You never said –'

Kevin took out a knife and pointed it at Nick. 'It doesn't matter what I say.' He moved it to face Winston. 'Now, old man, open the fucking till!'

Seeing the knife in Kevin's hand, Jamie gasped and went inside. 'What's going on?'

'I thought I told you to keep an eye out,' Kevin shouted.

'I didn't know you were bringing a knife!'

Winston took the opportunity to come out from behind the till. With the bat raised in the air, he ran towards the boys.

'Get out of my shop,' he yelled.

Kevin charged forward, and the knife went into the older man's stomach. Winston dropped his arms, the bat falling to the floor. His hands grasped his middle. Blood covered them in seconds.

'What the fuck have you done?' Nick ran to the door. 'We have to get out of here.'

'We can't leave him. He's bleeding too much,' Jamie protested.

But Kevin was in no mood to go anywhere. He stood over Winston and pointed the blade at him. 'I told you to give us the money from the till, but you wouldn't listen. Nick, get it now.'

'No way, I'm out of here.'

Kevin turned to Jamie. 'You get it then.'

But he was glued to the spot. With Nick gone, he couldn't get to the door without passing Kevin and he didn't want the knife in his stomach, too.

He had to talk him down somehow.

'Let's go now while we can,' he said. 'We can ring for an ambulance from the phone box on the corner.'

'Are you mad? He knows who we are.' Kevin looked down at Winston who was groaning in pain.

Before Jamie could stop him, Kevin dropped to his knees and stabbed Winston again. The old man's eyes widened in shock and disbelief.

It wasn't until the knife went in a third time that Jamie lurched forward to grab his hand. 'Stop!'

The knife fell from Kevin's grip. They both reached for it, but Jamie got there first and threw it behind the counter.

'What did you do that for?' Kevin shouted.

'Because you would have killed him.'

'I wanted to!' Kevin stopped a moment to catch his breath. Then he raced towards the door. 'You'll pay for this if I get in trouble.'

'Where are you going?'

But Kevin was gone.

Jamie was left in the shop on his own.

Winston groaned. Jamie stood up to find a phone. He saw one on the wall behind the till and rang for an ambulance. When he went back to Winston, there was no sign of life.

'Winston?' He nudged him. 'Winston.'

'What are you doing?' a voice said.

Jamie saw a woman who was about the same age as the shopkeeper.

'Winston, what's wrong?' She dropped to her knees.

'He's been stabbed,' Jamie explained. 'I've called for an ambulance.'

'Winston, wake up.' She shook him. 'Did you see who did it?'

'No, I...' Jamie's silence let him down, and she screamed at him.

'You did. Tell me who it was!'

'I didn't see, honestly.'

'Then how come you're still here now?' She gasped. 'Was it you?'

'No, I was trying to help.'

'I'll have the police on you for this. How could you do this to a defenceless old man?'

Jamie panicked and headed for the door.

'Where are you going?'

'The ambulance will be here soon.' He continued. 'They'll take care of him.'

'You won't get away with this! I'll tell the police everything.'

Sirens in the distance were getting louder as they approached. They brought Jamie back to his senses, and he ran from the shop.

He couldn't be here when the police arrived.

CHAPTER SEVEN

Having done as much as she could in Pepper Street, Allie drove back to the station to see if she could find out more about Brian Price. Perry had left with Sam and Frankie. Her team had covered the basics, uniform were out in force trying to locate Brian, and for now, Michelle was in the best place.

Allie sat at her desk, silent for a moment in the general noise of the open-plan office, taking a look to see if there were any complaints about the couple. Surprised to find there was nothing, she wondered why, seeing as Mrs Timmis seemed to have a catalogue of them.

Maybe it had never escalated enough for the police to be called out. Or Brian could have frightened Michelle so much that she didn't dare to contact them. It was often the case with these types of attacks.

Allie made a note to call in and see Grace Cole on her way home. Because once she was done here, she was determined to leave at a decent time. With working on the Shaun Green case, she'd been there well past eight p.m. for the past three evenings and wanted to spend some time with Mark and Poppy. She needed a bit of downtime, for sure.

The afternoon dragged without anything of interest coming their way. Sam checked with the hospital one more time to find that Michelle was out of the trauma unit but was being kept in for observation due to concussion. Allie was told to call again in the morning to see if Michelle was able to speak to them then.

As for Brian Price's whereabouts, police were searching for him, he was being hunted down. Regardless of Michelle's condition, there would be a press release going out. He needed to be found and brought to justice if he was still at large by then.

There was a knock at the door. Allie had an open-door policy, so DCI Jenny Brindley came into the office. Allie smiled, at the same time wondering why she was here. Usually, if there was a problem, Allie would be summoned to the top floor where Jenny's office was. So maybe this was a social call. She hoped so.

'I hear you've had a nasty assault come in,' Jenny said, sitting opposite her. 'I hope it wasn't too taxing for you.'

'I've seen worse,' Allie admitted, 'but I can't say it doesn't affect me, even after all this time.'

'And how is everyone on the team? Any more random notes or whatever I need to know about?'

Allie shook her head. A few months ago, she and her team had been targeted. Sam had photos left on her car windscreen of her and an officer who she was having an affair with. Perry had a petrol can and lighter, a note with the word "BOOM" written on it, left on his doorstep. Allie had received a note, too, advising her to watch her back, but it was Frankie who had come off worse when a car had been deliberately driven at his house, totalling his own vehicle and part of the garden and garage.

Since then, there had been nothing. Allie didn't know whether to be glad or worried there was a reason for it.

'We're trying to stay vigilant, ma'am,' she said. 'It's harder as time goes by as you get complacent, don't you? It slips your mind, and before you know it, you've put yourself in danger of being attacked. But life has to go on.'

Jenny paused before speaking again. 'I had a case, a few years back, when a man stalked me for three years.'

Allie's eyes widened. She had no idea that had happened.

'I kept it to myself as much as I could. It was someone I knew from my childhood, when I lived in Birmingham. We went to the same secondary school, but we were never in classes together. He didn't even talk to me, and when I left, I never gave him a second thought. I left for university in Manchester and joined the force, moved to Stoke and didn't see him.

'He turned up on a case I worked when I was a DI. He was interviewed as a witness to a fight in a pub where some poor soul got stabbed. He asked if we could go out for a drink; I refused, obviously. I was married then, too.' Jenny had been divorced and since remarried. 'That was when he started his reign of terror. He would appear wherever he could see me, any meetings I was at. I'd spot him loitering outside the station car park. He'd bump into me when I was out on lunch. And then he found out where I lived. I couldn't get rid of him.'

'What a prick.' Allie grimaced. 'Sorry, ma'am. It slipped out.'

Jenny smiled. 'He was a prick, and it took a court order for him to stop. In the end, he moved away when he was threatened with jail time if he didn't leave me alone.' She paused. 'The reason I'm telling you this is because no matter what I did or how many times I changed my routine to something different to fool him, he always caught up with me. I don't want you to feel responsible for your team. Be vigilant, all of you, but also be assured that you can't be in all places at once if anything does happen.'

Allie nodded her thanks. 'I must admit, even without the dreaded hot sweats, I do have trouble sleeping if I get something like that on a loop in my mind.'

'Well, this is to let you know that you're not on your own. If there is anything worrying you, come up and see me. It *could* be something or nothing, but it might also lead to much more. I'm here for *you*, Allie.'

'Thank you, ma'am. It's good to know.'

Jenny stood up. 'Right, I'd better get back to my own office. I'll catch up with you again in the morning. Let's hope Michelle Price is out of danger by then.'

With Jenny gone, Allie got back to work. But her mind wouldn't settle. She kept thinking what it would be like to be stalked. Of course, she'd had her own weirdo in 2015, when someone came after her, but it had been nothing like the ordeal Jenny had gone through. It must have been terrifying for three years. It was good of her boss to confide in her now.

And there she was this morning, thinking she knew all of her team inside out.

CHAPTER EIGHT

Tia Farrington walked home with a huge grin. The sun was warm on her face as she negotiated the traffic to cross the road to the estate she lived on. She was in her school uniform, but she hadn't been anywhere near the place for a few days now. Her parents didn't know, and she couldn't do it all the time, but Troy was on holiday from work for the week, and he'd wanted her to keep him company.

Unbeknown to her mum and dad, too, she'd been seeing Troy for two months. He was twenty-two, and they would go berserk if they realised she was sleeping with him. Of course she'd been careful. She was only sixteen, with exams to sit so that she could go to sixth form and then university. But the sheer thrill of having sex was one she was empowered with. Suddenly she was finding out more about herself, about the control she could wield and the joy she could receive.

Even so, neither of them would want her mixing with someone from the Bennett Estate. Yet she loved hanging out there with her cousin, Emily. Most of the teens went to their school, so there was always someone around to have fun with.

It was where she'd met Troy, too. Over a few nights, he'd

seen her when he'd called into the off-licence and started chatting to her when he came out. It took him a week to ask her out, and from there she had been smitten. Luckily, Emily was dating one of the boys from their class, so neither of them were left alone.

Her parents were such a pair of snobs, her dad more than her mum, though. He was a real hypocrite. His job involved mentoring troublesome teens, mostly male, helping them to find a way forward with positivity. He'd try and find them work in the area rather than see them end up in a prison cell and was constantly rallying support from local employers. Tia was proud of him really. He wanted to make a difference. But she did wonder why anyone without a future, or education, wasn't good enough for his little girl.

Tia and Troy. She giggled at how funny their names sounded when said together, like cartoon characters from a children's TV series. Troy was more of a man really, and the oldest boyfriend she'd had by several years. He had his own car, a decent job, and treated her well, always buying her gifts.

They'd ordered food in at lunchtime and had eaten a picnic in bed. Tia couldn't have been happier, even though Emily wasn't impressed. She didn't have a kind word to say about Troy, but at least she'd kept her secret from everyone.

Tia let herself into the house, removed her blazer and shoes, and stopped. The silence which greeted her was a little unnerving. She checked her watch: it was quarter past four. Her dad's car was on the drive, so he was home. Usually he'd have the radio on as he hated a quiet house, and often he'd be cooking something nice as Mum was working until nine. He loved creating his own recipes for her to try, comfort food with twists.

She went into the kitchen, expecting him to be there, perhaps reading a newspaper in the quiet. But the room was empty. She tried the living room. That was unoccupied, too.

'Dad?' she shouted up the stairs.

No reply. Perhaps he was in the shower, although she couldn't hear any water running.

In her room, she changed out of her uniform. Still no sight or sound of him, and there was no one in the main bathroom. The door to her parents' bedroom was closed.

Getting worried now, she knocked. 'Dad, are you in there?'

She hesitated, dreading walking in and finding him naked, ugh. She knocked again, but no reply.

She pushed open the door to see him tucked up in bed. He was lying on his side facing away from her. She moved forward to check on him. Perhaps he wasn't feeling very well.

His eyes were closed, and she wondered whether to wake him or not. But then she noticed the pallor of his skin. He looked like death warmed up. She gave his shoulder a gentle nudge, expecting him to wake from sleep.

'Dad?'

Still nothing.

Hairs rose on the back of her neck.

This was wrong.

She reached over to touch him again, this time on his face. His skin was cold.

She went around to the other side of the bed and stopped. There was a bottle of pills on the carpet. His arm was hanging over the side of the bed, a cut from his wrist dripping blood slowly, one drop at a time joining a small patch on the carpet. An empty bottle of Jack Daniel's lay next to it, a glass by its side with remnants that assumed it had been full at some stage.

Tia didn't stay long enough to see anything else. She was too busy running out of the room.

At the bottom of the stairs, she sat down before her legs gave way and took out her phone. Her hands were shaking so much that it was hard to operate it. All she could see was her dad's face.

Finally, she located her mum's number. The phone connected after three rings.

'Hey, Tils. Have you had a good day at –'

'Mum,' she broke in. 'It's Dad. It's... he's...'

'What's wrong with him, love? Is he not home yet?'

'I...' Tia burst into tears, unable to get her words out.

'Tia, what's wrong?' Her mum's voice was urgent now. 'You're scaring me. Can I talk to him? Is he there?'

'He's here, Mum, but he's dead. He's dead! You have to come home right now.'

CHAPTER NINE

JAMIE SANDERSON – AGED 16

When Jamie left the shop, he raced back to join the others, but he couldn't find them. The bench they'd been sitting on was empty. He glanced right and left, down the street, but they were nowhere to be seen. He clenched his hair in his hands and groaned. Where had they gone?

He ran home then, letting himself in quietly. He tiptoed upstairs, checking to see if his mum was asleep. She was out like a light, probably hadn't heard him come in.

He dashed downstairs, got out of his clothes, and shoved everything he'd been wearing into the washing machine. His trainers were caked in blood, but he couldn't throw them in as well. They'd make too much noise and might wake Mum. He needed her to stay upstairs so he could say he was here when Winston was attacked.

At the thought of what had happened, Jamie retched.

Covering his mouth, he raced through to the downstairs toilet, only just making it before he threw up. He sank to his knees.

What had happened back there? He'd got himself into something he wasn't able to get out of easily. He needed to see Kevin and Nick, find out why they'd left him there.

He got changed and went out again, keeping the hood up on his top. It was raining so the estate was quiet. He searched everywhere, but still he couldn't find them, nor Colette or Michelle. He wasn't brave enough to visit any of them at home. Besides, he only knew where Colette lived anyway.

Maybe he should have stayed in. He could have fudged the truth and said he was there all night, especially with his mum passed out. Kevin said there were no cameras in the shop, and it was late, so no one had been around.

He shook uncontrollably. What was he going to say if the police called?

Unless…

Jamie thought back to getting home. It was dark and raining, not many people out. Perhaps if anyone saw him, he could say he was with Colette. She would lie for him.

He walked near to the newsagent's to see what was happening. There were two police cars outside, and crime scene tape wrapped around two lampposts stopping anyone from going nearer.

Jamie crossed the road and stood behind the cordon, trying to look inside the entrance. But he couldn't see anything except blue lights flashing through the night.

'Terrible what's happened, isn't it?' a woman said as she joined two others.

'Disgusting,' said another. 'How someone could kill a man like Winston is beyond me. He was such a sweet soul.'

Jamie's head swam. Did she say that Winston was dead?

He waited a few minutes to make sure he'd heard right,

but the women said nothing else. They were too busy gawping.

Jamie walked away quietly. As soon as he was out of the street, he ran all the way home.

In bed, he let his tears fall. Winston Lowe was dead. He'd never forget seeing the horror on that woman's face. The wail of disbelief when she saw what had happened. He wondered if it was Winston's wife. If so, she'd been left without a husband, a man who she'd probably been married to for years. They might have children, grandchildren. They could have ruined the lives of them all. The knock-on effect would be huge.

What had they done?

But it was Kevin who had killed Winston. Not him.

Jamie would have to get his story straight before he went to school in the morning, act as if he knew nothing about it until he could speak to Kevin and Nick. He'd never been in trouble. No one would suspect him. And Winston had died, so he couldn't tell anyone what had happened.

Maybe he should go to the police first. But, even if he told them it wasn't him, he might be seen to be an accomplice, along with Nick, regardless. He'd heard about joint enterprise. He might get roped in for being there. After all, if they weren't thieving, Winston Lowe wouldn't have had to defend himself. Kevin wouldn't have used a knife to...

With jumbled thoughts scrambling around for attention, Jamie squeezed his eyes shut, hoping to get some sleep, but images flashed in front of his eyes.

Watching out for anyone who was about to come in the shop.

Glancing in to see Kevin with a knife in his hands.

Looking down to see Winston covered in blood, holding his stomach.

Seeing the woman appear, the horror on her face.

This was a nightmare. He would wake up soon. Because this couldn't have happened.

It just couldn't.

CHAPTER TEN

Allie turned into the main drag of the Bennett Estate. She kept vigilant to see if there was anything going on that she should know about. Not that it was her job nowadays to do the beat bobby role of policing, but sometimes with the least of intentions, she'd notice something that she could file for a later date. And often, she'd spot someone who she could have a chat to, even if it was inadvertently checking in to see how they were.

She had her favourites everywhere. Some of the residents had won her heart when she'd helped them out over the years. Some were not so fond of her. Some would love to share the gossip they'd heard at the local pub or queuing for a paper in the shop on the parade.

Sadly it was drizzling, the sky grey and heavy with the promise of rain to come. She saw nothing out of the ordinary, so a few minutes later, she parked outside Grace's offices on the far end of the estate.

Before she went inside, she reviewed her emails to see if anything needed her attention. There was nothing she had to do immediately, only a message that told her forensics had finished at the Price property, which she passed on to her team. A patrol car would guard the premises in case the husband returned, but for now, Pepper Street could get back to a little more normality.

Allie had sent apologies for the Safer Estates meeting she'd been due to attend that morning. Grace chaired it each month, so Allie should be able to get an update on business and actions needed while she grilled her for information about the Prices. She stepped inside the small reception area, smiling at the man behind the counter.

'I'm here to see Grace Cole,' she said, still not used to hearing a different surname. She had known Grace as Allendale until she'd married Simon, Allie's long-term friend, and senior crime reporter for *Stoke News*. It had been utter joy to see them getting on so well, both happy and in love.

She sat down to wait for Grace to come downstairs for her, scanning one of the leaflets on the noticeboard. But as soon as her bum hit the seat, the door to her right opened, and there she was.

'I'll let you off for getting out of the meeting this morning,' Grace chastised as they hugged. 'They are exceptional for sharing intel, but they don't half drag on as we have so much to cover. Wait until I tell you what the O'Connell family have been up to.'

They chatted amicably while they went upstairs and into an open-plan office similar to the one where Allie shared space with other teams. Grace pulled an elastic covered band from her wrist and pulled her loose hair back into a high ponytail. Along with the minimal makeup she wore, it had the illusion of taking twenty years from her. She was a keen runner and wore sporty trainers, along with a smart navy suit and cream blouse.

Grace pointed to a mug, steam coming off it. 'That's yours. No point in asking as you always say yes.'

Allie flicked out her tongue in jest. 'I seem to have drunk half drinks today, so this is very welcome.'

Grace rummaged round in her drawer and threw a chocolate bar to Allie.

She caught it and grinned.

'How is the woman who was assaulted?' Grace asked, tucking into one, too. 'Is she anyone I know?'

'That's what I've come to see, while you bring me up to speed with the Safer Estates meeting.' Allie told her all she knew about the Prices. 'I wondered if you'd had any dealings with her around domestic abuse.'

'The name doesn't ring a bell.'

'We also found details of a complaint, noise nuisance. Longton Housing Office are familiar with him. I spoke to one of the housing officers there, Peter Kemp, and he told me he'd been out to see the couple, and Michelle on her own, on numerous occasions. Nothing serious enough to call us, though. Brian Price said it was only banging doors and noise from the TV that was mistaken for Michelle crying. He said the neighbour next door was always whinging at him, and his exact words were he couldn't fart without her complaining.'

'Charming.'

Allie nodded. 'She was really sweet, more concerned about Michelle than having a go about the noise.'

'Let me have a look.' Grace moved her mouse to wake up the computer.

While Grace searched their database and then made a telephone call, Allie twirled from side to side in her chair. The office environment was like her own, taking a breather but ready to go at the first sign of trouble.

Grace's bunch were always good for intel, especially as the initiative of joint- and multi-teamed staffing had been taken on board. There were designated officers covering anti-social behaviour, domestic abuse, and coercive control, drugs-related issues, keeping an eye on the gangs and county lines.

There was a social worker and a housing officer, all covering the six towns in the city. It worked really well, Allie thought, since it had been put together a few years ago. And Grace had come into her own as the team leader, after taking Allie's place on secondment.

She sipped at her coffee, wanting food really, but a sugar fix would have to do. While she was finishing the chocolate bar, her phone rang. It was Perry.

'There's been a body found in a house on Norton Heights,' he said.

'Our suspect, you mean?' She sat upright, alert at the news.

'No, it's someone else. Control have received a call from a woman whose teenage daughter has found her father deceased. It's thought he might have taken his life, but it's sounding suspicious by all accounts.'

'I'm in Tunstall with Grace. If I leave now, I can be with you in twenty minutes. Meet me there.' Allie disconnected her phone and dropped her chin to her chest for a moment. Then she gave Grace a faint smile. 'No rest for the wicked. Off I go again.'

'Curry next weekend?' Grace shouted after her.

Allie gave her the universal signal for 'call me', hoping that she'd get time to see her and Simon soon. But with what was going on in Stoke right now, she'd be lucky to get a minute to herself.

CHAPTER ELEVEN

Lauren Farrington sat on the edge of the settee in her living room. The phone call from Tia had been the worst thing ever to happen to her. She'd had to fight hard to get her daughter to say much through her sobs, but then she'd left work and dashed home, needing to see for herself if it was true. She wouldn't – couldn't – believe it until then. Only half an hour ago she'd been telling Paul Dixon off as he'd arrived late for his shift yet again. Now her husband had gone.

She didn't understand. Nick would never take his own life. He'd said it was a coward's way out. Lauren was always arguing the point with him. In her opinion, it was a hard thing to do, even if it did leave others behind to pick up the pieces.

She'd seen him that morning. Everything had been as normal. It was early when he'd left, but he hadn't appeared worried about anything, nor had he the night before. They hadn't rowed, not even bickered. What were the last words he'd said to her? "Don't forget the window cleaner will be here today, so I'll leave the side gate open."

She hoped she wasn't about to find out he'd run up a

mountain of debt, remortgaged the house, and that she was going to lose everything they'd worked for. Because she didn't want to think about moving out and starting again. Without him.

And if she'd known he was going to do something so drastic, she would have spent time with him the evening before. She would have made Tia stay in and watch a movie with them, ordered in a takeaway and shared a bottle of wine. Although to be fair, the way Tia had been behaving lately, she doubted she would have stayed in with her parents. Tia had got in with a group of kids from the Bennett Estate, coming in later than her curfew and being a bit lippy when questioned about it.

Lauren had been proud that they'd brought up a kind and loving daughter, until she'd started to stay out late, coming home tipsy and making a nuisance of herself at school. Still, at least Lauren knew where she was when she was with her niece, Emily.

She cursed inwardly. Such useless things to think about, but it took her mind off the horror of the situation. It stopped her thinking how her life had changed in an instant. How her husband had been cruelly taken away from her, from Tia.

Because it would be up to her to tell everyone. Being left to pick up the pieces, perhaps she'd change her views after all. Maybe by the end of all this, she would think he *was* a coward. That he shouldn't have left her to fend for herself, do everything alone. With no future to look forward to, no hope. Just her and Tia.

Tia.

Lauren would have to be strong for her daughter. She needed to get them both through this. Sixteen was such a young age to lose a dad. Lauren had lost her own when she was twenty-two. She and Nick hadn't long been married, and she'd woken to a frantic call from her mother that time, who had found her father dead beside her. He'd been cold to the touch, having died in the early hours of a heart attack.

How was she going to tell her that Nick had died in bed, too, but of his own free will? It was bound to stir up painful memories.

Lauren assumed the police would want to question her, Tia, too, perhaps. She hoped they wouldn't think it was staged – that she had murdered him and tried to cover her tracks. You know, like they did on the TV in lots of programmes. Wait for the twist in the case.

She almost laughed aloud at her ridiculous thoughts. Why would she think he owed money to anyone? Why would the police think she would have anything to do with Nick taking a Stanley knife and slashing at his wrist?

The thing that hurt most was Nick knew Tia would be home first to find him. Why had he done that? Nick knew Lauren would be at work until nine, too, so had plenty of time to plan if so.

Or had something gone wrong and it happened too quickly? Had he wanted Tia to find him as some kind of cry for help?

Of course Lauren kept all this to herself. She wasn't guilty of his death. Their marriage was sound. She wasn't having an affair, and to her knowledge, neither was he. There was nothing they didn't know about each other.

Was there?

She turned to the window when she heard sirens approaching. Moments later, a police car pulled up outside the house. There were lights flashing. She went to answer the door, Tia close behind her.

Then, in what felt like a dream state, she showed the two uniformed officers where Nick was. She couldn't even go into the room.

Now, Lauren hugged her daughter fiercely. Tia was inconsolable, and the sound of her sobbing brought Lauren to tears, too. They held on to each other while they cried, united in their grief. They weren't – hadn't been – a close touchy-feely family, but she did love her daughter and would get her through this as much as she could.

All around, while the hustle and bustle continued, they sat in bewilderment. Lauren gasped as her gaze fell upon a family portrait of the three of them above the fireplace. She'd have to take that down as soon as possible.

Once the emergency services had given her their home back.

Once the police had stopped trampling all over her thoughts.

Once she had buried her husband.

A sob escaped her, and it was Tia's time to comfort her mother.

CHAPTER TWELVE

JAMIE SANDERSON – AGED 16

Jamie thought about everything well into the early hours of the morning, wishing he could turn back time. Praying it wasn't true. But when he slept, it became a nightmare, and he woke up screaming out.

He stayed off school, telling his mum he wasn't well. It wasn't a lie. He felt physically sick.

At half past ten, the doorbell rang, and Jamie almost jumped out of his skin. He peered around the curtains, so as not to alert anyone he didn't want to see that he was home. But it was Kevin and Nick.

Reluctant to let them in, he went out through the back door and around the side of the house. Neither of them were in school uniform. Instead, they were wearing leather jackets and jeans.

Although Nick seemed nervous, glancing up and down the street, Kevin stood there proud, all man about town rather than someone who only a few hours ago had put a knife in someone's stomach.

'All right, mate?' Kevin asked.

'No, I'm not,' Jamie cried. 'What the fuck happened last night? You said you were going to rob the place, not kill someone.'

'Keep your voice down,' Kevin warned. 'As far as the police know, I wasn't there. Nor was Nick. Neither were you, unless anyone saw you.'

Jamie said nothing about the woman he thought was Winston Lowe's wife. How could he? Knowing Kevin, he'd go and finish her off, too, so she couldn't identify him. Not that she'd known he was there. All Mrs Lowe had seen was Jamie. Oh, shit. This was so much worse than he'd thought.

'How long do you think it'll be before they haul us in?' He pointed in Kevin's face. 'It was your fault. You shouldn't have taken a knife with you.'

'You need to watch yourself.' Kevin squared up to him. 'The cops have nothing on us, so we keep quiet.'

'You killed the old man! How can I say nothing?'

'If you do blab, then I'll make sure you regret what you say.' Kevin raised his fist in the air, grabbing Jamie's jumper to pull him closer. 'And then I'll start on your old woman.'

'You leave my mum out of this.'

Kevin punched him in the stomach. '*You* keep your fucking mouth shut,' he said as Jamie keeled over. 'Or else there'll be more where that came from.' He glanced at Nick, who hadn't said a word. 'Cat got your tongue?'

Nick looked away. It was as if he didn't want to be seen here, with either of them. Jamie realised that there was no point relying on Nick to tell the truth. He was too scared of Kevin not to lie for him.

They left then, and Jamie went back into the house, holding on to his stomach where Kevin had hit him. Once more, he wondered whether to give himself up first, even though it meant grassing on Kevin and Nick. Or was it better to say nothing? Either way was going to be horrendous.

For the rest of the day, he thought about Winston, how his family must be feeling. Winston was dead, and no amount of wishing otherwise would bring him back.

Jamie didn't have much sleep that night either, and when nothing occurred the following day, he was hoping that the evidence the police had would point to Kevin and not him. But it was playing on his conscience, too. He was thinking of confiding in his mum, see what she would advise him to do. She'd hate him, of course, for getting into a mess. But someone was dead, so that was much worse.

He'd tell her after they'd eaten.

Even then, he couldn't find the words. He hadn't got an appetite so was pretending to eat his tea, sitting at the table, when the knock came that evening.

'Go and get that, love,' she said. 'It will probably be for you.'

Jamie was hoping it might be Colette. She hadn't been in touch, and he couldn't understand why. But when he saw two men in dark suits, and a uniformed police officer standing behind them, he almost felt the blood drain from him. Fear made him freeze to the spot.

One of the men in a suit leaned forward, holding out a warrant card. 'Jamie Sanderson?'

Jamie nodded.

'I'm arresting you for the murder of Winston Lowe.'

'What? No, wait, you've got it wrong.' Jamie struggled while the man read him his rights. Handcuffs were clicked into place around his wrists. 'It wasn't me,' he cried.

'What's going on?' Mum had come out to see what the commotion was.

'They're saying I killed someone. I didn't, I swear.'

'What are you doing?' She tried to push the officer closest away. 'Leave him alone. You can't just take him.'

'How old are you, son?' the man asked.

'Sixteen.'

He turned to her. 'As a minor, he needs an adult with him. You can accompany us to the station.'

'I haven't done anything, Mum,' Jamie said, his voice wobbling with emotion. 'I need to answer some questions, and they'll see.'

'But –'

'Get your coat, Mrs Sanderson. We're ready to go right now.'

Mum was crying as she searched for her handbag, but Jamie was more concerned with what was going to materialise. He'd thought of many things he could say, but he wasn't going to lie for the likes of Kevin and Nick. Sure, they'd beat him up when he saw them again, but he wasn't getting into trouble for them.

They went out to the police car, curtains twitching in the dark. Mr Grocott across the road was even standing on his doorstep having a good gawp. Well, let him, because Jamie would be home soon. He would have his say, and then things would be cleared up.

He hadn't done anything wrong.

CHAPTER THIRTEEN

Less than ten minutes later, Allie pulled up outside the address she'd been given. It was a large sprawling detached house that she'd passed many times. Set back from the main road, it boasted three floors and a separate double garage. There was a police car parked in front of it, alongside an ambulance. Several neighbours were out in their front gardens, no doubt wondering what was going on.

They walked up the drive and a uniformed officer came out. It wasn't anyone Allie recognised, a tall beast of a man who she hoped was a gentle giant.

'PC Ericson, ma'am,' he said with a nod.

'First name?'

'Gareth.' He pointed back to the house. 'My colleague, Dan, is inside. We were first on scene. I'm sure you know all this, but the call came through that someone had found a deceased male at home. It was called in as he'd taken his life, but I'm not so sure. He has bruising coming out around his neck.'

'Oh!' Allie updated Perry who had come across to join them after parking his car nearby. 'Which room is he in?'

'He's upstairs, second door on the left.'

'And his wife and daughter?'

'In the living room with Dan.'

She turned to Perry. 'Let's view first, and then we can see what we need to say to the family.'

They dressed quickly in forensic gear that Allie always carried in her car. Then she stepped inside another house with the same trepidation that she had in Pepper Street earlier that day. Behind her she could hear the occasional car driving past on the road. But inside, a young girl's sobs almost broke her heart.

The living room door was further down the hall, so she couldn't see anything as she made her way upstairs. Yet, thoughts of what might have happened flashed through her mind before she met with the family.

Was the schoolgirl telling the truth? Had she had a row with her dad, resulting in a fight, with something going drastically wrong? Surely she wouldn't be capable of staging a murder to look like a suicide?

Had there been anyone else in the house?

Had the man's wife got an alibi?

Were there any burglaries in the area recently that may have escalated?

Were there any signs of him trying, and failing, to hang himself? It was a horrible thought but one that needed to be investigated. Perhaps that was the cause of the bruising. Once a thorough sweep of the property had been done, that could be ruled in or out, depending on what they found. She knew it wasn't likely but could still be a possibility until proved otherwise.

At the top of the stairs, Allie glanced at the door in question, saw it ajar. She stepped towards it, pushing it wider, and then going into the room. Then she sighed when she saw what PC Ericson was referring to. It was clear Mr Farrington had been dead for a few hours. And that he hadn't taken his own life.

Someone had staged his murder.

'It's like buses,' Perry remarked, staring down at the body. 'Wait ages for one and then two come along at the same time.' He pointed at the victim. 'Gareth is right about the marks around his neck. He's been strangled, hasn't he?'

'Yes, and then put into the bed. A Stanley knife placed beside him to make it appear he's cut his wrist after downing tablets and alcohol. Toxicology will rule the last two in or out, plus the state of his eyes, but the knife wound is a whole new ball game. Are there any signs of forced entry?' She turned back briefly to Gareth.

'We checked every room, and there are no broken windows nor damaged doors.'

'So how did our killer get in?' Allie thought out loud. 'With a key? Or was he or she let in by Mr Farrington?'

'Whoever it is was also here long enough to stage the death,' Perry said. 'I wonder what time it happened.'

'At your service to let you know.' Dave Barnett appeared in the doorway behind them. 'Twice in one day, who would have thought it.'

Allie sighed quietly and whispered. 'There goes my early finish.'

It was a hazard of the job, and yet, already she could feel the adrenaline pumping around her body. The sense of someone needing justice for a loved one for a family torn apart in such a devastating way. She'd have to tell his wife and daughter the details soon. It wasn't something she was looking forward to. Their hearts were going to be smashed twice over.

Allie took another quick glance around the room. The decor was warm, kitted out in pale blues and cream. Curtains draped at the windows, artfully placed. A family photo in a frame next to a paperback novel on one side of the bed.

The blood spatter on the carpet alone was going to mar the tranquillity of it all. Mind you, Allie wondered if Mrs Farrington would ever go in there again. She knew she wouldn't want to.

She stepped into the en suite. It seemed as if no one had been in there. It was clear of blood and any signs of a struggle, but Dave would tell her otherwise.

Perry was riffling through a chest of drawers when she came out. Allie left him to it while she updated Jenny. Then a quick call through to Sam, and the rest of her team were tasked with what they did best. It was going to be another long night.

'Allie, you'd better come and see this,' Dave said.

'What is it?'

He held up a piece of lined paper, which had been folded in half. 'I found this under the duvet.'

Allie took it from him, opened it out, read the message on it, and frowned.

I LIED.

CHAPTER FOURTEEN

Downstairs again, with a deep breath, Allie knocked on the living room door to announce their arrival.

'Mrs Farrington, I'm Detective Inspector Allie Shenton, and this is Detective Sergeant Perry Wright.' Allie showed her warrant card, Perry doing the same. 'We're so sorry for your loss, and I apologise for doing this so quickly while we're still in forensic clothing, but we like to talk to you as soon as we can. May I ask you a few questions?'

The woman sitting on the settee with her young daughter nodded, tears brimming immediately. She wiped at them quickly, but more fell. She was in her late thirties at a guess, having her blonde hair cut in a quirky choppy style that suited her oval face. Her daughter's hair was longer, to her shoulders, and she had her mother's eyes. They clung on to each other in a heartbreaking manner, as if either didn't want to let the other go.

Shock was setting in, so Allie instructed Dan to make drinks for them, and once he was gone, she sat across from the women. Perry took the armchair in the bay window.

Despite the atmosphere, the room was light and airy and

appeared to be a space to gather in. There was a leather three-piece suite that she could imagine lounging on while watching TV. A bookcase full of fiction and non-fiction books to browse through, and a coffee table that was dressed with flair as well as seeming to have a day-to-day purpose.

What it showed to Allie was a family at ease. It wasn't too polished to convey either one controlling the other, and neither was it messy to show the state of a mind in turmoil.

'Can you run me through this afternoon, please?' Allie said, aware that this would be used as the first interview.

Mrs Farrington, first name Lauren, spoke for her and her daughter, Tia, explaining how they had both found Nick. Perry took notes as she did.

'Has anything happened recently that might attribute to his death?' Allie asked next. She wanted to see if Lauren had any thoughts of her own.

But Lauren shook her head. 'Not as far as I know. There was nothing troubling him, unless he kept it from me.'

'Do you think that's likely?'

'I can't be certain, of course, but I'd like to think we told each other everything. We were quite a close couple. I-I don't know what to think.'

Allie took a moment before she broke the woman's heart. 'Lauren, it's too early to tell for sure, but we believe Nick didn't take his own life.'

Both Lauren and Tia's eyes shot up to meet hers, alarm and confusion visible.

'What do you mean?' Lauren wanted to know. 'I don't understand.'

'There are bruises appearing around his neck which may suggest asphyxiation. Whoever might have done that has set the scene to look as if Nick was the one responsible. But bruising continues to develop after death, you see. They're coming out prominently now. I'm so sorry.'

'You mean someone did that to him?' Tia burst into tears again.

Lauren held her in her arms while she did the same.

Allie had to glance away for a moment, the scene too intense. But she had a job to do.

'I'm still not sure I understand,' Lauren said, once she'd composed herself a little. 'I mean, how did anyone get in without breaking a window or damaging a door?'

'We're investigating that. I have to ask more awkward questions now – of you both,' she said. 'I need to know where you've been today so I can –'

'You think one of us killed Nick?' Lauren gasped. 'How could you say that? We loved him.'

'I'm sorry to be intrusive, but we have to find out who did this to your husband, and doing that involves some things that may feel unpleasant. Lauren, you were at work, I believe?'

'Yes, I should have been there until nine. I'm a supervisor at Tesco, the Hanley store. My shift started at midday.'

'Thank you. And Tia, you were at school?'

Tia nodded.

'Did you go anywhere afterwards?'

'No, I came straight home.' She dipped her eyes momentarily.

Allie wondered why.

'Did you see anyone outside, or nearby when you got here?'

Another shake of the head.

It was a long shot. Allie doubted the killer would have hung around, but neighbours may have spotted someone recently, perhaps even watching from a car. It had happened before and was likely to happen again.

Lots of unanswered questions that would come out in the wash.

When she had asked all she could, Allie concluded the interview. 'Your home is a crime scene at the moment,' she told Lauren. 'We'll be as quick as we possibly can, but we will need to move you out for a while. Is there anyone you can stay with? Family, friends? If not, we can arrange for a hotel.'

'I can ring my sister, Yvonne. She only lives a few minutes away. She'll come to pick us up. I have to tell her anyway.'

'There's no need. I can let her know and then take you to her.' Allie gave a faint smile. 'Can I gather a few things for you both?'

'Can't I do that?'

'I'd rather you didn't because of the body being in the bedroom. I'll gather you enough for overnight. Is there anything in particular you'll need?'

As Lauren rifled off a list and where to find everything, Allie gave a subtle nod to Perry to leave. He could get the bag ready while she finished off here.

'I want you to know, Lauren, Tia,' Allie spoke to both in turn, 'that we will be working non-stop on this case to find out who did this to your husband.'

Lauren couldn't speak. Allie empathised, flashing a faint smile. But she hadn't finished yet.

CHAPTER FIFTEEN

JAMIE SANDERSON – AGED 16

At the police station, Jamie was processed and then put in a cell. His mum had to wait in another room until it was time for him to be interviewed.

It was the first time Jamie had been inside a police station, never mind been arrested. He'd watched so many TV dramas that he'd thought he'd be familiar with it, but in reality it was much worse.

When the door banged closed behind him, he pulled the blanket he'd been provided with over his head and cried.

When the door opened again, he was led along a corridor and through a further door to another part of the station. The uniformed officer who escorted him was in his early twenties, tall with some impressive tattoos showing on his arms. He was chatty, making Jamie feel at ease, until he was shown into an interview room.

The two detectives from earlier were sitting waiting for him.

Then his mum was brought in. He didn't know then who was more scared, her or him.

'Sit down, Jamie.' One of the officers who had arrested him earlier pointed to the seat opposite him. He then set up a recording and, once he was ready, spoke to Jamie, introducing himself by name as DS Hallam, his colleague DC Townsend.

Jamie's right knee bobbed up and down as he listened, beads of sweat appearing on his forehead. He felt as if he was about to faint, his nerves shattered by the intensity of the situation, the horror of why he was here.

His mum put a hand on his thigh, urging him to sit still.

Jamie glanced at her gratefully. He had to do everything he could not to seem nervous, as if he was hiding something.

'What were you doing two nights ago?' DS Hallam started the questioning with.

'I was out with my friends,' Jamie replied.

'Who would they be?'

'There were a lot of us.' Jamie stalled for a moment, not wanting to give names. But then he thought better of it and told them every one. 'We were messing around in the bus shelter on Moorland Road,' he said afterwards.

'Between what times?'

'I was there about seven and left about nine. I was in the house for half past, wasn't I, Mum?'

'I think so. I was out of it, if I'm honest. I've tried some new sleeping pills, and they really did the trick. I've been suffering from insomnia for the past six months and I –'

'Yes, thanks, Mrs Sanderson.'

'It's Marie.'

He paused for effect, the atmosphere dense with foreboding. 'Thing is, we brought all four of them in this afternoon, and all four said you were involved in the murder of Winston Lowe.'

'Dear Lord.' Marie burst into tears. 'Tell me that's not true, son.'

'It isn't, Mum,' Jamie told her. 'I swear.'

'That's not what they're telling us.' DS Hallam shook his head slowly.

Jamie listened to the detective, who was giving a completely different version to what happened. He cut in several times but wasn't listened to. Instead, the man talked over him.

When he stopped, Jamie managed to give his opinion. 'That's all lies. I didn't stab Winston Lowe. I couldn't do that.'

'They're saying that they didn't go into the shop with you.'

'They did! I was the lookout. Kevin and Nick were going to see what they could steal, but I turned round when I heard noise. I saw Kevin stab Winston, and that's when I went into the shop. You must have found the knife. It would have Kevin's fingerprints on it as well, but I tried to save Winston by getting the knife away from him.'

'We didn't find any of his fingerprints, but we did find yours.'

'That's not right.' Jamie tried to think back. Had Kevin been wearing gloves? He didn't think so. His heart sank at the realisation he had no one on his side, no one to speak out on his behalf. Then he remembered.

'Ask Colette and Michelle. They would know it wasn't me.'

'Again, they're saying it was you. They're all saying that.'

Jamie was shocked by this. Colette was his girlfriend. Surely she wouldn't lie about him.

'But it's wrong!' he said.

'All the evidence is pointing to you. We will be charging you with murder.'

'I didn't do it, I swear.' Jamie was crying by now, scared of what was being implied and its consequences. 'I didn't, Mum. You have to believe me.'

'I believe you, son.' Marie glanced up at the officers. 'Please, he wouldn't do anything like that. He's a good boy.'

'That's what they all say, Mrs Sanderson.' DS Hallam's stare was hard. 'But we have another witness, too. Mrs Lowe, Winston's wife.'

Jamie paled.

'She said there was only you in the shop when she went downstairs to check on Winston after hearing noises.'

'No, I –'

'She said you had the knife in your hand.'

'I didn't!'

'She said she didn't see anyone else and that you ran away when you heard the sirens.'

'I panicked because of how it looked.' Jamie sat forward. 'I went behind the counter to find a phone to call for an ambulance.'

'You went to find the knife to finish off the job.'

'No!'

'Well, how do you explain that she saw no one but you?'

'Because Kevin and Nick had left!'

'I think we'd better stop this,' Marie said. 'My son has a right to a solicitor, and you haven't even asked him if he wants legal representation.'

'I asked him earlier on, and he declined,' DC Townsend spoke.

'You're putting words into my mouth,' Jamie cried. 'You never asked me that.'

'It doesn't matter. It won't help as you've already admitted to his murder.'

'I haven't said anything!'

DS Hallam glanced at the clock on the wall and reached across the table. 'Interview terminated at eighteen-fifteen.' He stopped the recording. 'I think we have everything we need for now.'

Jamie dropped his head into his hands. No one was listening. He was going to prison for something he hadn't done.

This couldn't be happening.

CHAPTER SIXTEEN

'What was Nick like?' Allie continued questioning Lauren after a short break. 'I hope you don't mind me asking, but it's good to know the backgrounds of victims from those closest to them.'

'It sounds cliché, but he was my soulmate. We met in secondary school. I've practically known him all my life. We got married when we were twenty.'

'What did he do for a living?'

'He's a youth leader for a charity, Hilton's Heroes. They work with underprivileged kids and run workshops to help them achieve more, think about what they want to do in the future instead of accepting they'll do nothing good. He was very well respected in the field.'

Allie had heard of the organisation. She commended anyone who'd do that type of role. Even though she spent her time with adults who should know better, teens were hard work. Especially the ones she came across – ones who were being groomed without knowing, used for carrying drugs, lured into sex and so much more. It was great to hear of someone like Nick who had made a difference. She imagined he was going to be a huge loss.

The people he worked with needed to be spoken to as well.

'And were you happy?' she went on. 'I'm sorry I have to ask, but it's –'

'Yes, we were fine.' Lauren rubbed at Tia's back as the young girl's sobs slowed down.

Allie nodded her understanding. 'So no problems as a couple?'

'No. We were so comfortable around each other. I suppose that's because we've been together so long.'

'You never argued?'

'Of course we did. I'd have a right old moan about him to my sister. But it was simply that, letting off steam to someone. We loved each other.'

'So can you think of anything, no matter how small, that may have resulted in his death?'

'No. He was a bit of a tearaway at school, but when he left and got a job, he seemed to grow up. Like most of us do, usually. He enjoyed helping young teens in the city. He was settled with what we had, you know. Happy with me and Tia.' Her eyes brimmed with tears. 'I'm going to miss him so much.'

'And you have no idea who would want to harm him?' Allie posed the questioned again. Sometimes people were more forthcoming once they'd got used to her talking to them.

'Not in the slightest,' Lauren replied.

'It could be someone he knows.'

Lauren looked up with a frown.

'As you know, there was no forced entry to the property, so either Nick let someone in, or someone got in with a key. Did you give a spare to anyone?'

'My sister has one. No one else.'

'Are you close to your sister?'

'Yes. Our parents moved out of Stoke a few years ago. Dad died shortly after. There's only our mum now.'

'I'm sorry to hear that. What about friends?'

'We have a few, but mainly we're always busy. I work shifts and am often called in at short notice to cover, so we ended up using that as an excuse.'

Her questions finished, Allie stood up. 'Thank you for the information. If you remember something I should know, please don't hesitate to contact me.'

Lauren stood up, too. 'Will you excuse me for a moment?' she said before running out of the room.

Lauren locked herself in the downstairs cloakroom. She sat down on the toilet lid, head in her hands, and cried. Gut-wrenching sobs as she wondered how much more she could take. She couldn't even go into the bedroom and lie on the bed. The police and forensics people would be in there for hours yet.

So would Nick.

Even seeing him for a fleeting few minutes was enough for her to keep replaying the image over and over in her mind. Glazed-eyed, the blood dripping from his wrist as the life had seeped out of him. The empty whisky bottle, the glass with its remains. The bloodied knife on the carpet. Now she'd been told his death was suspicious, it all made sense.

Who would do that to him?

There was a knock on the door.

'Lauren, are you okay?' Allie said. 'We need to leave now.'

Lauren wiped her eyes and went to the door. 'I'm not going anywhere,' she told her emphatically. 'So if you have to have someone on watch outside, then fair enough, but I'm staying put.'

'I can't allow that, I'm sorry.' Allie paused. 'I know it feels insensitive for us to ask you to leave, but it's not just for us to gather evidence and find out who did this to your husband. It's so that we can check through every room to see what we can find, try and piece together exactly what happened. That isn't going to be nice for you to see, and the investigation here will go on for hours. I promise we will take care of Nick and move his body as quickly as we can. And Tia will be better away from the home, too.'

'I could stay in the kitchen.' Lauren pleaded. 'I won't get in the way.'

'That won't be possible.'

'Why?'

'It's best if you stay at Yvonne's.'

Shoulders drooping, Lauren accepted the situation. 'Will it only be for tonight?'

'I think so, but I can't be sure. It will depend on what we find.'

Lauren nodded. 'Okay. I'll go and fetch Tia and get it over with.'

'If you don't want to stay with your sister, we will arrange something for you?'

'Oh, I didn't... I meant leaving Nick... upstairs, like that.' She hugged herself.

Allie placed a hand on her arm. 'It may not feel like it as I have a job to do, but I'm here for you. Please reach out if you need to. I am genuinely sorry about Nick, and my team are the best, even if I do say so myself.'

Lauren could see that the detective was trying to make her smile, ease the pain of the situation. It was kind of her to try, but nothing was going to be the same again.

CHAPTER SEVENTEEN

Allie's car pulled up outside Lauren Farrington's sister's address. She lived on the Bennett Estate, on a main drag. The house was small compared to the Farringtons', Allie noted. A semi with enough room for one car on the frontage at the expense of a garden.

Lauren shuddered as she removed her seat belt. 'I'm not sure I want to go back to the house now I've left.'

'I never want to,' Tia was adamant. 'How can we, when we know what's happened in that room?'

Lauren squeezed her daughter's hand. She held on to it tightly while they walked along the path. The front door was opened by a woman Allie didn't need to be told was Lauren's sister. She was her double, a few years older perhaps.

'Lauren, Tia,' the woman cried and burst into tears, hugging them both together.

A younger version of Tia dashed downstairs and joined in the hug, tears streaming down her face. Allie thought she could almost be Tia's twin.

'Can I go with Emily to her room?' Tia asked afterwards, tentatively.

Lauren nodded, and the two girls shot indoors and up the stairs.

Allie introduced herself to Yvonne.

'A family liaison officer will be briefed about the situation in the morning and, if it's okay with you, Mrs Leyland, will be on hand until Lauren and Tia can go home.'

'Yes, of course,' Yvonne agreed. 'I'll help with anything I can.'

'Thank you. For now, it's imperative the forensics team do their job. Evidence will be with us shortly, and we'll be able to move quicker then. I expect we'll know more tomorrow.'

'Will he be... there long?' A sob caught in Lauren's throat. 'At the house, I mean?'

'It'll be a few more hours yet, but the coroner has been informed. Once they can remove his body, he'll be taken to the mortuary. There will need to be a postmortem, to establish the cause of death.'

With her sister's arms still around her, Lauren sobbed. Even though she'd been crying before, it was as if the bulk of it had been held in until that moment. It was obviously a comfort to be with her sister. Allie could understand that, even after so long without Karen.

She tried to block the thoughts from invading her, not let it creep under her skin. She knew it would. She always took her work home, the grief, the pain, the sorrow, the angst. The anger, the questions.

She waited until she felt able to leave them. Afterwards, she drove to the station. It was nearing eight-thirty when she walked across the room to join her team.

'What a day.' Allie's shoulders drooped. 'Two cases coming in so close together is quite a rare thing, thank goodness. Let's hope the people of Stoke sleep sound in their beds tonight and none of them cause anymore mayhem.' She plonked herself down in Frankie's vacant chair. 'Anything come in I should know about?'

'Brian Price seems to have gone to ground once he was picked up on ANPR in Trentham.'

'And we don't think he drove onto the M6?'

'No. We have teams searching the area. There are barriers at Trentham Estates, so he can't hide in there, although the security team are keeping an eye out in case.'

'He could park up anywhere in this city, travel by foot to hide somewhere. But we'll still find him. Especially come morning. I wouldn't be surprised if he handed himself in before that, though.'

'Let's hope so. One less thing to think about.'

Allie yawned. 'One hour, folks, and then we're off for the night. We can't do much until the morning now.' She spotted Frankie coming back. 'Ah, the very man. How do you feel about being lead coordinator on the Shaun Green murder while we look into the two cases that have come in today?'

Frankie's face breaking out into a smile gave her the answer.

'You can start in the morning. I think we all need a bit of beauty sleep.' She yawned again, covering her mouth with her hand.

But Sam smirked when she caught her eye.

'I'll stay for a bit longer, boss. I'm making waves with the socials, seeing what's coming in. There are a lot of people who know Nick Farrington on Facebook – his settings are minimal, so I can lurk. It's going to take a while to sift through, but I'll search through his posts for the past six months for starters and see if I can spot any known names. There's also a page for Hilton's Heroes, too, so I'll cross-reference that as well.'

'I'll sort out the search team, see if there are leads we can follow up tomorrow.' Perry nodded in the direction of their team leader, Malcom Stern, who was walking towards them. 'There's also going to be a lot of trawling to do if anyone has CCTV et cetera.'

Allie waved to Malcolm before sneaking off to her office. If there was anything to tell her, someone would let her know. For now, she wanted a bit of thinking time by herself.

It seemed they would all be late leaving that evening, regardless of her trying to send them home to get some rest. But it was great not having to chivvy them along to work. Detective hours were always long when a murder case came in. They knew it and yet they thrived on the chance to find suspects and charge them with heinous crimes. They were faces to be there for the public to talk with – hopefully easing their concerns rather than being abused for not doing enough. Most people assumed everything could be carried out as quickly as the fictional detective TV shows portrayed. Some tasks were easy to tick off the list. Others had a longer time period to hinder them.

Luckily she had Dave as her secret weapon. He had never let her down yet.

CHAPTER EIGHTEEN

Colette Ryland shot up from her chair the moment she heard her husband, Kevin's, van pull up in front of their house. They had no garage, no drive either, so it was a bonus to get somewhere to park immediately outside the front door. It always meant the difference between Kevin being in a decent mood or a foul one, especially when he had to park a distance away and the weather was bad.

She opened the front door and rushed out to the pavement. Kevin was opening the rear doors to get his coat and bag.

'What's up?' he asked.

Colette couldn't believe he was so calm. 'You mean you haven't heard the news?'

'One of the machines on D run broke down, and I've had my head inside it since dinner time. It's been a bloody nightmare. It's always me who has to sort it out, not that tosser who owns the company. I'm the lackey lad, as usual. One of these days I'll punch his lights out and walk. I swear to –'

'Nick Farrington's been found dead at home this afternoon.'

'Oh no. What happened? I only saw him last month, and he seemed fine.'

'The police are saying there's foul play. They're looking into it as a murder investigation.'

'What?' Kevin's eyes widened in disbelief.

They moved inside. After taking off his coat and boots, Kevin went into the kitchen, grabbed a bottle of lager from the fridge, and joined Colette in the living room. She was sitting on the settee, her face ashen. He flopped down next to her and took a large mouthful.

'What's being said about it?' He reached for the TV remote to turn up the volume. It was already on a news channel, although the ticker tape across the screen wasn't saying Nick's name. 'Do they know how it happened?'

'I've been watching it for an hour. They're reporting the same thing over and over,' Colette explained. 'I suppose they haven't got much evidence yet.'

'What about online?'

'All speculation really. Lots of people saying how well liked he was.'

Kevin huffed.

Colette gasped inwardly. Kevin had always been envious of Nick and how well he'd progressed. Kevin said he hadn't done a day's hard graft in his life. He called Nick's job a namby-pamby office role, pussyfooting around teenagers who couldn't be bothered to get out of bed and get a job.

Yet Nick would always contact him every few months to meet up. Kevin would mostly say he was working until Nick persisted. They'd go out for a drink, and Kevin would return in a foul mood. He'd go on about Nick's new car or his latest holiday. Said he chucked his wealth down his throat, bragging about everything when Colette knew Nick would have done nothing of the sort.

When Nick and Lauren had moved into their latest

home, Colette wouldn't have been surprised if Kevin's skin had turned green. He couldn't understand why he wasn't doing so well; said Nick's parents had obviously helped him out. Colette was sure it was nothing to do with anyone but Nick being such a nice guy. She never said anything, though. Kevin couldn't hold his temper. She wasn't going to be his punch bag.

'When did he die?' Kevin broke into her thoughts.

'They said he'd been found this afternoon. I tried to ring Lauren, but she didn't pick up. I wonder if she's still at the house with the police.' She shuddered. 'Brian has attacked Michelle and gone missing, too. It's been a crazy day.'

Kevin's brow furrowed again. 'Come again?'

'She rang me first thing after he'd been violent towards her last night. I said I'd go round to see her, but I couldn't get in the street for a police cordon. I found out that Brian was seen getting in his car and tearing off like a madman, just before the ambulance came. You remember their neighbour next door? Well, she told me. She got my phone number from the noticeboard in Michelle's kitchen.'

Kevin clearly couldn't get his head around all the information Colette was giving him. After a hard shift, it was no wonder, she realised.

'What happened there, same old, same old?' he asked.

'Probably. Brian was on nights. Came home and beat two barrels of crap out of her. Then he left her, lying on the kitchen floor and covered with blood. She had terrible head injuries, the bastard. The neighbour said it must have been him and that was why she saw him leaving in a hurry. I know he's been using his fists on her lately.'

'Did she tell you that?'

'Michelle did, yeah.' Colette didn't want to say anything to drop herself in it. She told Kevin most things, but Michelle had only confided in her about the abuse she was getting. 'I'll punch his lights out myself if I ever see him again. He's hurt her one time too many.'

'She should have left him years ago. Is she still at the hospital?'

'Yes. I've rung twice, but they won't tell me anything as I'm not family.'

'I want to know more about Nick.' Kevin paused. 'Try Lauren again.'

'I don't think –'

'I'll do it.' Kevin took out his phone and tapped on the screen. A few seconds later, he sighed. 'It's gone to voicemail. Hi Lauren, it's Kev Ryland. I'm so sorry about what's happened. Ring me when you can, yeah? If not, we'll pop over first thing in the morning.'

'She'll have enough to deal with, let alone us visiting,' Colette remarked as he disconnected the call.

'Like I said, he's our mate.' Kevin's hands formed fists. 'What the hell is going on, Col?'

'Do you think –'

'I'm not even going there.'

His tone warned her to stop. She would send another message to Michelle before she went to bed and try Lauren again in the morning.

Because she wanted to know what was going on as much as Kevin.

CHAPTER NINETEEN

JAMIE SANDERSON - AGED 17

Jamie arrived at juvenile detention a nervous wreck. He'd heard tales of borstals and boys coming out of juvie worse than when they'd gone in. But once the evidence came back to say it was Kevin and not him who had killed Winston, he'd be getting out of there. So he wasn't majorly concerned about it at first.

He'd hated it from that first night, but he settled in quite well, even though some of the boys were rough with him. He tried to be friendly with everyone, making the most of a bad situation. He'd always been known for his positive outlook at school.

Yet, it had tested him because he'd had to wait five months before facing a jury. During that time, he'd tried to keep his spirits up, but it got harder every week. There were visits from his mum, but no one else. He'd expected Colette to come, but she hadn't. She'd obviously chosen to forget about him. He wondered who she'd be seeing now. A girl like her wouldn't be on her own for long.

He wasn't happy that she hadn't stood by him. Nor how she'd lied. But she must have had a reason. He'd be able to ask her soon, once he was out. He couldn't wait to see her.

So he was glad to hear that it would all be over soon.

His solicitor was saying he might be best to plead guilty, to get a lesser sentence. But Jamie had refused. Why should he when he hadn't done anything wrong? All he was guilty of was being an idiot for getting involved with Kevin and Nick, that was for sure. They'd set him up to take the rap for their part in things, and now Jamie would be able to have his say.

But in court it all went wrong. The evidence was overwhelmingly against him, the jury shaking their heads and tutting as the case went on. With each day that passed while he sat in the dock waiting to be set free, his faith and confidence dropped. The prosecution were giving a picture of him that wasn't true. They were portraying him as a monster. They were lying about it. And when it was his turn to take the stand and have his say, he'd been tongue-twisted and manipulated into saying things to make him appear guilty.

Seeing Mrs Lowe, sitting with her family, had been the worst part of it all. It had taken him two days to even glance in her direction, and when he had, she'd caught his eye and glared at him. He wanted to tell her how sorry he was, yet he knew that Kevin was still out. He hadn't been charged with anything, and he didn't know why.

But at least his mum had been there to support him.

Once all the evidence had been heard, the jury went out to deliberate. Jamie sat in a side room, thinking about the first thing he'd do when he got back home. He'd have to readjust, maybe get stick off some people who might think he was guilty, but he'd stay calm. He was going to see Kevin and then

Nick to see what had happened, too. He couldn't understand why he was the only one taking any blame.

The jury were back in five hours with a unanimous decision. Jamie had stood up in the dock, his head down, unable to meet anyone's eye. The spokesperson, a man who was old enough to be his granddad, had spoken loud and clear.

Guilty.

'No!' Jamie cried, standing up. 'I didn't do it! I didn't. You have to believe me.'

He was taken down and led back to the holding cells. He sat with his head in his hands. Things had gone from bad to worse. A not-guilty verdict had been the only thing to keep him going since the night he'd been locked up. Now, he wasn't getting out? They'd got it wrong.

It had been hard to deal with now Jamie was looking at life imprisonment when he got sentenced. It also meant he'd be going to an adult prison when he was nineteen. He wasn't cut out for that life. It would ruin him.

But he had no choice.

When he went back to court three weeks later, he was a different Jamie to the one before. He had resigned himself to a life he shouldn't be a part of. No one was listening to him when he said he hadn't killed Winston Lowe.

He was given life with a minimum of eleven years. This time there'd been no emotion from him. He'd accepted no one had believed him, so he wouldn't give anyone the satisfaction of seeing him crack.

But he would bide his time, and once he was out, he was going after Kevin and Nick, Colette and Michelle. That copper, too, Hallam. They had all betrayed him.

After all, he had plenty of time to plan how he would get his revenge.

CHAPTER TWENTY

Allie turned off the car engine, home at last. The hour had morphed into several more as things started to come in as they were about to leave. Malcolm had updated Perry with the search team's findings, but there was nothing of interest yet.

Dave Barnett rang twice to give them his interim findings. He'd logged the evidence from Michelle Price's assault. Both of them were hoping it wouldn't get any more serious by the morning.

He'd also got going with some of the evidence from the home of Nick Farrington. Christian Willhorn had told him he was doing the postmortem and would have his initial report ready by breakfast.

'I'll have to do a lot of grovelling when I next see you both,' Allie had told him.

'Cakes will do.' Dave chuckled down the line.

'Ah, I can't make cupcakes like your beloved wife, Dave. I'm not sure you'd enjoy shop-bought ones, which is my only option.'

'Any cake will do, but don't tell her indoors.'

Having two serious cases within one day obviously made double the work for Allie and her team, and with an outstanding murder to solve, too, they would be pushed. For now, she wanted to be sure to follow up on every lead, to make sure they missed nothing.

Dave would have his work cut out, although she knew he'd always try and rush their urgent stuff through. He was such an asset to her wider team of professionals, and she was glad they got on so well.

Calling in favours, which meant he had to work long hours, too, was another key element. Hopefully he would have more for them first thing in the morning – which was today, actually. Will, too.

Now it was nearly midnight, and the street she lived in was silent. Most people would be in bed or getting ready to retire for the night, and she hadn't even seen her family. Both Mark and Poppy would no doubt be in deep sleeps, so she'd need to creep in.

She let herself into the house quietly, the hall light illuminating the way for Dexter as he came padding towards her.

'Hey, bud,' she greeted, another yawn overtaking her. But even though she was worn out, she needed something to eat. A bowl of cereal would suffice, along with a mug of tea. She hadn't eaten anything since four p.m., and that wasn't anything substantial.

She let Dexter out in the garden and got together her meal and drink. She sat down at the kitchen table, rubbing at her neck to ease its stiffness. A fifteen-hour day would do that to you.

Dexter came in, ball in mouth. He dropped it at her feet, wagging his tail in anticipation of playtime.

'Not right now, Dex,' she whispered. 'Can't make a noise. Don't want to wake anyone now, do we?'

Despite the dog going back to his basket, there was movement from upstairs. A flush of the toilet, footsteps on the stairs. Mark appeared in the doorway, hair dishevelled, yawning as she had done minutes earlier.

'Sorry, I tried to be quiet,' she said with a grimace.

'I heard your car. You know I can't sleep until you're home.'

She smiled. 'How's Poppy?'

'She's good. She has a part in the school play. Well, they're doing several musicals and films rolled into one. It took me all my time *not* to roll my eyes. I bet you'll have a case on then, so I have to sit through it all.'

'You love it really,' she teased. 'What does she have to do?'

'She's going to be Mary Poppins. I hope she doesn't ask me to spell supercalifragilisticexpialidocious.'

'God, no. I have a hard job with some of her spelling tests at the moment!'

Her cereal all but gone, she watched Mark switching the kettle on.

'Might as well have a brew while I'm here.' He took out a mug, placed a tea bag in it. 'How are things? You haven't had two cases in one day for a long time.'

'I'm glad of that, because double the work means I am bushed. I'm getting too old for it.'

They shared a mutual smile, both knowing that no matter how tired she was, she would be up early again to continue.

She loved her job, even the long hours when a case came in, the thrill of the chase, so to speak. Justice getting done for bereaved families. Heading a team that did most of the legwork was a privilege no matter what.

'I don't think you'll be retiring any time soon. Look at you.' Mark pulled out a chair and sat across from her. 'You might feel knackered but you're positively glowing.'

'It's adrenaline,' she teased. 'Or maybe a hot flush due to hormones.'

'So romantic.'

Allie snorted. 'How's work with you?'

'Same old, same old. Barry has gone.'

'No way!'

Barry Hargreaves was Mark's nemesis. Mark had been snubbed a few times for certain roles, that he could do better in his sleep, due to Barry being the son-in-law of the boss.

'Seems like karma bit him on the arse at last.' Mark raised his mug in salutation. 'He's been living on the edge for a while now. No one can take the piss as much as he does. Just because he's family, he never gets strung up for anything.

'Anyway, he was in the meeting room when I popped in this morning, and when he came out, he slammed the door so hard we all thought the glass was going to break. His face was beetroot with rage. It was quite the sight.' Mark grinned. 'Like I say, karma.'

'Well, maybe things will get easier now he's not there to carry anymore.' Allie tried to hide a yawn behind her hand. 'I'd best get to bed.'

'I take it that's not a proposition?'

'It's definitely not.'

'Shame. The table is clear, and Poppy is asleep.'

'As much as I admire your stamina, old man, and your humour,' Allie teased, 'it's still a no.'

CHAPTER TWENTY-ONE

FRIDAY

Early next morning, Allie was in the briefing room with her team and a group of uniformed officers who had been seconded to help out.

'Okay, listen up, everyone.' She clapped for attention. 'It was a busy day yesterday with a serious assault and a murder. Firstly, let's get up to speed with Michelle Price.' Allie went through what they knew so far. 'Anything on Brian Price's whereabouts, Sam?'

'Nothing.' Sam shook her head.

'I'll be heading to the hospital after this briefing. Until we've spoken to Michelle, we'll be none the wiser where he might be. He's twenty-four hours ahead of us regardless.'

'He must have heard the news that she's still alive, if he thought she wasn't?' Frankie queried. 'It was reported from lunchtime yesterday.'

'Either way, there's an officer stationed outside her room

in case he comes to finish what he started. But for now, I hope he stays away.' Allie checked her notes. 'Last night we had a male deceased at home, Nick Farrington. Wife's name is Lauren. Their daughter, sixteen-year-old Tia, found him. Lauren was at work, so her alibi should be easy to check out, and Tia was at school, so someone needs to make sure of that. Also, while I think about it, Lauren's sister, Yvonne, who they've gone to stay with, has a spare key, so we need to check her whereabouts and rule her in or out.

'When Perry and I attended, at first it looked to be no more than a suicide. A man in his early forties had slashed a wrist after downing half a bottle of Jack Daniel's, and a fair dose of codeine pills were missing from a bottle.

'On further investigation, it became suspicious when bruising appeared around his neck which seemed conclusive with strangulation. So the whole thing was set up. What we need to figure out is who killed him, why, and then why a staged death.'

'Maybe someone didn't think his bruising would come out after death,' Sam said. 'So perhaps an amateur.'

'It's a possibility. Will is checking for booze, narcotics or painkillers, or anything else in his system. We'll know more after the PM, which he assured me would be here first thing.'

Allie scanned her emails. 'Ah, here we go. Initial findings briefly are death by asphyxiation. Wound on his wrist was more than likely done after death. Toxicology shows no signs of anything in his system. Hmm… so why were the pills missing?'

Allie glanced at her notes next. 'When the house was searched, a note was found under the duvet. It simply said, "I LIED."' Now we know Farrington's death wasn't by suicide, what is our killer wanting to tell us when he left it?'

They brainstormed a little more, and then Allie turned to Frankie for an update on Shaun Green.

'Forensics have found blue fibres on Shaun's jacket,' he told them. 'No traces of anyone else's blood but his. The stab wound punctured his stomach.'

'God, that's tough. I believe stomach wounds can be the most slow and painful way to die.' Allie shuddered at the thought.

'I've spoken to his wife again, and his work colleagues,' Frankie went on. 'No further information from any of them. There's no more evidence to report on at the crime scene. A few shoe prints in the mud for a size ten foot which we knew already. Neighbours are angry about it, you know, the usual. Not expecting it to happen on their doorstep bollocks.'

'Good work, keep at it for now.' Allie rounded up the meeting then. 'Let's crack on and have a good day. And stay safe out there, people.'

CHAPTER TWENTY-TWO

JAMIE SANDERSON – AGED 19

For the two and a half years Jamie had been in juvenile detention, he'd kept his head down. He'd got on well with most of the other boys, occasionally getting into scraps which were never of his doing. But he'd survived quite well, considering.

Male prison was a totally different beast.

For starters, the men were of all ages. Most were rougher. There were so many who tried to get him to be part of their gangs, but he wanted to be alone.

When he'd been in juvie, he'd long ago stopped telling anyone who would listen that he was innocent. No one believed him. No one wanted to listen. They accused him of whining.

So when they heard what he was in for, most gave him respect and never questioned him. In the end, Jamie went along with it, often using it to his advantage. He hated doing it, but it was for survival reasons only.

Yet, it began to backfire as there was always someone waiting to prove him wrong, make out he wasn't the hard nut he thought he was. And it happened every time new inmates came onto the wing.

Jamie was tired of it yet had no choice but to knuckle down and get through it. At least his life would begin again once he got out, not like Winston Lowe.

He often thought of Winston and his family, what it would have been like for them to lose a man like him, being the breadwinner and life and soul, no doubt.

But he thought more about his so-called mates and how they'd betrayed him. It ate at him every day he was inside. Why was it that Kevin Ryland and Nick Farrington had not been charged with anything? Why hadn't either of them come to visit him? Or Colette, or Michelle? It didn't make sense. He didn't have a friend to his name. Not here, or outside.

It was when Shaun Green arrived that everything began to get worse. Even though he was from Stoke, Shaun had it in for Jamie the moment they met. In no time at all, he became the wing's golden boy. The one inmates went to about everything. The one who found out information from the wing and had special treatment from the governor for letting him know about it.

Shaun was nothing more than a grass, but he didn't see it that way. Neither did his cronies, or else they were too afraid to say anything. Of course, Jamie would never join in with anything, so he knew it was only a matter of time before he'd be singled out.

It was school bully tactics. Not letting him sit in an empty chair or telling him to move from one so Shaun could lounge in it. Saying he wasn't welcome to play pool or rapping the cue across his hands when he was about to take a shot.

Jamie often went to his cell to get away from it. But it was when he was ambushed in there, and took a beating from Shaun while two others watched the door, that he saw red. He needed to do something about the situation.

He was sitting in the canteen when Shaun next had a go at him.

Shaun plonked himself down on the bench opposite Jamie. 'You happy with that shit you're eating?' He pointed to it.

'It's okay.'

Shaun dipped his finger into the middle of Jamie's scrambled eggs and stirred them around his plate. Then he hawked loudly and spat in the food.

Jamie put down his knife and fork and stood up.

'Aren't you going to eat that?' Shaun wanted to know.

'No, I'm not.'

'I think you are. Sit down again.'

Jamie stayed where he was, and a competition of wills began.

'I told you to fucking sit down,' Shaun spoke through gritted teeth.

Jamie didn't move, staring long and hard at him. But when Shaun reached across to grab his plate, Jamie anticipated what he was going to do.

He turned the tables and shoved the eggs into Shaun's face, hitting him hard with the plate.

Shaun was caught off guard, and for a moment, the room went quiet. The plate clattered to the table, and Shaun wiped his face with the sleeve of his sweatshirt.

'You're fucking dead.' He rushed forward, jumping the table with fists flying.

Jamie dodged the first one, and the second, and landed a

punch of his own in Shaun's gut. Then he pummelled Shaun to the floor.

The men around jeered, urging him on while the prison wardens stood and watched. Jamie hit out again and again. By the time two of them decided to make their way over to split things up, Jamie was being pulled from Shaun by an inmate who was sure he wouldn't stop until he'd done some serious damage.

Jamie didn't want to stop.

All that pent-up anger which had festered over the years finally exploded. He was tired of living a lie. He was sick of being told what to do. Being bullied by men who were nothing, when all he wanted was a quiet life. He had a lot of years to serve yet, and he knew more men like Shaun would come along to try and spoil things for him.

He had to start doing things on his own terms. That didn't mean keeping quiet, getting on with things and not complaining. It meant retaliating.

A new Jamie emerged that day. And Jamie found he quite liked him.

From that moment, the majority of the bullying stopped. Sometimes things were awkward between them. There was a lot of name-calling from Shaun, resulting in the odd scuffle, but for the main, they kept away from each other.

Jamie was determined to survive his sentence, keep his head down, and get out. He hardened up, both mentally and physically.

No one was ever going to walk over him again.

CHAPTER TWENTY-THREE

While Sam continued manning the inquiry, gathering evidence and logging it all as it came in, Perry went off to visit the mortuary with the Farrington women. Jenny had been on to Allie about press releases, and a conference was being held that afternoon with details of the murder investigation.

For now, Allie decided to take Frankie with her to the hospital to see if Michelle Price was able to tell them anything more. Allie had rung earlier but hadn't been able to get through. With the staff so busy nowadays, it was often easier to make a visit while they were out.

Depending on traffic, it would take them anywhere from fifteen minutes to half an hour. She hoped for the former.

'What's with the soppy smile?' she asked Frankie, once they were seated in the car.

'Happy, that's all.'

She stared at him until he relented.

'We're trying for another baby.'

'That's great news! I hope you haven't jinxed it now.'

'I don't care. We're enjoying the practicing.'

'Too much information!' Allie smiled.

They dealt with so many lives cut short in their line of work, so it was extra nice to hear about plans for the future.

'Sorry, I'm excited. Actually, Isla is pregnant – only six weeks, so we're not telling anyone yet. But as you can see, I'm having trouble keeping it to myself!'

'Ah, that is wonderful,' Allie chimed. 'Congratulations. I am so pleased for you both.'

The baby talk continued until they were in Hartshill. At the Royal Stoke, they managed to find a parking space in double time, shooting into one that just about accommodated a car.

'We need the emergency ward,' she told him after she'd paid for a ticket.

They made their way into the building and up to the first floor. At the nurse's desk, they showed their warrant cards and explained why they were there. They were told to take a seat.

'Doesn't seem good that they're not taking us through straightaway,' Allie said after they'd been there for a few minutes. 'Might grab a cup of hot chocolate from the vending machine. Want one?'

'I'd love one, please.'

She stood up, but a nurse came walking over.

'Sod's law,' she muttered to Frankie.

'Detectives.' The man nodded a greeting. At a guess, he was in his late twenties, dark-skinned, with a razor-sharp goatee and a thick head of black hair. His smile lifted the atmosphere in the gloomy corridor. 'I believe you're after an update on Michelle Price.'

'Yes, please.'

'She's doing well, considering. Do you have a suspect?'

'At large for now. Will she be able to talk to us, so we can establish what happened to her?'

'I think so. Her vitals are improving by the hour now. I suggest you check back either late this afternoon or first thing in the morning. She's still under observation, but she's definitely on the mend.'

Allie tried not to show her disappointment. It was good that Michelle was getting better, but she desperately wanted to talk to her, to see where Brian might have gone to ground after the attack. Find out what brought it on, if it had happened before. She also needed to see if Michelle was capable of fighting back, not literally, but in the sense that Brian would be found and arrested if necessary.

As they returned to the car, Allie's phone rang. It was Perry.

'I had an interesting chat with Tia when her mum popped to the loo,' he told her. 'She admitted that she wasn't at school yesterday. She took the day off to spend with her boyfriend.'

'Ah, so at least she has an alibi. We'll need to check it out with him.'

'It's Troy Menzies.'

'What on earth is she doing with that dipstick?' Allie couldn't help herself.

He was one of the known mules on the Bennett Estate.

'Yeah, my thoughts, too, and I managed to keep them to myself. She was more worried about her mum finding out. But we'll have to tell her, right?'

'Well, technically we could leave it be if it checks out. But seeing as it's one of our friendly neighbourhood drug dealers, I think a quiet word is needed, at the right time. And you're taking them back to her sister's?'

'I think so. Should I check to see if the property is clear for her to return beforehand?'

'No, let them go to Yvonne's. I'll take a trip to Tunstall

and see if Troy is home. Having a day off, my arse. He hasn't done a legal day's work in his life.'

'Love's young dream.' Perry laughed. 'I think she can do far better than him, though.'

'Who are we to say who we fall in love with?' Allie was at the car now. 'Head back to the station, and I'll catch you in about an hour.'

Arriving at the Bennett Estate twenty minutes later, Allie pulled up and stopped the engine once more. 'I won't be a minute. I need a quick word with Mr Menzies. I'll shout if I need you.' She pointed to the phone in his hand. 'Ring Lyla and see how she is.'

There was that big smile again. Allie couldn't help but return it.

Allie banged on Troy's front door, hoping he wouldn't recognise her copper's knock. She glanced around at the state of the garden while she waited. A pile of soggy cardboard boxes with a car tyre slung on top of them stood in the far corner. The hedges and grass needed a good trim, and the mountain of black rubbish bags next to the bin seemed as if they'd been there forever.

She was about to knock again when the door opened.

When Troy saw it was her, he smirked and took a stance with an arm above his head while he crossed his feet at his ankles.

'What do you want?' he asked when she'd done nothing but glare at him.

'I'm taking in how ugly your face is and yet how it's going to get a lot worse if I start telling tales on you.'

'Come again.'

'You and Tia Farrington. She's a minor.'

'She's sixteen, and believe me, all woman.' He licked his lips suggestively.

Allie held in her disgust. 'She's still at school. It won't look good, especially if I let it be known that you're grooming her.'

He frowned, his arms dropping to his sides. 'I'm not a paedo. I don't do that sort of thing.'

'So you're not buying her gifts to encourage her to work for you?'

'I'm not a pimp either,' he protested.

'Whatever.' Allie held up a hand. 'All I'm saying is keep away from her.'

'You can't make me.'

'Else I'll be doing some damage limitation of my own.'

'You can't do that.'

'I can, and I will. I'm sure some of the regulars in the pub will be furious if they find out you're messing around with a young girl. You know how much this estate hates paedos.'

'I am not a –'

She shrugged. 'How am I supposed to know what you are, or you aren't, when you're giving off the vibe?' She turned to go and then stopped. 'Her dad has been killed, and the last thing she wants is to become infatuated with you. So stay away or else I'll start some rumours around the estate.'

'People know I don't do that sort of thing.' He stood defiantly now he realised she was leaving.

'Mud sticks, my friend,' Allie taunted.

She did leave this time, chortling to herself at the cursing that was going on. Allie called that a friendly warning. The next time she wouldn't be so calm. She'd haul him in for questioning about something or other, and make sure everyone knew about it.

CHAPTER TWENTY-FOUR

After the press conference she'd attended with Jenny, Allie left the room behind her. Still questions were being fired at Jenny. Why did they think she was going to say anything more when she'd told them she wouldn't?

Still, at least she'd got away with Will Lawrence from *Staffordshire News* getting on her case as he hadn't been there. His remarks could be quite cutting at times, always taking a pessimistic overview of them not catching who they were after. Well, tough luck, Will, she mused. Not today.

Once she was in the corridor, a message came into her phone. She glanced at the screen to see it was Simon Cole. He'd been in the room on the front row.

Quick coffee? I have some information for you.
Ten minutes? Usual place.
See you there.

Allie glanced at the clock on the wall. Quarter to midday. Close enough to lunchtime, she might as well take the opportunity to grab lunch while she was out.

At the coffee shop in Piccadilly, Simon was sitting down when she went past the large window that overlooked the pedestrianised walkway. She grinned when he pointed to two mugs already in his possession.

Inside, she made her way past the long counter with its small queue of customers, squeezed through the mother-and-baby group who had commandeered three tables and most of the aisles, and back to where Simon was thankfully in a corner by himself. It was bound to get busier soon, but for now, they were free to chat without fear of anyone overhearing them.

'I wasn't sure how long you could stay or else I'd have nabbed a couple of wraps for us,' he said as she got to him.

'I have time to eat.' Allie smiled, sitting down opposite him and removing her coat. 'Well, I'm making it, because a woman can't survive the day on caffeine alone. Do you have time?'

'Definitely.'

They perused the menu and gave their orders.

Allie removed the cutlery from the napkin wrapped around it. 'So, what is it you wanted to see me about?'

'I needed you away from the baying mob, especially Will. But he wasn't there today. He must be on leave.'

'Probably, but I'm not complaining. Things are so much nicer when he isn't around. Anyway, I digress. I received this earlier, from our post. It's been in a few hands until it got to me. But it was hand-delivered.'

'Is it evidence?'

Simon grimaced. 'I don't know. It came first thing, but I didn't clear my in-tray until ten-thirty. So I brought it with me rather than call you.'

Allie got out a pair of latex gloves and popped them on. She then took the envelope from him and pulled out a sheet of paper. The words written by hand were in capital letters.

WORKING FOR THE ENEMY IS NOT A WISE THING TO DO.

Allie's eyes widened. Simon knew that earlier in the year there had been a few timely things happening to her team. Allie trusted him enough to share the details because she knew he would keep them to himself. Plus she was worried whoever it was might come after other people close to the team, too. Her theory had been right.

'Shit, Simon. That means whoever is playing with us is doing the same with you. Unless you have other ideas who it might be?'

Simon huffed. 'In my line of work, it could be anyone, the same as you. I thought I'd show it to you so that you'd know what to do about it. I haven't told anyone at work.'

'I'm not sure if that's wise. They might want to do a risk assessment on the kind of jobs you report on.' When he went to protest, she held up a hand. 'I know it's not ideal. I hate getting babysat, too, but your safety is far more important than your pride. And you have Grace to think about. She's police, too.'

'I haven't thought about anything else since I got it.'

'I'll send it to forensics and see if they can get anything.'

'Do you think it's connected to all that crap you had a few months ago on the Katy Frost case?'

'It's possible.' Allie didn't want to be reminded of that. She didn't want to think of either her or her team in danger. 'I'm assuming now you've shown me, you want to take this further?'

Simon shook his head. 'I don't *want* to, but I feel I need to. I'd never forgive myself if anything happened to Grace.'

Allie nodded, immediately recalling one of her cases that

Simon had worked on with her team. She'd been kidnapped and bundled in the back of a van. It was only when she got away that she realised the man was going after Mark. Luckily, he hadn't managed to do anything to him. But it had been the scariest few hours of her life. So she sensed how Simon would be feeling. She needed to put his mind at rest.

Having said that, Simon had been beaten badly during one of Grace's murder cases. He'd been given a warning of the brutal kind. So maybe he was fearful because of those memories, too.

'Let me take this, show it to Jenny, and then at least we can put a plan in action, or think ahead if anyone is going to come after us. I can't be sure these threats aren't real when they involve you as well. For all we know, it's an idiot out there trying to scare us without wanting to inflict any real harm. But equally, there could be someone who's planning something big.'

'Scary stuff.' Simon shuddered.

'I'll get someone to take a look at your CCTV footage. See if the person who delivered it can be ID'd. I doubt it will be that simple, but if so, we can bring them in for a chat.' Allie reread the note before popping it back in the envelope and then pulled off her gloves with a snap. 'I think you need to tell work, to cover yourself.'

It was Simon's turn to sigh. 'I think you're right.'

CHAPTER TWENTY-FIVE

JAMIE SANDERSON – AGED 21

Jamie walked into the visitors' room, waving when he caught sight of his mum. His smile faltered a little while he tried to keep his features neutral of anything other than happiness. Marie was so pale. She'd lost weight since her last visit, and that had only been two weeks ago. She was in her early forties and yet she looked like death warmed up.

'Jamie, lad. How are you, duck?' Marie held her arms out for him.

'I'm good, Mum.' He gave her a quick hug before sitting down across from her at the small table. Now he was closer, he could tell there was something wrong. 'Are you all right?'

'Nothing a couple of nights' sleep wouldn't put right, son.' Marie laughed, although it didn't reach her eyes. 'I'm finding my tablets aren't doing their job nowadays, which in turn affects my rhythm for a few days.'

Jamie sensed she wasn't telling him everything but didn't

pry anymore. Instead he asked about their dog, Freddie, who was getting on for twelve years old now. His thoughts went into overdrive before she'd had time to reply. 'Is Freddie okay?'

'He's fine and dandy.' Marie smiled. 'He keeps me on my toes, although he's not enjoying the longer walks anymore. His legs are playing up a bit. Old age, comes to us all.'

'Hark at you,' Jamie protested. 'You're barely in your forties.'

Marie said nothing, so he filled in the silence, asking questions she could answer. About her job (she was sick of shift work), about the neighbour next door who had bought an electric guitar (thankfully he's got fed up of it quickly, hardly uses it at all now), and whether people were still talking about what he was supposed to have done (it's been five years, son. You're old news.).

Still, Jamie waited apprehensively for her to tell him what was on her mind. It came with ten minutes to go before visiting time was over. She reached across the table and covered his hands with her own.

'Son, I have something to tell you.'

He watched as her eyes filled with tears. 'You're getting married to that idiot, aren't you?' He joked because he didn't want to hear anything bad. 'I knew it.'

'Mike Kent?' Marie laughed it off. 'Don't be daft. He's not for me.'

'Then what is it?'

'I...' She squeezed his hands. 'There's no way to tell you this, but I have... cancer.'

Her words played around in his head until he could ignore them no more. 'Cancer? Where?'

She pointed at her chest. 'I found a lump, before my last visit. I didn't tell you then because I was waiting for tests, but when I got back home, there was a message from the doctor's surgery. I had to go straight to A and E for tests and then to the cancer centre the next day.'

'But they found it quick enough, right?' Jamie squeezed her hands this time. 'You can have chemo, or whatever it is they need to do?'

Marie shook her head. 'It's too late. It's spread to my bones. I wasn't even unwell, so there were no signs for me to worry about.'

'But there are lots of new drugs on the market nowadays. They can try things, can't they?'

She said nothing, tears welling.

Jamie wanted to ask her, desperately needed to know, but he couldn't say the words. But Marie obviously knew what he was thinking.

'Six months, son. It could be longer, it could be less. No one will know for sure. I suppose it depends on my body.'

'No, this can't be happening.' Jamie's eyes were teary now. 'I can't do time while you're... dying.'

'I prefer not to be pampered, you know that.'

Her tone was jovial, but he didn't see the fun.

'This isn't pampering!' He lowered his voice because people started to look their way. 'You need someone to take care of you, Mum.'

'Fiona from next door but one said she'd help me out. Her husband, you remember Trevor from the garage down the road? Well, she married him two years ago, and they've been so kind to me while I've been on my own. And Shona next door says she'll help with shopping and cleaning. Margaret, you know, from number seven. She's been an angel and says she'll accompany me to as many appointments as she can. It's so nice of everyone.'

'It should be me.' Jamie's teeth were gritted now, emotions pouring out of him that he struggled to keep under control. '*I* should be taking care of you.'

'I know it's hard for you, son. But I'll be okay, honestly.'

'I won't have any time to be with you because I'm stuck in here!'

'Don't worry about me. Just keep your head down and get out as soon as you can. That's all I want you to think about now.'

'How can I when I want to be with you?'

That night, alone in his cell, Jamie broke down. The years had been cruel to his mum. First his dad left with no warning. Then she got ill with depression and anxiety. It must have given her many sleepless nights since he'd been sent down, too, and now this. What had she done to deserve such a life? Not to be able to reach the age of forty-five?

He lay on the top bunk in his cell, alone due to his last inmate going home. He wanted to scream out in frustration. He wanted to bang on the cell door, keep everyone else awake for a change, as he thought about a world without his mum.

Even though he couldn't be with her regardless, there was always the thought of her waiting for him when his sentence was over. He had family, a home to return to. Now, he wouldn't have either.

He buried his head under the blanket. At least he could cry without trying not to be heard.

Life was so cruel and yet, it could have been so different if it wasn't for his past mistakes.

CHAPTER TWENTY-SIX

After a quick bite to eat, Perry and Frankie went to Nick Farrington's workplace. It was only a few minutes on foot for them as his base was in Stafford Street. They walked up Piccadilly, chatting about the cases they were working on.

A man worse for wear sidled over to them asking for spare change, but they politely refused. Perry sighed. It was getting much too often for his liking, but the area was set out for people to sit around. It wasn't, however, made for the druggies of the city to harass the general public.

It wasn't even a wise idea to make a mental note for a PC to patrol the area as it was a full-time job. Still, he'd got away with any aggro today. Mainly he used his warrant card as a deterrent if necessary.

The offices of Hilton's Heroes were on floor one, over a KFC takeaway. Perry was glad he'd eaten or else he'd be diving in there. He was quite partial to their chicken burgers.

'If I worked in this building, I'd be downstairs far more than I should for something to eat,' Frankie said, pushing on the door to take them to the stairs.

'I was thinking the same thing. Maybe because it's so near, it's not used as much by the staff up here, though.'

'Perhaps. Mind, I'd never get fed up of a pint if I was near a pub.'

'Yeah, you would.' Perry pulled himself up by the banister as the stairs rounded a corner. 'How often do we go into Chimneys nowadays?'

Chimneys was the pub a stone's throw from the station.

'Ah, that's an age thing.' Frankie chuckled. 'Can't take your drink more like.'

Their banter came to a halt when they found themselves in a reception area. A woman behind a desk gave a welcoming smile. This time Perry did show his warrant card.

The woman's face dropped, and she became a little teary. 'It's so hard to believe. I was only talking to Nick on the same afternoon. He was looking forward to watching the football match that evening.' She reached for the phone. 'I'll get someone to you. I won't be a moment.'

Frankie and Perry chatted to her while they waited, gleaning more information about Nick Farrington. The woman didn't have a bad word to say about him. He was a team player, positive, bubbly. A great mentor for the teens who used the service.

'He's going to be a huge loss.' She finished when she saw a woman coming towards them. 'This is – was – his line manager.'

Perry waited for the other woman to join them. They were shown into a side room where she spoke about him in the same manner as the receptionist.

After a few minutes of the usual questions to see if she knew anyone who might harm him, or if anyone had a grievance about Nick lately, he asked if he could speak to a few of the service users. She took them through to a room where there were several males. They were sitting huddled together, long faces and unhappy demeanours.

'You take the ones next to the coffee machine,' Perry told Frankie, 'and I'll speak to the guys over by the pool table.'

As Frankie made his way to the group, Perry introduced himself to the two lads. They were in their mid-teens, casually dressed but had at least made an effort to wear clean gear. Neither of them stepped away when he said he was police, which was a good start. They told him their names – Charlie, and a nickname in the case of Spud. Perry assumed this was because of the shape of his head, accentuated by his close-cropped hair.

They surprised him by talking about Nick Farrington with a fondness similar to the receptionist.

'He was sound,' Charlie said, shaking his head. 'I can't believe he's dead. Do you have anyone for it yet?'

'We're working on it,' Perry told them. 'Which is why we're here today. We're putting together a picture of Nick to see if we can figure out why this has happened to him. It seems people have a genuine respect for him, so we wanted to know if there was anything you could tell us, anything out of the ordinary, that happened recently. Had Nick upset anyone, for instance?'

'Not that I know, although I don't come every day.' Spud took his phone from his pocket when it beeped and then put it back again after reading whatever was on the screen. 'He was so likeable, trying to include us in things, you know? He was keen to get us talking, always there to listen. Not that I ever told him anything.'

'Do either of you know Troy Menzies?' It was worth a shot, Perry thought, especially as he was secretly dating Nick's daughter.

Spud shook his head.

Charlie nodded. 'I saw him in here a couple of times last week.'

'Can you recall what days?' Perry took out his notebook.

'I don't really want to get involved.'

'I won't need to use your name. I'm curious to see if he's known to Nick, that's all. Did they speak to each other, did you notice?'

Charlie shrugged. 'Nick only spoke to him as much as he did anyone. Troy did ask me about Nick, though.'

'Oh?'

'He wanted to know where he lived and bragged about dating his daughter, Tia.' Charlie smirked. 'I think he was lying about that. Because if so, he was punching way above his weight. Tia is gorgeous.'

'She's also still at school.' Spud grimaced. 'He's older than her, too.'

'But you don't know of any animosity between the two men?' Perry reigned them in before the conversation went too off course.

'No, like I said, Nick got on with most people. I didn't see anything wrong.'

Frankie came across to them, a slight shake of the head telling Perry he hadn't learned anything of significance either. He thanked the lads, and they went out into the corridor.

'Get anything useful?' Frankie asked. 'My lads thought a lot of him.'

'Same here. I did find out that Troy Menzies has been hanging around. I wonder if he scouts here for runners. He can be very friendly and persuasive until he gets you under his thumb.'

'Or maybe he was rubbing Nick's nose in the fact he was dating his daughter without his knowledge?'

'I'll bear that in mind.' Perry pointed along the corridor.

'It doesn't seem as if anyone had a grudge against him or threatened him in any way. Let's split up and do a few of his work colleagues, and if we get the same answers, we can call it a day.'

CHAPTER TWENTY-SEVEN

Allie had got back from lunch with Simon when she took a phone call from the Royal Stoke. 'That was the hospital,' she told Sam. 'Michelle Price is able to speak to us.' She checked the clock on the wall. 'I'll head up there now.'

In the car, Allie blasted out The Jam. It always served to put her in a good mood, remove the gloominess she often got at this stage in a case. Not enough happening, leads going dry, evidence still being fast tracked. So a dose of 'Going Underground' was called for.

She got out of her car, paid for parking again, and went into the building. It was quieter now, the earlier rush of the day easing. Visiting hours were almost over as she made herself known. At the ward, she was shown through to a side room.

Michelle was lying in bed, her eyes closed. There was bruising to her face, a bandage covering most of her blonde hair. She had a couple of broken fingernails on the hand sticking out from beneath her bandaged arm, several plasters on small cuts, too. Defence wounds, Allie supposed.

'Michelle?' she said softly.

The woman turned towards her.

Allie held up her warrant card. 'How are you doing?'

'I survived.' Michelle glanced at the bedcovers. 'I'm glad of that. I thought I was going to die.'

'Mind if I...?' Allie pointed to a chair and sat on it. 'Can you talk me through what happened? We can take it slowly if it's too upsetting, but I'd like as many details as you can recall.'

'I was in the kitchen when I heard the gate open. The back door was unlocked because I'd stepped out to get some fresh air to clear a headache and that's when he... he rushed at me. I fell to the floor, and by the time I'd managed to scream, he was on top of me. He had hold of my wrists and was telling me to be quiet. I fought him... I didn't know what else to do... I wondered if he was drugged because his eyes were so wild.' Tears welled in her own, and she wiped at them.

'You're doing great, Michelle,' Allie encouraged. 'I know it's hard to relive, but it really will help us understand what happened. Would you like a glass of water?'

'No, thanks.' Michelle continued. 'I tried so hard to get away from him. I wouldn't give in, and he kept wrestling me down. He grabbed my hair and pulled it tight in his fist and banged my head on the floor. He did that a few times, and then I began to lose consciousness.'

She took a breather, and Allie gave her time.

'I reached for his eyes, trying to scratch at them,' Michelle went on. 'And it was then he... he tried to stab me and caught my arms. Luckily, they were superficial wounds. The surgeon said my thick dressing gown saved a lot of damage.'

Allie shuddered inwardly at what Michelle had been put through. And that bastard had run?

'Were you conscious at any time yesterday?' she wanted to know.

'I can't remember getting to the hospital. I woke up there, and it surprised me in more ways than one. I was convinced he was going to kill me.'

Allie gave her a moment to compose herself. She only had a few more questions and she would be on her way.

'Has Brian done anything like this to you before?'

'What do you mean?'

'You last saw him yesterday morning, is that right?'

'No. He was due home after a night shift, but I didn't see him.'

Allie frowned, wondering if Michelle was still suffering from concussion. She paused. 'The man who attacked you wasn't Brian?'

'No. We've been having some problems lately, but he would never do this to me.'

Allie was totally confused now. Had they all jumped to the wrong conclusion? That was unacceptable if so. She had to be sure.

'Brian was seen leaving your home shortly afterwards in a great hurry by car.'

'It wasn't him.' Michelle pointed to her eye. 'He did this to me the night before. I thought it was him returning to say he was sorry. I-I was on the verge of leaving him. My friend was coming over to see me. She's been trying to get me to find somewhere else to stay.'

'Are you certain? You're not saying this to make sure he isn't in any kind of trouble?'

'I'm not.'

'Do you know who it was?'

There was a gulp before Michelle spoke. 'It was Jamie Sanderson. I haven't seen him in years, not since I was in my teens, but I'd recognise him anywhere.'

'That must be... at least twenty years ago?'

Michelle nodded, tears running down her cheeks again. 'I was scared he was going to kill me.'

'Is there a reason why you'd think this?'

'No. But there is something you need to know.' Michelle was openly crying now. 'I found out about Nick Farrington, and I know him. So does Jamie Sanderson.'

Allie sat up a little straighter. 'How?'

'We went to school together.'

'Do you keep in touch?'

Michelle shook her head, then looked away.

'So why would Jamie Sanderson do this to you?'

'I-I don't know.'

Allie sat in silence while she digested her thoughts. Michelle didn't say anything more, so Allie was none the wiser minutes later.

But she did know one thing.

The case had turned on its head.

The door to the room opened, and the uniformed officer on guard popped his head around the frame. 'Can I have a word, please, ma'am?'

'What is it?' Allie asked when she joined him.

He pointed to a man sitting a few metres away with his head in his hands. 'He tells me he's Brian Price and wants to see Michelle.'

'Thanks.' Allie strode down to stand in front of him. 'Brian Price? I'm DI Shenton. Me and my team have been searching for you.'

CHAPTER TWENTY-EIGHT

Allie sat down next to Brian Price. She wasn't being unkind when she thought he was nothing to look at. He was weighty, with red, greasy cheeks, his greying hair needed trimming, and his teeth were like a man in his nineties. She wondered if he had an underlying issue, alcohol perhaps. It might understand his anger towards Michelle. Although it wouldn't be an excuse for it.

He glanced at her for a moment, then his attention flicked to the floor. 'How is she?' he asked eventually.

'She's doing all right,' she told him. 'It was a good job the emergency services were called and were able to attend to her swiftly.' Her anger building, she dialled it down. Maybe this was her opportunity to get a handle on what had been happening before Michelle was attacked. 'What's been going on between the two of you?'

'Couple stuff, you know.'

'If you think that blackening her eye and splitting her lip is *couple stuff*, then I don't agree with you.' She sighed inwardly. So much for keeping her anger at bay. But it always hurt her to see a woman abused by a man.

Brian waited for a moment before speaking again. 'What happened to her?'

Allie told him all she could. 'Does the name Jamie Sanderson mean anything to you?'

'No. Is that who attacked her?'

'Michelle believes so. She told me you and her had an argument the night before and she thought it was you returning from work.'

'How did he get in?'

'The back door was unlocked. Michelle had stood on the step for some fresh air, hoping to clear her headache a little.'

Brian had the decency to blush. 'We haven't been getting along lately.'

'That's something we'll have to address. You'll need to come to the station for questioning.'

'But I didn't do... that.' Brian pointed to the floor.

Allie imagined he was seeing the images of Michelle in their kitchen. She was certain they'd be etched in his mind for some time, if not forever.

'What happened this morning doesn't excuse what you did,' she said. 'So why did you run? For all you knew, Michelle could have been close to death.'

'I panicked when I saw all the blood. I thought I'd get the blame.'

'Why? Is that kind of thing between you and her a regular occurrence?'

He gasped in horror. 'I would never hurt her that much.'

She rolled her eyes, trying not to swear. 'So the odd punch and slap every now and then, you think, is okay?'

'I get carried away. I'm sorry.'

Allie wasn't interested in apologies. 'Why didn't you call an ambulance?'

'I-I thought it was too late.' He bowed his head again, ran his hand over his face. 'I realised then how much I loved her and what I was doing was so wrong. I thought I'd never have the chance to tell her how sorry I was.'

'It's a little too late for that,' she snapped. 'What you did to Michelle is nothing to what Jamie Sanderson has done, and we will deal with him accordingly, too. But don't water it down. *You* assaulted a woman. You had no right to do that.'

'I know. Can I see her before we go?'

'I'll ask her. Unfortunately, I can't tell her what to do, or personally I'd suggest she never spoke to you again.' Allie pushed herself to standing. 'Do I need to cuff you while I wait for someone to take you to the station, or will you behave yourself if you sit there?'

'I'll behave.'

'Good. You can stay with the officer on the door for now.'

Allie popped back into Michelle's room and then beckoned Brian in once she'd agreed to see him.

'I'll keep the door ajar,' she told him. 'But I won't listen in.'

Brian nodded his acknowledgement.

Allie took a moment to ring Perry and relayed what she'd learned.

'So the two of them know each other and we've been searching for the wrong man. That's a turn-up for the books.'

'It seems so.'

'Why did Brian run?'

'He thought he'd get the blame. Their relationship is volatile.'

'Sounds like a coward to me. Did Michelle tell you why Sanderson came after her?'

'She wouldn't say. I don't know if she's scared of repercussions from him or worried about telling us something. Brian said he thought he'd killed her.'

'But he left her there.'

Allie could hear the anger in his tone, similar to her own.

'He must have thought we'd blame him because Sanderson did a runner.'

'But now we have evidence that tells us differently.'

'Indeed. Let's get on to the press, see if we can do some damage limitation. Speak to Simon, see if he can help. But first, can you arrange for someone to collect Brian? He needs his rights reading to him as well. Under the circumstances, even though I despise what he did to Michelle, we have at least put his mind at rest that she's still alive.'

'And Sanderson?'

'Get Sam onto finding out as much intel as she can. I'll be back in the station in half an hour. Are you hungry?'

'Do bears –?'

'Yeah, I get you.'

Allie disconnected the call, smiling at two medical staff who walked by. She needed to clear her head after the recent discussion. How had they jumped to conclusions so quickly? In their defence, the evidence so far had pointed at Brian, but his DNA would have been all over the home anyway. They had to find Sanderson, and quick.

A few minutes later, Brian came out, gaze to the floor, shoulders drooped.

'It didn't go well?' Allie queried.

He shook his head and sat down next to the officer again. He wasn't forthcoming, but she hoped Michelle had told him to sling his hook.

Maybe a lesson had been learned by some during this incident after all.

CHAPTER TWENTY-NINE

Colette finally received a message from Michelle and drove straight to the Royal Stoke after work. It was busy due to it being visiting hours from half past six. It took her an age to buy something from the shop situated in the foyer. The queues at the self-service tills were huge, but she bought chocolates and a couple of magazines. She wasn't sure how long Michelle would be staying on the ward or else she'd have bought a paperback. Michelle was an avid reader.

Even so, Colette couldn't help wanting to know everything she could about Jamie.

She and Michelle had been friends since they'd met when they were in nursery class. They'd both grown up on the Bennett Estate, three streets apart, and had been joined at the hip through primary and secondary school and worked at the same place for their first Saturday jobs. Colette's unexpected pregnancy when she was barely through her GCSEs had thrown a spanner in the works for a while, but Michelle had remained as supportive as she could.

Michelle had been there for her when she'd told Kevin, and then her parents, that she was keeping her baby. It wasn't an easy thing to do, but she'd been determined to give her daughter the best she could. And she'd done all right by Hannah. She was twenty-five now, working in Derby as a HR advisor.

She pushed the door on the room she'd been told Michelle was in, smiling when she saw her sitting up in bed. Her face was a mess, but she was alive. Even so, Colette's eyes brimmed with tears at the sight of her friend. She placed her gifts down on the bed and leaned close to give Michelle a gentle hug.

'You blagged a side room!' she said with a chuckle, knowing how lucky that was. 'How are you?'

'I'm sore.' It was Michelle's turn to cry. 'I thought he was going to kill me, and I never did anything to him.'

'I know.' Colette pulled up a chair and settled in beside the bed. 'I was so upset when I heard. I called round like we'd arranged but I couldn't get anywhere near your house. And you weren't answering your phone – obviously – so I was worried sick until your neighbour, Irene, rang me. And then I didn't know what to think.'

'The police thought it was Brian until I spoke to them. Can you believe he left me on the floor, covered in blood and unconscious? If it wasn't for Irene finding me, I might have died. I hate him so much.'

'So you definitely think it was Jamie Sanderson?'

'I'm certain it was. He spoke to me, said my name. He said he'd waited a long time to come and see me.' Michelle gnawed at her bottom lip. 'I haven't told the police any of this, so you mustn't either if they ask. I told them I can't remember what happened.'

'I promise not to say anything. I would have done the same. But don't you think they'll find out sooner or later about Jamie? They'll see what he did and –'

'What *he* did. We weren't there to see.'

'I know, but don't you ever wonder about it all?'

'I don't think about it now. It was years ago.'

'Why would he come after you, and do that to Nick, too?' Colette grimaced. 'You do know about Nick, don't you?'

Michelle nodded, her eyes brimming with tears again.

Colette handed her a tissue, watched as she dabbed gently at her cheeks. Waited for her to gain her composure before going to speak again. But Michelle beat her to it.

'How's Hannah?' she asked. 'Did she get that job she went for? I was going to ask you about it yesterday.'

'Yes, she did. Starts next month.' Colette smiled, sensing that Michelle wanted to change the subject. 'I wish she lived closer, but it is what it is. Truth be told, I think she's glad to get away from us. Kevin can be a right pain when he's on the warpath over something and nothing.' She stopped, a blush appearing on her cheeks. 'Sorry. I didn't think.'

'It doesn't matter. I know we both chose wrong ones and would have done differently if we had our time again. But you had Hannah to think about.'

'I did.' Colette didn't want to talk about the daughter she'd had as a gymslip mum. Not now. It didn't seem right.

'That night, back then,' Michelle said suddenly. 'Did you ever doubt it was Jamie who –'

'Not at all,' Colette cut her off. But she had thought about it a lot over the years since it had happened.

'It's weird why he would do this after all this while.'

'Kevin said that, too. There's no logic to it, is there? Not unless we're missing something.'

A nurse came in to take Michelle's blood pressure, and once she'd gone and they were on their own again, and their talk had dried up. Both women were left with their thoughts.

'How have you left things with Brian?' Colette said, staying on mutual ground.

'He wanted to see me. I refused at first, but when I was

told he was going to be arrested, I said okay. I needed to say my piece anyway. He told me he was sorry and that it wouldn't happen again. You're damn right, I told him, because I want a divorce.'

'Well done, you. I'm sure you'll be better on your own.'

Michelle smiled, even though Colette could see she was in pain.

'No, you see. That's where you're wrong, because I have you.'

Colette beamed. 'Why don't you come to stay with us for a few days when you get discharged?'

'Thanks, but I'd rather go home. I'm getting the locks changed on the house. Brian is moving out. It's the least he can do for me.'

CHAPTER THIRTY

As soon as Colette left the hospital, she couldn't get to her car quick enough. Drivers were circling the car park searching for spaces, but she got in and stayed where she was. Much to some of the glares thrown her way by disgruntled drivers, she had to ring Kevin.

'I've been to see Michelle,' she said before greeting him. 'She told me it wasn't Brian who attacked her. Kev, It was Jamie Sanderson.'

'What the – is she sure? None of us have seen him for twenty-odd years. He must have changed a lot since then.'

'You're easily recognisable from your school photos, and I'm often told I haven't changed a bit.' Colette's dark hair had always been one length with a block fringe, her frame small. She dyed her roots every few weeks and was liberal with the wrinkle cream, but that was all for keeping age at bay.

She thought of Kevin. His hair was shorter, and there were grey hairs appearing here and there, but his physique hadn't changed either. He still had that cheeky-boy image, the lopsided grin, and the bright-blue eyes amid the crow's feet. They would both be recognisable, so Jamie might be, too.

'Do you think he'll know we're married?' she went on.

'I doubt it. It's not as if any of us kept in touch. Has Michelle said anything to the police about him?'

'She mentioned she knew him from school, that's all.' Colette paused, almost not wanting to ask the question. 'You don't think he'll come after us next, do you?'

'Of course he won't.'

'But why would he do that to Michelle? And it must be him who killed Nick. It's too much of a coincidence.' Colette gasped. 'Oh God. I can't breathe.'

'Relax, he won't come after us.'

'How do you know?' She couldn't understand how calm he was.

'Sanderson was released from prison fifteen years ago. If it is him, why would he leave it so long?'

'He's been in and out of prison since then, too.'

'How do you know?'

Colette gnawed at her bottom lip. 'I kept an eye on him, in case something like this happened.'

'You never said.'

'I didn't think he'd come after Michelle and Nick!'

'We were kids back then.'

'Even so…'

'Even so?'

She wasn't about to say anything else. She didn't want the wrath of him when he got in from work. 'You're sure he won't come after us?'

'Not now the police are chasing him. I think he's done enough to get himself put back in jail for the rest of his life.'

'That's if the police catch him before he does anything else.'

'He was always a scatterbrain. I bet he'll slip up soon.'

Colette watched a man come within an inch of her front bumper and then reverse into a space that had come vacant across from her.

'Have you ever seen him around?' Kevin wanted to know.

'No.' She was being truthful. She didn't think much of Jamie nowadays. 'Have you?'

'I thought I'd spotted him every now and then, but who knows if I was right or not. I think I'd have known if it was him, though. Col, I have to go. It will be fine. No need to worry. I'm finished in half an hour. I'll pick up a chippie tea on the way home, save you cooking.'

After the call was finished, Colette thought about their conversation. Were they really safe if Jamie was out there, on the loose? He'd tried to kill Michelle, and it was only by pure luck that Brian came home when he did and stopped him in time.

So to her mind, there was a lot to worry about. Because if he wasn't caught soon, she thought he would strike again, and it could be either her or Kevin he came for next.

She'd talk to Kevin about going to the police when he got home. It wasn't a subject she could bring up over the phone.

Kevin had come out of the main work area into the corridor to take the call, the only place he'd be able to hear above the noise of the machinery. Now, he leaned on the sill of a window, glancing down at the road below. Rows of taillights, traffic lights, pelican crossings. Everyone was rushing somewhere. On their way for a night shift. Out to see friends. Home to family. He'd join them soon, but for now he could only think about Jamie Sanderson.

What was his game? Why now, after all these years, had

he suddenly appeared? Wasn't it enough that he'd murdered Nick and terrorised Michelle?

He thought back to what Colette had implied. Would he come after the two of them? He'd have to stay vigilant until the police caught him. Because this couldn't be over so soon. She and him were connected to what happened to Jamie. It seemed like he was back for revenge.

CHAPTER THIRTY-ONE

JAMIE – PRESENT DAY

Jamie kept his head down as he walked along Waterloo Road and onto Maple Street. Making sure there was no one around, he dived into the entry halfway down. It took him to the back of a row of terraced houses.

He trod carefully through the cobbled area, making sure not to step on anything that might make a noise. It wasn't particularly busy at any time of the day or night nowadays, but he didn't want to alert anyone to his comings and goings.

The houses to his left were derelict, boarded up mostly, some with steel doors. The row to his right were lived in. He could see lights at windows, upstairs and downstairs, imagining families getting together, parents putting their kids to bed for the night, having friends round for wine and nibbles.

At the fifth gate, he hurled himself over the six-foot wall and landed in the yard with a thud. He took out his phone to use as a torch, allowing him to move swiftly to the window, which he had broken the glass on a few nights ago.

After seeing the police checking the building was secure, when he'd had time to make off before they saw him, he'd had to use a different way of getting in. On his exit, he'd lodged a large piece of wood on the sill to cover it up. The property might get checked again, but in the meantime, it would be just his luck to get pounced on by the local Neighbourhood Watch busybodies.

He pushed himself through the opening, being careful not to snag himself on any of the tiny shards left around the edges and stepped lightly over the remnants on the kitchen floor. Either kids, vandals, or druggies had made a mess of it, and he expected from the state of it that no one had been in here for a while regardless. As well as the glass now littered everywhere, the worktop must have an inch of dust on it. The cupboards were dated and mouldy, the paintwork a nasty nicotine colour.

In the front of the building, through a narrow hallway, was where the newsagent's used to be. Jamie stepped into the room now, standing on the spot where his life had changed in a flash. If he closed his eyes, he could still see it all, as clear as anything.

Kevin attacking Winston.

Winston on the floor, dying.

There had been so much blood.

He hadn't been savvy at sixteen, not how he was now. Not how he had been made to be, due to all his time in prison. He'd seen so much violence since then. Most of it had been unnecessary.

How had he found himself as part of that world? He'd never fitted in with it, and yet, here he was now, fully appreciative of its power. How it made him feel invincible not guilty.

Jamie didn't stay in there long. He needed to be in and out as quickly as possible, so he went upstairs. He was getting things ready but without being too obvious. He didn't want anyone to identify him because he'd been seen too much in one place. Not before his plan was executed to the full anyway.

He stared through the window. There were no lights on, so no one would see him. It was a desolate area, one that suited him fine. One that described his life, too. One big fuck-up.

He pulled out the photo he'd folded up and put in the pocket of his jeans. There were five teenagers on it. He was in the middle, laughing with his arm around Colette's shoulders. She had played him well back then.

They had all ruined his life. Now it was time for him to destroy theirs.

He left shortly afterwards, arriving back at his flat some twenty minutes later. He went into the kitchen, opening the fridge to see a couple of bottles of water, a can of lager, and a pack of cheese. Opening a cupboard door revealed a few biscuits and two tins of soup.

He emptied the shopping he'd fetched from the Co-op on his way. All quick and convenient food as he didn't feel like cooking. A sandwich, a bar of chocolate, and a bag of crisps as part of a meal deal, despite the late hour. A sausage roll that he could eat cold for breakfast if he didn't want it now.

He ate while he caught up with the news on TV. He couldn't believe how he'd screwed up yesterday. Of course he couldn't have known that Michelle's old man would come home early so he'd been unable to finish her off. But he was annoyed that in his rush to get away, he'd forgotten to leave the note that was tucked in his pocket. It would have linked her to Nick Farrington, so that the others would know he was onto them.

Jamie wanted them to be terrified he would turn up and do the same to them.

At least when he'd killed Nick, it had all gone to plan.

He'd got into their property quite easily in the end. He'd looked around it the day before and found no likely access, plus a house alarm. So plan B was to hope that Nick got home first, as usual. That way he could knock on the door and push his way in.

He'd watched him for a few weeks to see what time he got home, plus his daughter and his wife. So when he was ready to attack, he chose the same day as Michelle because he wanted to be out of Stoke as quickly as possible.

He planned on staying no longer than three more days. All the time he needed to get his revenge and slip out of the city. Because Jamie Sanderson didn't exist anymore, and he was ready to be someone else.

CHAPTER THIRTY-TWO

Back from the hospital and sitting with her team, Allie wanted to hear what Sam had found out about Jamie Sanderson first. She was hoping they'd get an address so they could bring him in for questioning. Maybe, if he cooperated, they might get an understanding of his reasonings. Had he been there to kill Michelle Price, and if so, why? It was hard to tell, seeing as Brian came home and disturbed him.

'Okay, Sam, what have you got for us?' she asked.

'When Sanderson was sixteen, he murdered sixty-two-year-old shopkeeper Winston Lowe. It seemed as if Sanderson was set to rob the place, Winston reacted, and he was stabbed in the torso several times. According to her statement, his wife came downstairs while he lay dying.

'Sanderson was behind the counter and said he was after a phone to call emergency services. Mrs Lowe said Sanderson denied it was him who had attacked her husband and then did a runner. But she ID'd him from a lineup, plus his prints were on the knife.

'A group of teenagers also said he'd lied when he told the police he was with them, too. Due to his age, he got eleven years. Served them all – three in juvie and the rest in a male prison. But get this. One of the teenagers was named as Michelle. I have a surname of Whalley, so it could be worth seeing if it's Michelle Price.'

'Great work.' Allie was genuinely impressed. She often missed the nitty-gritty side of working a case now she was a DI and could delegate.

'There's more,' Sam went on. 'Nick Farrington was interviewed, too.'

'And they all said they weren't with Sanderson?'

Sam nodded.

'So, what do we think? Is this a crime of revenge?' Allie pouted. 'If so, for what? If not, why attack Michelle? Was it to warn her about something, threaten her, maim her even? Was the outcome supposed to be her death?'

They chatted between themselves, throwing in questions and answering them to rule them out or think more about.

'Sanderson's prison record is pretty grim,' Sam commented. 'Since leaving prison at twenty-seven, he's spent more time back inside than on the outside. He's been involved with petty theft mostly, but he has a record for the odd assault.'

It was a pattern Allie abhorred but equally understood. Some prisoners felt lost on the outside, and most of the time weren't given enough help to rehabilitate themselves.

Some got out of prison in the morning and went on to commit crime that very same day, ending up in a cell for the night as they had nowhere to go. No one to return to, no family who wanted to know them. No loving home to rest in.

The system was dire, and now the government were releasing prisoners early because the prisons were getting full, there didn't seem to be a day when someone appeared in the news when they'd committed a further crime and got sent back inside.

'So, for now, there's a tentative link between Michelle Price and Nick Farrington as they knew each other and gave statements to the police, but there is no evidence to suggest Sanderson killed Nick.' Allie drummed her fingers on the desk.

'And there's only one note?' Frankie offered.

'Which begs the question, what does Sanderson think he's lied about? Did something happen that made Jamie turn on his friends who were spoken to at the time?'

'Because they grassed on him?' Perry suggested.

'Which if so could mean he wasn't responsible for Winston Lowe's death.'

'But murdering them all?' Sam questioned. 'It takes guts to kill someone never mind several people, even if planned.'

Allie sat back in her chair. 'We need to find Sanderson, especially now that Brian Price is in the clear for attacking Michelle.'

'Do we think Sanderson meant to kill Michelle?' Perry waited for confirmation.

'If this is linked to Nick Farrington, I think so,' Allie replied. 'Brian coming back probably saved her life, as ironic as that now sounds.'

'Wait a minute.' Frankie held up a finger. 'I think I've found a link to Shaun Green and Jamie Sanderson.' He clicked the mouse on his desk and brought up a file. 'It might be something and nothing, but they were both in prison at the same time.'

'If it was Sanderson who murdered Green, maybe he's getting revenge for something that happened inside?'

'Interesting. When we find him, we can question him about his whereabouts when Green was killed. Frankie, can you run through everything again and then check with the prison? It's a long shot due to how many years ago they were locked up, but something might have been logged if there was a problem between them.'

'Will do.'

'Is your copper's nose twitching, boss?' Sam asked, a knowing smirk on her face.

'Maybe.' Allie yawned. 'But I think it will have to wait until tomorrow. Let's call it a night and start afresh in the morning.'

With her team gone, Allie grabbed a quick coffee and sat in her office to have a think about the day's events. There was something odd about all of it. Sam was right about her having a gut feeling. So first thing in the morning, she was going to look into Jamie Sanderson and the murder of Winston Lowe as well as Sanderson being the killer of Nick Farrington, and now another tentative link to Shaun Green. Then she would get her officers to go through everything in Sanderson's file, too, to see if anything was amiss.

She also needed to speak to Grace, see if she could help her out with anyone knowing Jamie from the community. His last address had come up as he was no longer there, he'd moved on from his bail hostel several months ago, so he could be anywhere.

Finally, she sent Jenny an update, explaining that the two cases may need to be assigned to one operation. Then she switched off her computer, and the lights in her office, and set off for home.

Allie got back at a reasonable half past ten. She'd missed Poppy, but Mark was up, so it was good to spend a bit of downtime with him.

Yet, in bed later, she found herself still awake at two a.m. She couldn't switch off, afraid she was missing something, a crucial item or note that would blow the case even further open.

It had been a revelation to learn that the two cases had a

link, even if tentatively for now. But it really was likely that it was all connected to Jamie Sanderson.

One thing she was definitely doing was going to talk to Michelle again. She was hiding something, and she needed to coax it out of her.

'Are you awake?' Mark spoke quietly beside her.

'Sorry. Do you want me to go in the spare room?'

'No.' He pulled her closer, spooning up against her back. 'I wish I was twenty years younger and could ravish you so that we'd both get to sleep afterwards.'

'Hey, speak for yourself.' She reached a hand round to him. 'I'm game if you are. I need something to take my mind off things.' When he didn't reply, she whispered his name. Then she grinned. He'd fallen asleep on her, bless.

He wouldn't even remember the conversation in the morning, yet she was going to tell him all the same. However, all the hinting at sex was his way of saying he needed her. It was nice, and they would reconnect soon. It had been a while since they'd made love. A couple of weeks, perhaps. But she would welcome it all the same.

If she wasn't so tired.

She sniggered quietly, closing her eyes to try and settle down again. Otherwise she would be good for nothing in the morning. And that wouldn't do at all.

CHAPTER THIRTY-THREE

SATURDAY

Colette left the supermarket and headed to her car. It was a mild day for October, but hardly a soul around as it was so early. She hadn't been able to sleep so had got up and decided to do the weekly shop. It wasn't even seven a.m. yet.

As she walked, she spotted a man coming towards her. Was that... it couldn't be.

It was.

Jamie Sanderson.

She gasped, umpteen questions running through her mind in seconds.

Should she pretend she hadn't recognised him, then get out her phone and call for the police?

Had he found out where she lived? Waited for her to come out and followed her?

Would she be better running back to the store and alerting security, or getting in her car and driving off?

Colette's smile was faint while she figured out what was best to do. There wasn't time left to do anything but panic. She'd have to act as if she didn't know he'd attacked Michelle, and more than likely murdered Nick.

'Long time no see,' Jamie said when he reached her.

Her breath caught in her chest. Age hadn't been kind to him. His skin was sallow, face and body thin like he needed feeding up. His clothes were messy, a little whiffy, and he wore a woollen hat showing no hair. What had happened to that teenager she'd fancied? Now it was like looking at a... tramp.

His eyes unnerved her. He was staring, as if he was ready to pounce.

'Is that you, Jamie Sanderson?' she said, trying to stay calm.

'The very one. I haven't seen you in years. How are you?'

'Fine, thanks.'

Her breathing ratcheted up further. She wasn't going to start a conversation. After what he'd done to Michelle, he could do the same to her. It would be over before anyone could get to her.

'I was wondering if you'd seen the news lately.' Jamie stepped closer to her.

Colette moved back, glancing over his shoulder. There was no one she could see to shout to, but should she scream? Or would it be quicker to run back and alert a security guard?

Somehow she was rooted to the spot regardless.

'The news?' she said eventually, her voice almost a whisper.

'About Michelle, you remember her? I know you were friends back –'

'I know what you did to her. Please, leave me alone.'

'I'm not going to hurt you now.' Jamie shook his head. 'I wanted to give you something.'

He walked nearer, and still her feet wouldn't move. Her mouth felt like it was stuffed with cotton wool, her tongue swollen to double its size. She prayed her bladder wouldn't give way.

Jamie had a piece of paper in his hand, and he held it out in front of her. 'Go on, take it.'

She did as he said.

'I want you to give this to the police. I didn't have time to leave it when I... saw Michelle again.'

'What... what is it?'

'It's a note. Want me to tell you what it says?' He didn't wait for her to reply. 'I lied. Do you know what I'm referring to?'

Colette's teeth chattered. 'No.'

'Oh, I think you do.' Jamie stared pointedly at her. 'Anyway, it's *so* great to see you again. Keep in touch, yeah?'

Colette sighed with relief, resting a hand on her chest.

But then Jamie turned back.

A man drove into the car park but went past them to another row. She kept him in her peripheral vision. If she could get him to see who she was with... Jamie's photo was all over the news. He was pushing it not to be seen.

'I nearly forgot.' Jamie's hand dived into his jacket, and he pulled out an envelope. 'Here you go. This one is for you.'

She took it from him. Then he gave her a wave and walked away. This time he kept going.

When he was out of sight, Colette ran to her car, getting in and locking the doors. She wiped away tears that had fallen, her fear real as she expected him to come back and harm her.

With shaking hands, she managed to put in her key and start her car. Then she screeched off and out onto the road, only slowing when she was sure she wasn't being followed.

Pulling up outside her house fifteen minutes later, she finally sobbed with relief. She had got away.

The envelope was on the passenger seat. Was it another note, meant for her? She opened it and removed its contents.

There was a photograph and a slip of paper. The photo was of the five of them. Colette remembered it being taken as if it were yesterday. Michelle had bought one of those disposable cameras that were all the rage back then and asked a man walking past to take their picture. She and Michelle were sitting on a bench, and Nick, Kevin, and Jamie were behind sitting on its back. They were laughing because Jamie had nearly fallen off, and then they'd struck a pose.

Nick's face had been scraped out, a line was across Michelle's, and there was an ink circle around her and Kevin.

Colette covered her mouth with her hand. It seemed so final, and yet there were three of them left. Was Jamie saying he had meant to kill Michelle? And *was* it him who'd murdered Nick?

And where had the photo come from? Had he been through Michelle's things at her home and stolen it? Or had he found it online and had a copy made? She and Michelle shared so much without thinking. But then again, why would they have ever thought something like this would happen?

With trepidation, she read the note next.

YOU LIED, TOO.

CHAPTER THIRTY-FOUR

Kevin was awake, having a lie-in. He stared at the bedroom ceiling, annoyed at the wallpaper peeling off in the corner. So many times he wished he didn't live in this crap little house in this crap little street with its imbecile neighbours. Carter Street was the pits, and he'd lived there for most of his adult life.

Nick's house was all over the news. It was impressive to say the least, although Kevin had never been inside it. Nick had always met him in a pub. He'd often wondered about the snobbery behind that. But then, again, Kevin had never invited Nick to his house. It was too embarrassing.

Nick's was privately owned. Kevin couldn't help being envious. To think that *he* hadn't ventured further than the town he was brought up in pissed him off big style. It was as if life was rubbing his nose in it. He felt as faded, or was that jaded, as the wallpaper.

The front door opened and then closed with a bang, making him jump.

'Kevin!'

He heard Colette bound upstairs. The door flew open as she came into the room.

'What's up with you? You look like the cat's peed in your handbag. Not that we have a cat.' He smirked.

'I saw him,' Colette replied, a whimper in her voice. 'Jamie Sanderson. I saw him!'

'Where? Was he here?' Kevin sat up abruptly, swivelling around as if Jamie was going to magically appear behind him.

'He was outside the supermarket when I was going back to my car.'

'Did he say anything?' Kevin bristled. 'Did he hurt you?'

'No, he said he wanted me to give this to the police.' She handed him the note. 'He said it should have been left with Michelle, but he didn't get time because he was disturbed.'

'"I LIED."' Kevin's brow furrowed. 'What's that supposed to mean?'

'He gave me one that said I lied, too, and then this photo.'

Kevin couldn't believe it when he saw what Jamie had done to the image of the five of them. He was sending a message, wasn't he? That he was coming after them next. Fuck.

'Does this mean it definitely was him who killed Nick?' Colette spoke in a whisper.

'I don't know.' He didn't want to spook her.

'I'll call the police and let them know I've seen him.' Colette reached for her phone. 'I can give them the note that was meant for Michelle. It has to mean he killed Nick.'

'No!' Kevin sat up quickly. 'We can't do that.'

'But they're searching for him. He'll be arrested before he can –'

'Kill us, too?' He pulled on some clothes. 'If I see him again, I won't wait around. I'll go for him first.'

'Don't say that after what he's done. He's not going to stop. We have to call the police.'

'If they catch him, you know what this will be about. We'll have to go over everything again. You don't want to be questioned now?'

'I was thinking it must have something to do with Winston Lowe. Yet no one but Jamie did anything wrong.' She paused. 'Did they?'

Kevin glared at her. 'Not this again. You've always thought I was lying. You of all people should trust me.'

'I do! But I can't understand why he's killed Nick after all this time. And now we know he was planning on murdering Michelle. It was a good job Brian showed up!'

'He could have got to you today and yet he didn't.'

'That doesn't make me feel any safer.'

Kevin got out of bed and took her in his arms then. 'You're overthinking as usual. Nothing's going to happen to us.'

He was trying to convince himself as much as he was his wife. Jamie, like this, out of the blue, was worrying him. But if he touched Colette, then he'd get what was coming to him. Kevin wouldn't stand by and let anything happen to his family.

This had to end.

'Let's have a cuppa.' He stopped the conversation, rubbing his stomach comically. 'I fancy a bacon butty. Shall I make us one?'

'I can't eat.' Colette shook her head. 'I feel sick.'

'Well, let me get you a cup of tea and put the shopping away. Then we can think what's best to do.'

'Okay. I'll clean my face up first. I must look a right mess.'

Downstairs, Kevin went into the kitchen and lit up a gas ring. Checking to see if Colette wasn't near, he placed the first note over the top of the flame.

The second one had almost disintegrated when Colette caught him.

'What are you doing?' She rushed forwards.

'We don't want the police to get their hands on them.' He pushed her away as she reached for the cooker knob. Then he threw the photo on top of the ring, too. 'Nor this.'

'That's evidence! You should have saved it.'

Kevin said nothing until the photo was gone. The air was filled with the smell of singed paper, burnt ashes scattered all over the cooker top. He turned back to Colette, his lucky-go-happy mood disappearing in a second.

'You better keep this to yourself. No mention of it to the police, nor Michelle. Not a word, do you hear?' He squeezed her arm. 'Not a fucking word.'

'Ow. You're hurting me.'

He realised his grip and turned away. 'I might pop to see Michelle, see how she's doing. Lauren, too. She must be going through hell.'

'I'll come with you when you do.'

Kevin said nothing. He would go on his own and then tell her afterwards. He wanted to know if Lauren knew about Jamie Sanderson. And what Michelle had said to the police.

CHAPTER THIRTY-FIVE

As soon as Allie got into work that morning and had made a mug of strong coffee, she was back investigating Jamie Sanderson, hoping to establish, or rule out, further links. Some of the casework was now online, some on paper, which she had accessed and was going through.

She was sitting in her office. The door was ajar so officers knew they could come and go, but she was trying to shut off the general noise. There was always someone on the main floor, no matter what time of day or night, but at least there weren't phones ringing yet, conversations being had.

All she wanted to concentrate on was the case of Winston Lowe, the man who had been stabbed to death after a robbery went wrong.

She'd skimmed through statements from several people she'd heard about the night before. Michelle Whalley, who she assumed was Michelle Price, Nick Farrington, and two others were the group of friends who were questioned the day after Winston's tragic death. The other names were Colette Trent and Kevin Ryland.

Now, reading the statements altogether, she found they

pretty much spouted out the same lines, almost as if they'd been rehearsed. As if they'd been told what to say, perhaps? The girls said they hadn't seen anything. The boys said they hadn't gone into the shop with Jamie, didn't realise what he was about to do. It seemed a bit cut and dry, but there was no evidence to back up otherwise.

Next, she read the forensic reports on the knife found at the crime scene. Sanderson's prints were all over the handle, but there was also an unidentified half thumb print. As well, there was the faint etching of a bloodied palm on the glass that was above the counter. She read up on notes to say that this had been brought up in Jamie's defence and dismissed. Allie supposed it didn't mean there was someone else with him just because they'd found a print, but the palm was never identified.

There was a lot of circumstantial evidence, but to her mind nothing concrete.

Jamie was telling them one story, about being keeping watch outside and seeing Kevin stab Winston Lowe and then do a runner with Nick.

Nick Farrington and Kevin Ryland were adamant they weren't in the shop.

Colette Trent and Michelle were none the wiser as they hadn't been present, and yet their words were taken as gospel that it was Jamie who had killed Winston.

It didn't make sense. Surely someone would have seen that at the time.

She picked up her mobile and pressed a familiar number. The call was answered almost immediately.

'What do you want?'

'Charming, Dave. No "Hi, Allie, how are you?"'

'That's for my friends.' He chortled.

'I'm not too early for you?'

'Of course not. What can I do for you?'

'Well...' Allie filled him in on the case. 'I was wondering if you could take another look at some of the evidence. It's over twenty years ago, so the good thing is all the new techie stuff you have available now. The bad news is it's twenty years ago, so swings and roundabouts.'

'Want to *swing* it by me?'

'Superstar. Are you at work?'

'Yes. I'll put the kettle on.'

'Even better, although I need to be back for eight-thirty for team briefing.'

She was with him in twenty minutes. He took her through to the staff quarters, into a small kitchen with a large table at its centre. Allie's eyes widened when she saw a cake tin on the table. Dave's wife, Sue, made the most delicious cupcakes.

'Go on,' he said. 'You know you're dying to see what's in there.'

Allie removed the lid, her shoulders sighing as a whiff of vanilla caught her nose. 'Did I ever tell you how much I love you?' She took out a cake, pulled down the wrapper, and bit into it. 'Heavenly breakfast.'

Dave made tea while they chatted about the case. Considering he was in his sixties now, he had a great head of salt-and-pepper hair, and black thick-rimmed glasses gave him a fun appearance. Even so, she saw him rub at his back after getting milk from the fridge. He seemed tired, and she wondered:

'Has the grandson arrived yet?'

'No.' Dave rolled his eyes and handed Allie a mug. 'He'll definitely be here next Wednesday, though, as they'll induce, so not long.'

He sat across the table from her while she told him her thoughts.

'I can certainly test some things again,' he said when she'd finished. 'There's a new one we can use for fingerprint analysis. Perhaps that palm print might be more accessible now, too. We can run it through the system afterwards. That's dependent on its owner being on there, mind.'

'It's a start. 'I'm going to get in touch with Colette Trent and Kevin Ryland, too. All their statements were a tad polished to me. I'll see if Michelle Price knows of their whereabouts.'

'You have a hunch?'

'I don't think Sanderson was given a proper chance to tell his side of things. The detective in charge assumed he was guilty from the get-go. Gary Hallam, do you know him?'

'I worked with him until he finished all of a sudden.'

'Oh?'

'Said he'd had enough of the job. Shift work, daily abuse, blah, blah, blah.'

'We need a word with him once I have your report. You never know, he might be in danger, too. Especially if there was anything corrupt going on.'

'Back then it was rife.' Dave shook his head. 'It'll be good to prove something wrong if I can find it.'

'You'll be my hero if you do.' She smirked. 'Obviously, you're my hero anyway. Goes without saying.'

'You are a wise one,' Dave replied. 'Want to take another cupcake with you for later?'

CHAPTER THIRTY-SIX

After a quick catch-up with her team, Allie decided to go and see Michelle Price on the off chance that she would tell her more. Michelle was still on the same ward, but thankfully, when Allie saw her she was brighter than the day before. Her pallor had improved, and she'd managed to get her hair washed.

'Hi, Michelle.' Allie smiled. 'How are you today?'

'Better, thanks. I'm being discharged soon and going home, alone. Me and Brian are over.'

Allie nodded in understanding. Only time would tell if Michelle was brave enough to go through with that. People in coercive relationships were often battered and bruised on the inside as well as their outer body, so it could be hard for her to leave her husband. Michelle could be dependent on him, needing somewhere else to live, or be unwilling to go in case he hurt her more.

'There are people I can connect you with.' Allie gave her a contact card. 'Please call me if you ever need help.'

Michelle took the card from her. Then she glanced away, as if nervous as to what was coming next.

'I've been thinking about our last conversation,' Allie began. 'I can't help feeling that you had more to say about Jamie. I've been going over his file of Winston Lowe's murder back in 1999. I came across a Michelle Whalley. Would that have been you?'

'Yes, that was my maiden name.'

'So are you still unsure you don't know why he would attack you?'

There was an uncomfortable break before she spoke again. 'I hung around with him for a while. There were five of us – me, Jamie Sanderson, Colette Trent, Kevin Ryland, and Nick Farrington. Kevin was always a wild one, and he got Jamie to be a lookout for him when he was going into thieve some stuff from the newsagent's. We were only kids then, sixteen at the most, and it was a bit of excitement. I'm so ashamed of it now, but me and Colette never got involved.

'All three of them had been gone for twenty minutes when Kevin and Nick came running back to say that Jamie had stabbed the old man and he was dead. Well, we all panicked and legged it. When Jamie was arrested, I couldn't believe it. He never seemed the type to do anything like that, but you don't know, do you?'

Allie kept it to herself that what Michelle had told her didn't tally with her statement. 'So he went to prison for the murder of Winston Lowe. And you hadn't seen him since then?'

'No, not until he attacked me.'

'Do you keep in touch with any of the others?'

'Me and Colette have always been friends, mostly through the socials now, mainly Facebook.'

'What about Nick Farrington?'

'I haven't seen him in a good while.' She shook her head. 'I still can't believe he's dead. What did Jamie do to him?'

'We haven't concluded the enquiries as to his involvement

yet. We're waiting for evidence to confirm if it is him.' It was a white lie so as not to give her too many details. It might make her feel worse. Survivor's guilt was almost as much of a killer as the real thing. 'Did any of the others see Nick Farrington? What about Kevin?'

'I think they used to go out for a drink every now and then. Colette is married to him, you know?'

'To Kevin?'

'Yes.'

Allie thought that was interesting but kept it to herself. 'One more thing. Did you ever get to speak to Jamie after he killed Mr Lowe?'

'No.'

'What about the name Shaun Green? Does that mean anything to you?'

Michelle paused while she racked her brain. 'I don't think so, unless it was someone from school that I've forgotten about. Who is he?'

'It's fine if you don't know him.' Allie wasn't going to disclose anything to her. 'Okay, we'll leave it there for now. Could I have Colette's phone number from you, please? I need to call and see both her and Kevin.'

Michelle seemed uncomfortable but picked up her mobile and read a number out. Allie jotted it down. Then she asked a few more basic questions about what Michelle could recall from her attack, to see if she'd remembered anything further. But there was nothing else that she hadn't already mentioned.

'Do you think he'll come back and hurt me?' Michelle wanted to know then.

'We can't be certain. So I'd prefer it if you went to stay somewhere else for a few days. Is that possible?'

Michelle gasped.

'It's just a precaution.' Allie put a hand on her arm. 'But he is a dangerous man. Not knowing his whereabouts is a problem for us. We don't have the resources to put a watch on everyone. Do you have anywhere you could stay?'

'I could speak to my mum. She's offered already.'

Back at the station, Allie updated the team about her chat with Michelle first. 'I'm not sure why her story is different from back then. It could be a memory lapse. But I'll be interested to see what Colette and Kevin Ryland have to say about it. See if their recollections are the same or different from their statements.' Then she mentioned seeing Dave. 'He's running tests on some of the forensic evidence back then.'

'What are you thinking, boss?' Perry wanted to know.

'Somehow I don't think Jamie Sanderson killed Winston Lowe.'

'I agree. But there was evidence to prosecute and charge him for it.'

'Yes, and plenty of it.'

'So either something was missed or –'

'Something was tampered with to make him seem guilty.'

'A cover-up?' Sam suggested.

'I hate to say it, but it's looking likely.' Allie sighed dramatically. 'Let's go through it all again and find out.'

CHAPTER THIRTY-SEVEN

'Would you like me to come in with you straightaway or do you want a little time alone?'

Lauren Farrington turned to DI Shenton. 'I'm not sure.' Her features crumpled at the thought of what she was about to do. But then she stepped forward. 'I need to do this alone first. Tia, would you mind staying here for a few minutes?'

Tia seemed upset, but she drew her eyes away.

Eventually her daughter spoke. 'I'll be right outside if you need me, Mum.'

Lauren let herself into her home. She held her breath, half expecting Nick to come running down the stairs and throw his arms around her, tell her it had all been a joke – or a bad dream, even. But wishing wouldn't change things. Hoping wouldn't bring him back.

Yvonne had wanted to come with her, but Lauren had talked her out of it. She needed to do this by herself. She was the one who would have to come home to this empty house every day. So too would Tia, but Tia wouldn't feel the loss as much as she did. She wouldn't physically ache for a part of her life that had disappeared in a blaze of whys and wherefores.

She closed the door behind her and leaned on it, unable to move another step right then. Nick's coat was at the bottom of the banister. The number of times she would have told him to move it, hang it up not leave it lying round.

She tried to recall if it was the coat he'd worn on the morning of his death. He had two he used for work. A lightweight one and a thick, black coat to his knees. It was the thick black one that he wore the most.

It was the one that was over the banister now. He must have come in, taken it off, gone upstairs and...

She gulped away a sob threatening to erupt. Did he know he was going upstairs to his death? And how did his killer get him up there? Was he showing someone something?

But in the bedroom?

It didn't make any more sense now than when she'd first been told it was a suspected suicide.

If Nick had taken his life, it would have meant he'd done everything himself. Now that he hadn't, it shed a whole new light on things.

Someone had got him up the stairs. Not carried him, but coerced maybe? But then why set up the alcohol and the tablets? Surely the knife was enough.

She turned back towards the front door. Whoever had got in must have known Nick. If someone had come to the door who he didn't recognise, even if he'd answered it without thought, he would have fought to keep them from getting in.

And things would be out of place, and they weren't. Everything seemed as it was when she had left it that morning. The morning her whole life was about to change.

Slowly she went upstairs. Even in her state of mind she moved a little to the right on the step that creaked. The house was pre-war, built in 1936. Lauren reckoned each one of them knew noises and bumps, and creaks and groans as the house settled around them every night. She wondered if she would find this a comfort or if she'd be running to check the door every time she heard a noise.

Would the person who came after Nick come after her next? Was she even safe? Well, she might be scared but she was damned if she was going to let anyone run her out of her home. So this had to be done.

At the top of the stairs, she hesitated for a moment before practically running along the landing and into their bedroom. She knew if she didn't that she would turn and go back downstairs.

She had to face her fears and go in that room again. That room was her future. It was what her whole life depended on.

Would she move from here? Was she strong enough to stay here knowing what happened in there, or did she never want to live in the house again?

This part was up to her, nothing to do with Tia, or Yvonne, or her family. Her decision.

In the room, her tears fell as she gazed at the bed. Still she had the image of him lying there, on his side, one arm out, dripping blood. She could still see the knife on the floor, the emptiness of his face.

She removed her shoes and lay down on the bed. The covers had been taken away as evidence. She wouldn't be able to smell either of their scents. But at least the mattress had remained. There had been talk of the police taking that for forensics at one time, although she'd get another one now anyway.

She curled up in a foetal position where Nick had last lain. What would have been going through his mind? Would he have realised that someone had attacked him? Was the slash of the knife quick, unexpected, therefore he wouldn't have been able to stop it anyway? Here, too, there was no sign of disarray.

What the hell had happened?

CHAPTER THIRTY-EIGHT

Allie gave Tia a reassuring smile, deciding now would be a good time to have that chat. But Tia went to sit on the wall. Immediately, she started scrolling on her phone. Undeterred, Allie went to sit next to her.

Tia could easily pass for eighteen. Thick foundation covering a cluster of spots, black eyeliner, perfectly applied lipstick. She had an air of maturity about her, yet strip away the layers, and she was a vulnerable young woman.

Allie despised how today's teenagers grew up too quickly but equally realised that she had been the same when she'd been sixteen. She'd always wanted to be the same age as her sister, Karen, who had been four years older than her. When Allie was fifteen and still at school and Karen was nineteen, working and driving her own car, having a steady boyfriend, four years seemed such a lot.

'My sergeant told me that you weren't at school the day your dad was killed and that you were with Troy Menzies.' Allie stared at her. 'Have you been seeing him long?'

Tia's eyes widened. 'About two months,' she said quietly. 'You won't say anything, will you? Mum and Dad don't let me out on my own much at night.' The tears fell as she realised what she'd said. 'I mean...'

Allie rested a hand on Tia's forearm. 'I knew what you meant. It will take a while to get used to this, I know.'

'No, you don't,' she snapped. 'You haven't lost your dad.'

'That's true, but I did lose a sister when I was younger.' She paused. 'So, where did you and Troy meet? Was it through your dad at the centre?'

Tia shrugged, not forthcoming with anything that might get her into trouble.

'He's a lot older than you.'

'Only six years.'

Her tone was defiant, but Allie could hear a tremor in it. What wasn't she telling her?

'I'm curious as to why you chose to spend time with him rather than go to school.'

'I like him, there's nothing wrong in that, is there?'

'Of course not. As long as he treats you well.'

'He does. He's always buying me things. He likes me.'

The word "grooming" sprang to Allie's mind, but she kept it to herself. However, she did want to warn Tia off if she could.

'You do know that he's a drug dealer?'

Tia wouldn't look at her. 'I haven't seen him with anything.'

'So you've not been in his car while he's gone into someone's house?'

'No.'

'Or seen him come out of anywhere with parcels?'

'No.'

'Been with him when he's dropped off or collected someone from the train station?'

'No! What is this?' Tia folded her arms. 'I thought you

were trying to find the man who murdered my dad, not interrogating me.'

'I'm *trying* to keep you safe. You're not so silly that you don't know what he's up to. Troy is known to us, Tia. I obviously can't say any more than that, but be careful he doesn't get you into something you're not keen on. Something that will get you into trouble, with me, for instance.'

Allie knew the young girl would catch her drift. Really, she wanted to tell Tia that Troy was drug-dealing scum who'd let someone else take the rap if he could get away with it.

'I know what I'm doing,' Tia said after a pause.

It was said like a sixteen-year-old who hadn't lived life yet, not mature enough to know when things would go wrong. Allie was about to go into lecture mode when she heard a scream.

Both she and Tia froze.

It wasn't one of fear that might send Allie running into Poppy's room, afraid the young girl had had a nightmare.

It wasn't a scream of pain that someone had been in an accident.

It was the scream of grief, as someone realised that their life had changed forever.

'Wait here,' Allie told Tia.

'But I want to –'

'Please, give me a moment.'

The teenager did as she was told. Allie jogged upstairs and stopped by the open bedroom door, almost in tears at what she saw. Lauren was lying on the side of the bed where her husband had been found.

There was nothing she could do. It was too raw and personal for her to intrude. Allie knew she would be making matters worse if she went into the room. This wasn't her pain to live with. Lauren needed to deal with the grief herself.

She knocked quietly on the door. 'Just checking you're okay. I won't come in unless you need me to.'

There was a beat of silence before Lauren replied. 'I'm fine, thanks, but I'd like to be alone for a while longer.'

'I'll be here when you're ready.'

Tia was at the bottom of the stairs, worry etched on her face. 'Is she okay?'

'I think she needs a few minutes. Let me make you a cup of tea.'

CHAPTER THIRTY-NINE

Allie knocked on the door of the Ryland household. Earlier she'd spoken to Colette on the phone and arranged to come to see her and Kevin. Both seemed nervous as she and Frankie entered the house.

They were shown into the living room, the house a pretty standard layout for the majority of council-owned properties on the estate. But it was neat and homely, decorated well with a modern touch. A pale-coloured settee and a matching armchair. Striped wallpaper and a TV over the fireplace. A selection of family photos on one wall, including a baby morphing into a young girl and then a woman.

'Have you found out who killed Nick Farrington yet?' Kevin asked as soon as they'd introduced themselves.

'We're waiting on forensics, so I can't tell you any more than that right now.'

'But you know that we knew Jamie Sanderson?'

'Yes.'

'So you don't know what he's going to do next?'

'There's a logical pattern, but we can only work on assumption. Which is why we're here to have a chat with you.

We're trying to establish a motive for Jamie to attack Michelle, and to murder Nick if we find evidence linking him to that. So my team have been going over the murder of Winston Lowe from 1999.'

The blood dropped right out of Colette's face, and she sat down. Kevin glanced at her surreptitiously and then did the same. Allie and Frankie followed suit.

'We saw you were both interviewed by the police at the time,' Allie went on. 'Is that correct?'

'Yes, but we didn't have anything to do with the murder,' Kevin stated.

'I never said you did.' Allie glanced surreptitiously at Frankie before continuing. 'Can you tell me what was asked and what you answered?'

'Don't you have a record of it?'

'We do, but I'd like you to tell me in your own words.'

'I can't remember what I had for my tea two nights ago, let alone that many years.'

Allie frowned. Was Kevin stalling, or was there more to this conversation?

'Please try,' she urged, looking at Colette. 'Can you remember anything while Kevin has a think?'

'We weren't there,' Colette told her. 'Jamie went to the shop, but he never came back. We waited for a while and then went home.'

'And you, Kevin? Is that similar to what you remember?'

'Yeah. That's right what Colette said. It was the next day we learned what had happened to Winston. Shame, he was a nice man.'

Allie knew what Michelle told them was now contradicting what they were saying, but for now she kept quiet.

'Can you think of a reason he would come after Michelle like he did?'

They both shook their heads.

'Or to kill Nick Farrington?'

Colette burst into tears. 'This is too much. If Jamie is responsible for both, he might come after us next.' She turned to Kevin. 'He might, might he?'

'I don't know!'

Shocked by his raised voice, Allie changed the subject slightly. 'Do you have children?'

'A daughter, Hannah. She's twenty-five, lives in Derby.'

'Is she due to visit you soon? I'd be wanting to defer that.'

'You think he'd come after Hannah?' Colette covered her hand with her mouth.

'We don't know what he's going to do next, if anything. We're simply trying to stop anyone getting hurt if that is his intention.'

'Why haven't you caught him yet when you know his name?' Kevin said. 'He could be anywhere.'

'We are sharing as much as we can, and widely.'

'Why aren't the press and TV channels shoving his image into every house in the city? That would catch him.'

'It's not as simple as that, Kevin,' Allie told him.

'Why not? If people can get cancelled in a matter of hours, then I'm sure you could find a killer among us. It's madness that you haven't already.'

Allie kept it to herself that his insinuations were ridiculous. 'We're doing everything we can,' she appeased.

'Yeah? Well, it's obviously not enough.'

'Why are you so angry?' She posed the question to Kevin. 'We're trying to solve a murder and find the man who attacked your friend. We're now warning you to be vigilant, and yet you're quite sharp with us.'

'Sorry, a bit tired, that's all.' Kevin grimaced. 'And we're both worried about the situation. Jamie murdered someone when he was sixteen, and it seems he's never stopped. We want him caught.'

'I understand. Do either of you know a man called Shaun Green?'

'No.' They spoke in unison.

By their lack of reaction to the name, Allie sensed they were being honest.

'Should we?' Kevin asked. 'Who is he?'

Allie didn't answer his question, posing another instead. 'We can't be certain, but we believe Sanderson may target either one of you next. So I need you both to take precautions.'

'He's always been not right in the head,' Kevin spat.

'Will you let us know when you hear something?' Colette asked.

'We will. We'll show ourselves out, thanks. Just be mindful.'

Outside, out of hearing range, Allie glanced at Frankie as she opened the gate. 'That was an odd conversation.'

Frankie raised his eyebrows. 'It was awkward to say the least. I wonder what's going on?'

'Colette's also remembering it wrong – or right if her original statement is wrong.'

They were level with her car, but before they got in, Frankie spoke again. 'Why do you think Kevin was so hostile?'

Allie leaned on the roof, thinking for a moment. 'Maybe we said something that was too close to home.'

'There's definitely something they're not telling us.'

'And it's our job to find out what that is. I'm going to do more digging.'

CHAPTER FORTY

Michelle had been back from the hospital a mere half an hour when the doorbell rang. She hoped it wasn't a reporter from *Stoke News* because she didn't want to talk to anyone.

She was shocked when she saw who it was.

'Hi, Michelle!' Kevin cried. 'I wanted to see how you are. I heard about what happened and I'm glad you're on the mend.' He held out the flowers. 'These are for you. Colette sends her love.'

It was like stepping back in time, seeing a ghost, in fact. Michelle hadn't seen Kevin in what, ten years now, it must be. He was dressed casually, jeans and checked shirt showing under a black parka-style coat. He'd hardly changed at all – more age lines and wrinkles, a little less of his dark hair, and it was a lot shorter.

Michelle studied him surreptitiously while he glanced around the room. She wondered if he was taking in the tatty wallpaper.

'How did you know I was home… from the hospital?' she asked when he stepped inside.

'Colette messaged me after we had a visit from the police,

so I thought I'd call. I couldn't believe it when I heard what had happened.' He sat down uninvited. 'Is no one with you?'

'I'm waiting for my mum to pick me up. I've split with Brian.'

'Well, I'm not sorry to hear that. I thought it would have been that good-for-nothing idiot of yours, but it was Jamie Sanderson. Are you sure?'

She nodded.

'And you had no warning? You hadn't seen him around?'

'No, nothing. Have you?'

Kevin shook his head. 'Nick of all people – murdered. Have the police said anything to you? Have they any idea who could have done that? Do they think that was Jamie, too?'

Michelle shrugged. 'They're saying there's not enough evidence back yet, but it has to be him, doesn't it? Although I don't know why now after all these years. He could have got to us when he first came out of prison.'

'That is, if it is him.'

'Do you think it was?'

'I'm not certain,' he fibbed. 'We'll have to keep an eye out. If he contacts you again, let me know before you say anything to the police.'

'Why?'

'Because I say so.'

Michelle wasn't sure that was the only thing he was worried about. Back in the day, Kevin could be very persuasive. She'd always had her suspicions that he was more involved in the night than he said. But he'd told her and Colette that it was only Jamie who went in the shop. That he and Nick were across the road, so they hadn't mentioned it to the police. Jamie must have grassed on them all, because they'd been questioned, but each one of them had stuck by what Kevin had told them to say.

It must be the truth. How would she ever know different?

Only the three of them knew what really happened. And now, Nick was dead, mostly likely killed by Jamie.

'How's Lauren coping?' she asked. 'Have you been to see her? I shall pop over once I feel well enough.'

'I'm going to see her this evening. It will be weird without Nick around.'

'Does she know Jamie is back?'

'Not unless the police told her. I haven't said anything. I haven't spoken to her in a while.'

'Do you want me to go with you? I might be able to tomorrow.'

'No, I only want to pay my respects. They won't release Nick's body for a while, will they?'

'The detective inspector told me they were struggling to find any witnesses, not much CCTV footage around, nothing on door cams except a man walking calmly away, but you can't see his face.'

'I suppose most people would be going past in their cars. How many would have spotted anything out of the ordinary driving past in their rush to get home?'

'Something might jog someone's memory if the police talk about it, though.' A sob escaped Michelle.

Kevin's hands clasped over hers. 'Make sure you stick to the original story if the police question you about what happened on the night Winston Lowe was killed.' He squeezed her fingers. 'Okay?'

She grimaced. 'Okay.'

'You still need to keep your mouth shut. You haven't said anything to the police about that night, have you?'

Michelle shook her head vehemently. She wasn't about to tell Kevin that the police had already asked her.

'Good, let's keep it that way.'

The doorbell rang, and she hobbled to the window, thankful to get away from Kevin. There was a man carrying a bouquet of flowers. A florist van was parked up, too, so she went to open the front door.

'Flowers for Mrs Price,' the man said, smiling as he passed them to her.

Michelle took them from him and went through to the kitchen, picking out the small envelope to see what soppy message Brian had written. He wasn't going to win her back with a bunch of roses, that was for sure. Still, it was nice to receive them unexpectedly.

'Who are they from?' Kevin asked.

'I don't know yet. Probably Brian.' She opened the envelope and read the message, paling when she took in the sender's name.

Hope you get better soon. Jamie.

Michelle gasped. She held on to a chair before her legs gave way.

'What's up?'

'Oh, nothing.' She composed herself quickly. 'Brian thinks being all soppy will win me over. But it won't.' She popped the flowers into the waste bin and wiped her hands. 'That's where they belong.'

Kevin nodded. 'I'll be off now then. You keep in touch, yeah? You know where we are. Especially if the police come sniffing again.'

Michelle let him out, sighing with relief once she closed the door behind him. Then she burst into tears at the thought that Jamie was behind the flowers. Would he come after her again?

She rang her mum, glad when she answered the call

almost straightaway. 'Mum, I was wondering how long you're going to be?'

'No more than ten minutes. I'm in the little Tesco. Thought I'd get you something nice for tea.'

Michelle went to wait in the front window until she could see her car pulling up. She wouldn't feel safe until she knew Jamie Sanderson couldn't harm her again.

CHAPTER FORTY-ONE

Allie knocked on the door of Gary Hallam's house. Shoulders straight, she blew out a long puff of breath when an outline of a figure appeared at the other side of the glass door.

'Despite what's going on, I'm not looking forward to this,' she told Perry who was by her side this time.

'Me neither.'

The door opened, and a man in his early sixties gave them a welcoming smile.

'Hi, it's Allie Shenton. This is Perry Wright. We spoke earlier on the phone.'

'Hello, nice to meet you.' Gary offered his hand to them.

They followed him into the living room. It was a quirky property, if a little dated and worn in places. A detached house, with large bay windows and a picture rail and fireplace that seemed original. But there were no family photos in this one.

'What can I do for you?' Gary smiled. 'Happy to help in any way.'

From first impressions, Allie wondered why he was being

so jovial with them. Did he not suspect what they'd be here for? He must have seen Jamie Sanderson's face on the news.

Gary pointed to the settee. She and Perry sat next to each other while he took the armchair nearest to the fireplace.

'You mentioned I'd worked on a case you'd like some details on.'

'Please.' Allie took out her notebook for reference. 'It was in 1999, the death of Winston Lowe. He ran a newsagent's over in Parker Close. A sixteen-year-old, Jamie Sanderson, stabbed him, and he died on the shop floor.'

'Ah, yes. The guy in the news. That case was brutal. I've never seen so much blood. It was everywhere.'

'Can you tell us about the investigation?'

'You don't have any notes?'

Allie shook her head. 'Paper ones are always going missing. I have a file but only bits in it. I was hoping to elaborate more with you as to what happened.'

'I'll try and remember. I was a new detective, so eager to learn. The case was the first murder I was involved in. We got a shout from Control – an anonymous phone call to say a shopkeeper had been stabbed.'

'Did you ever trace the call?'

'I don't think so. Things weren't so sophisticated back then.'

'Tracing technology was introduced in October 1998.'

'Oh, right. Maybe it wasn't working as good as it should then. Anyway, when we got there, the man was dead, his wife kneeling beside him, crying and holding on to him. It was hard to prise her away, I can tell you. I'll never forget that sound. She was traumatised. But we had to contain the crime scene.'

'The evidence on file suggests that there were at least two people at the scene but only Jamie Sanderson was interviewed and then subsequently charged. Was the other person not known to us?'

'I can't recall all the details, but I believe not.'

'When you interviewed Mr Sanderson, did he say he worked alone?'

Gary's gaze started to flick around the room, landing anywhere but on theirs. He shrugged. 'It was twenty-five years ago.'

'Let me help. He said he was with his friends, and he gave you their names.'

'Like I say, I don't know, but we would have done all we could to identify anyone else if that was true.'

'Did you speak to the people he named?'

'At the time, yes. They said they weren't out with him.'

'What I can't understand is where the teenagers came from? I mean, there must have been plenty of kids hanging around at that time of night. Did they offer information to you?'

'I can't recall.'

'So what made you interview these four in particular?'

He shrugged. 'Someone must have given in their names. Maybe it was Sanderson.'

'According to the dates and times on the statements, they were interviewed before he was arrested.' Allie paused for effect. 'So with no witnesses, Jamie took the rap.'

'You know the CCTV footage and cameras weren't a patch on what they are nowadays.' Gary's face reddened. 'There was no evidence other than his.'

'We believe there was someone else's prints on the knife,' Perry joined in.

'A partial,' Gary said.

Allie smirked: he could remember some things, then. 'Were the teenagers fingerprinted?'

'I don't think so.'

'Why not?'

'Because they said they weren't there.'

'But that fingerprint meant there was someone else with Sanderson, surely? It had Mr Lowe's blood on it. As did a palm print that we're having retested, too.'

'What are you getting at, Detectives? Because I don't like your tone.'

'As you must have seen from the news, one of the men was murdered two days ago,' Allie stepped in again. 'But there was a woman attacked and left for dead on the same day. She was able to identify it was Jamie Sanderson who came to her home. Both were two of the four teenagers you interviewed as part of the investigation into Winston Lowe's murder. We're obviously searching for Jamie, but we're also wondering if he will come after anyone else.'

Gary stood up quickly. 'You mean me?'

'I didn't say that. But we can't be certain. If you didn't treat him well, which it seems may be the case –'

'You have no right to say that!'

'He may hold a grievance against you and –'

Allie's phone rang. When she saw who the caller was, she stood up. 'I have to take this. I won't be a moment.'

She left the room and dashed outside. It had started to rain while they'd been inside, so she stood on the step, hoping the canopy would shield her from the brunt of it.

'Dave!' she cried. 'Please tell me you have exciting news for me.'

CHAPTER FORTY-TWO

'You do, don't you?' Allie said. 'I need to get to the bottom of why Sanderson is doing this.'

'The palm print with Winston Lowe's blood matches someone on our records. The extra fingerprint on the knife is the same person's, too. He has a criminal record, imprisoned twice, but after this event, so he wouldn't have been in the system in 1999.'

'Name?'

'Kevin Ryland. Ten out of ten for your intuition that something wasn't right.'

'So Sanderson *was* set up.' Allie pinched the bridge of her nose. 'This doesn't look good.'

'But you can tell the press about it, once you have Ryland in custody, of course? The public need to know, too.'

'We'll be sure to, but I expect Jamie will have gone to ground after what he's done recently.'

'He'll have a phone.'

'Most likely, but it will be a pay-as-you-go.' Allie sighed. 'We have no idea where he's living. He has nothing registered to him online, no social media accounts. It's like he's a ghost.'

'To all intents and purposes, he is. Someone who has been forgotten, even though protected by the system.'

'He didn't commit murder when he was sixteen. *Someone* made him into the monster he became.'

'Maybe so, but it was still his choice to come after the others. It's sad to think all this could have been avoided if the person responsible had owned up.'

'But unless Kevin Ryland cops for it, we'll never know if it was him or Nick, or even if it was Jamie who killed Winston Lowe. Kevin might say it was Nick now he can't speak for himself, although there isn't evidence that puts Nick there.'

Dave coughed, clearing his throat before continuing. 'I'm sending the knife for further tests. But other than that, he can be charged with perverting the course of justice, perhaps?'

'It's possible. I expect Colette and Michelle were told it was Sanderson by Ryland and Farrington. So now we know it wasn't him, it could have been either of the boys.'

'Do you really know it isn't him, though? His prints were on the knife.'

'I know, but he says he picked it up to throw it away from Kevin.' Allie groaned. 'It's not making sense. And why did Sanderson go after Michelle? She wasn't even there. Or maybe she was and she's covering up, too. I'll have to speak to all three of them again.'

'If it was Nick or Kevin who murdered Winston Lowe, maybe Sanderson will think Colette and Michelle were in on it. He'll think they lied so that Nick or Kevin could get away with it when really it might be nothing of the sort.'

'This is great work, Dave, and thanks for the chat. It'll be interesting to see what Hallam says about this new evidence. I'll caution him and then get uniform to bring him in, stick him in a cell, while me and Perry head over to Ryland's place.'

Allie went back inside Hallam's house. Gary was sitting

with his head in his hands. When he looked up, she noticed he'd been crying, and there were fresh tears running down his cheeks.

'I've cautioned him, Allie,' Perry told her. 'You need to hear this.'

Allie sat down, wondering when to share the content of the phone call. She thought maybe it was best to let Gary speak.

'What's going on?' she said when no one spoke.

'Kevin Ryland is my son,' Gary said.

Allie couldn't speak. She felt as if she'd been punched in the stomach. So not only did those teenagers lie about what happened to Winston Lowe, a grown man, a *detective*, corroborated their story enough to make sure the heat was taken away from his son? No, she couldn't believe what he was saying.

It had to be the truth, though, because all the niggles she'd been having were suddenly starting to make sense.

'He's my stepson really,' Gary continued. 'But I've been his dad since he was two years old. That's when I met his mum, and we married when he was four. His real father was never on the scene. I don't know where he is.

'Kevin was never an easy child to raise. He was in and out of trouble for most of his teens. When he came to me that night, he told me that Sanderson had stabbed Mr Lowe, that he'd been inside the shop when it happened, getting some sweets and cans of Coke. He said there was no reason to think Sanderson would do what he had, and that he'd panicked and ran.

'He asked me for help. He'd told his friends to say they hadn't been in the shop, but when two sets of prints came back, he confessed everything to me. I... made it go away for him.'

'You...' Allie closed her mouth before she said something

she regretted. Everyone had their own versions of what was right and wrong. Most people had a moral code, a line they wouldn't cross. And yet here she was, listening to a man who should have known better going against everything she believed.

'Did you do anything else?' she said instead.

'You were right. I took the statements from the kids who were with Kevin that night and made sure they said what I wanted them to.' He lowered his eyes momentarily. 'I'm ashamed of what I did, especially when Kevin continued getting into trouble. It was as if he'd got away with it once, he thought he could do what he wanted, and I did blame myself for that.

'At one time, he threatened to tell the force what I'd done if I didn't bail him out of a situation where he owed a lot of money. I'd had enough by then, but when he got sent down for grievous bodily harm, I left my job.

'My marriage broke down as the guilt put a strain on our relationship. I never told his mum what I'd done, but it split us up eventually anyway. She died two years ago. I haven't spoken to Kevin since then, not much before to be honest. So I know what it's like to have your life ruined. I've lived with this for years.'

'And yet you could have confessed at any minute,' Perry said quietly.

Gary's eyes dropped again. 'It had gone too far.'

Allie held in a sigh as she got to her feet. 'Stand up, please, and hold your hands out in front.' She read him his rights, unable to find an ounce of sympathy for him. There had been times during her career, and she was sure there would be many more, when she'd almost felt sorry to arrest certain people. When revenge had been taken on someone she thought deserved it.

But she would never, ever, have done anything like this.

. . .

Once transportation to the station had arrived, and Gary was in the back of a van, the door closed on him with his head in his hands again.

Allie turned to Perry. 'What a wanker. All that crap at the beginning as if he'd done nothing wrong. And such a selective memory. He let Jamie Sanderson rot in a cell, not caring how he'd perverted the course of justice to get him there.'

Perry too was in disbelief. 'You hear of corruption going on all the time, and yet it still punches you in the gut when it comes to light.'

'I'm glad I never got to work with him.' Allie buckled up and started the engine. 'Anyway, enough of the chatter and feeling pissed off about things. I need to speak to Jenny first, see what the process is regarding arresting Kevin.'

CHAPTER FORTY-THREE

Jamie made his way to the cemetery. He'd have to be quick because if the police were onto him, then there could be surveillance around the places they thought he might visit. But he wanted to see his mum's grave, talk to her one last time. Besides, how would they know where she'd be?

He laid the flowers he'd bought in front of her headstone. It had been purchased by their neighbours, friends who didn't want her to die without a resting place. It was nice of them, he thought now, as he gazed down at the words.

His name was on it, as a loving son. Of course he had always been that, but he'd let her down and he hadn't been able to see her on the outside to make amends.

'I'm so sorry, Mum,' he said quietly. Then, after taking a quick glance around, he made his way out. He'd wait until it was dark before going back to the flat. It was risky, and he wouldn't be there much longer, but it was home for now.

He called in at a small shop and bought a sandwich, along with a bottle of whisky and a coffee to go, then picked up a copy of *Stoke News*. Nick Farrington's murder was front-page headlines.

He kept his head down, but the shop was too busy for anyone to notice him. He wasn't much like his prison photo anyway. The last one had been taken about six years ago. He was safe for now as long as he stayed in the shadows.

Outside, he sat in his car and ate his sandwich. It was getting darker by the minute, so he didn't need to stay here for much longer.

He flicked through the newspaper, catching up with what the police had about him so far. It seemed like they were getting closer but not getting nearer either. They knew his name but not his address. They knew what he looked like but hidden under a hood with a scarf across his face, he could be anyone. They didn't know what car he drove, so he was inconspicuous right now, even though in plain sight.

Half an hour passed, and the night had drawn in enough. He started the engine and made his way to Parker Close. He needed to get ready for tomorrow.

Even though the shop had been derelict for years, it held too many memories. Jamie wished he could make amends for what happened to Winston Lowe. Kevin never should have taken his life. He had a wife and a family. All he was doing was trying to provide for them.

He started to gather together all the rubbish he could find in every room. There were lots of empty cardboard boxes and piles of newspapers and magazines. He trudged up and downstairs while he made a pile in the back bedroom.

With that task done, he went to his flat. Lying on the sofa, he drank some of the whisky, enough to relieve the tension, but enough to be alert if he had to move quickly.

He took out the list he'd made and held it up. There were only three more names on it. He was getting close to the end.

If he survived until then, of course. Because he was not going back to prison.

. . .

Kevin knocked on Lauren Farrington's front door. The flowers he held cost a fortune. What with getting a smaller bunch for Michelle, he was well out of pocket today. But they were good decoys.

It surprised him to see someone else answer the door. She was a woman in her late twenties with blonde hair.

'Can I help you?' she asked.

'I'm here to see Lauren.'

'And you are?'

'I'm... I was a friend of Nick's.'

'Let me see if she's up for a visitor. I won't be a moment.'

Annoyed to be left on the step, he snapped back at her disappearing back, 'And *you* are?'

'PC Joy, family liaison officer.'

She didn't even turn around, but Kevin was glad. She couldn't then see his expression. He hadn't thought of police still being there.

The woman was back in a minute, beckoning him in. 'Lauren will see you if it's a short visit?'

'Oh, yeah, of course.' He followed her through to the living room.

It had been a long time since they'd seen each other, and even then he could count the times on both hands. He stood in the doorway, then cleared his throat to speak.

'Hi, Lauren. These are for you, from me and Colette. How are you?'

'I wish people would stop asking me that,' she muttered, taking them from him.

'This place has changed,' he said, stamping his foot quietly. 'Nice floors. Did Nick lay...'

'You can say his name. I won't burst into uncontrollable tears. That's Tia's job.'

'How is she?' Kevin sat down at Lauren's request.

'Devastated, as am I. But we shut it out. Every now and again it comes bursting through, but we push it down.'

Kevin smiled faintly, wishing he'd never come. He couldn't say anything in front of the police, but it was vital he found out what, if anything, Nick had told Lauren.

'It's so ghastly to go through,' Lauren offered into the silence.

'That's understandable.' Kevin sighed. 'I honestly don't know how you're coping with it all.'

'I put a brave face on. It's even worse when the killer, that Sanderson, is still out there. And people coming and going, all the time. Sometimes there's so much going on, so many officers at the house that I want to scream at the top of my voice, tell them to leave me in peace. Other times, I can't stand the quiet of the house for only a few seconds, and I turn on the TV in every room we have them. Just to hear someone else speak. But now they are covered in news about Nick.'

'Do you know when they will – when the funeral is yet?'

'They can't release the body.'

'Have the police told you it was Sanderson?'

'No, I'm assuming.'

Kevin decided to come out with what he wanted to know. 'Did Nick ever mention him to you?'

'No. But then again, he never talked about his school days. It was as if he wanted to blank them out. I've often wondered why. Do you know?'

Kevin shook his head vehemently, knowing that was his cue to leave. Once back in his car, he thought about where Sanderson could be hiding out. He needed to find him before he caused any more damage.

CHAPTER FORTY-FOUR

Later that evening, Jamie stood in front of Kevin and Colette's house. From the pavement, he could see straight in, the idiots not bothering to close the curtains. It wouldn't matter anyway, as they'd be out soon.

The two of them were seated, one on the settee and one on the armchair, glued to the widescreen TV that took over most of the room. There didn't seem to be much conversation going on. They were like a couple of zombies.

He might have guessed Kevin wouldn't live in anything better than this. Nick he could believe making something better of himself. Jamie had never had him down as anything but a sheep, so perhaps they'd lost contact once they left school. Nick was always easily influenced by Kevin, but people change when they grow up. If they grow up.

He hadn't expected Kevin to be married to Colette, though.

He wondered how their marriage was holding up. Did Kevin treat her well, or had his temper followed him into their relationship? How had they got together? When had they got married? All questions he'd never get an answer to, but each would keep him awake until his task was complete.

He slid an envelope underneath the windscreen wiper of a cheap white van that had seen better days. His final act was to bang on the bonnet so the car alarm would go off. If it had one.

It did. Showtime.

He leaned against the driver's door, arms folded, until he noticed a light go on in the hallway.

Kevin opened the door and marched towards him. 'You've got some nerve showing up here.' He swung an iron bar at his side. 'You'd better fuck off right now or I'll –'

'You'll call the police? Sure, I'll wait for them to arrive. Then what?'

'You'll get arrested for what you've done.'

'Maybe. But you might, too. Because I'm sure they will have been looking into why I attacked Michelle and killed Nick. I'm sure they'll connect the dots back to Winston Lowe.'

'After what you've done, do you think that matters? Why did you kill Nick?'

'No comment.' Jamie's laughter was cruel.

His reply infuriated Kevin. 'What do you want?'

'Justice.'

'For something we did when we were kids?'

'You killed someone, and I got blamed for it.'

'I was sixteen.'

'So was I! Did you tell Colette and Michelle to say that they hadn't seen me that night? That you and Nick weren't even there?'

'We couldn't trust the girls not to blabber, so only me and Nick knew as we were in the shop.'

'Yeah, didn't work out well for him eventually, did it?'

The iron bar went up in the air. 'I'm warning you, get away from my property.'

'Your property?' Jamie huffed. 'It's privately rented shit. I see you've not made much of yourself either.'

Jamie stood up when Kevin came at him with a roar, bar raised in the air. He moved to one side, dodging it on its descent and smirking when he saw the dent it left behind as it hit the side of the van.

Kevin's face was a picture. He came at him again.

This time, Jamie grabbed the bar and pulled it from Kevin's grip. With as much force as he could muster, he backhanded it across Kevin's face. Blood from his nose spurted in mid-air.

Kevin dropped to his knees and Jamie raised the bar again. This time it hit him under the chin, his head flying back. He flopped onto the pavement.

Jamie walked slowly towards him as Kevin cried out in pain, crawling away. He brought the bar down on him, again and again.

The top of his legs.

The middle of his back.

Across his shoulders.

Then directly to his head.

Kevin stopped crawling immediately.

But Jamie didn't stop.

The bar came down again and again.

'Jamie! No, please! Stop.'

Jamie felt a tug of his arm and turned to see Colette, tears pouring down her face. He stared at her, and then down at Kevin's lifeless body. Having done what he'd set out to do, he walked away, leaving Colette screaming.

At the bottom of the street, he turned for one last look. Colette was sitting at the side of Kevin, sobbing while she tried to get him to wake up. People were coming out from every door. It was a pity he couldn't stay to watch the fun, but he had other things on his mind. Like the final steps of his plan.

'Wake up, Kev.' Colette rolled her husband onto his back and shook his shoulder, even then knowing there would be no response. The blood pouring from Kevin's head was pooling rapidly. She had to go inside to get her phone, call for the police and an ambulance, but didn't want to leave him.

'Get my phone,' she yelled to a neighbour who seemed to be glued to the spot. 'It's in the kitchen.'

'I have mine. I'll call for you.'

'No, I need to do it.' She held out her hand, and the woman passed it to her.

'Police, what's your emergency?'

'My husband.' Colette's words came out staccato. 'He's been attacked outside our house. I don't think he's breathing. Please, you have to come quickly.'

'Let me take your details and get people on their way and then stay on the line. Can you do that for me?'

'He's dead! He's not moving.'

'I understand. What's his name and the address?'

Colette told them.

'There's an ambulance allocated to you. It should be with you shortly. Now, is he still not breathing?'

'I can't tell.'

'I need you to put your hand on his chest and start pressing down on it. Not hard enough to hurt him, but enough to give him a jolt, okay? Count to five with me and then breathe into his mouth.'

'How the hell can I do that?' Colette sobbed. 'Half of his face has gone.'

CHAPTER FORTY-FIVE

After speaking with Jenny, Allie and Perry were on their way to the Rylands' address to pick up Kevin when a call came in over the airwaves.

'All units, assault on male outside twenty-two Carter Street. Ambulance en route. Possible life extinct.'

She and Perry glanced at each other, eyes widening.

Allie flicked on the blues and twos, putting her foot down when she reached a straight road. 'Please don't say Sanderson got to Kevin before we could.'

Perry picked up the handset. 'We're minutes away. Show us responding. Any further details?'

'Call came from his wife, Colette Ryland. Victim is her husband, Kevin. The male is suspected to be Jamie Sanderson, who left on foot.'

'He must be in the vicinity, although he could have a vehicle parked nearby,' Allie remarked. 'Keep your eyes peeled, Perry.'

When Allie turned into Carter Street, updates were still coming through. She parked next to the ambulance. There were people on the lawn and a paramedic crew around someone.

Allie could see Colette and raced over to her. 'What happened?'

Colette stood still as if she hadn't heard her.

Allie touched her arm. 'Colette,' she said gently but firmly.

Colette glanced at her, as if seeing her for the first time. 'He's... he's dead.'

Allie stayed with her while Perry made a call to Control. He took over as more officers arrived.

The paramedics were working to revive Kevin, but she knew it wasn't going to work. He lay limp, the bottom half of his face unrecognisable. The amount of blood behind his head was huge. There was no way anyone could survive that.

They stayed as they were until the paramedics pronounced no signs of life. Colette gave out an almighty scream, and Allie tried to comfort her. She couldn't blame Colette when she slapped her arm away.

'This is your fault,' she yelled. 'You should have stopped Jamie.'

'Did Jamie do this?' Allie had to confirm it.

'You should have caught him before he could hurt us. You let Michelle down, too.'

'Was it Jamie?' she repeated.

'Yes! You let Nick down and you let me down. You're the police. You're supposed to protect us!'

Allie waited for her to get everything off her chest before speaking again. 'Let's go inside. There's no more you can do out here, and we will need to start searching the area.'

'I can't leave him.'

Allie shepherded her into the house. They went through to the kitchen, and she sat Colette down at the table. She pulled out a chair, sitting next to her, instantly seeing the blood covering Colette's hands. They'd need to process her, as well as her clothes, later that evening. It wasn't going to be easy.

She sighed inwardly, realising they could have been minutes away from stopping this. Sanderson seemed hellbent on getting to the couple. Yet she couldn't understand why he hadn't done anything to Colette. He'd attacked Michelle in the hope of killing her, so why spare Colette after he'd butchered Kevin?

'I'm so sorry for your loss,' Allie began. 'But I need to ask you a few things while it's fresh in your mind. We need as much information as we can.'

Colette nodded.

'Did Kevin say anything to you?' she asked after Colette had gone through what had happened.

'He didn't have chance. We heard the alarm on the van going off. Kevin went out to switch it off. I didn't know anything was going on at first, until I heard shouting.'

'What about Sanderson?'

Colette flinched when she said his name.

There was a knock on the door. Perry opened it. 'Boss?'

'I won't be a moment,' she told Colette.

In the hallway, Perry held up an evidence bag. Inside was a handwritten note, all in capital letters. 'It was under the windscreen wiper on the van.'

Allie took it from him to scrutinise it. '"IT WAS ME." Is Sanderson saying what we think? That Nick lied, and it was Kevin who killed Winston Lowe?'

'It would match the fresh evidence we have. But then why didn't he do anything to Colette? She was part of the original group of friends.'

'My first thought was murdering her husband in front of her was enough.' Allie glanced at the closed kitchen door. 'So it seems Jamie came to the house to leave that note and to be seen. Kevin came out to him brandishing an iron bar that indirectly led to his death.' She shook her head, trying to rid it of the images she was conjuring up.

'Grim,' Perry admitted.

She left him to it then and went back to Colette, hoping to get as much information as she could. But Colette spoke first, her comment completely taking Allie by surprise.

'I have to tell you something,' Colette started. 'This wasn't the first time I've seen Jamie.'

Allie remained calm and quiet while she heard about the notes and the photo that Sanderson had given to Colette. She groaned inwardly hearing that Kevin had destroyed them. He had no right to do that. It was evidence that might have led them to Sanderson sooner or linked cases quicker. Now Kevin was gone. It beggared belief, but it had happened.

'I'm sorry.' Colette's body began to shake. 'I told him to come to you, but he wouldn't.'

She broke down again, heartbreaking sobs that ripped through Allie. A feeling of failure washed over her. They hadn't been quick enough to stop this. And yet, they'd been going full pelt since Michelle Price had been attacked. Intel gathering was one of the hardest and lengthiest jobs. Her team were good – she was good. There *was* no fault on their behalf.

Seeing the woman in her grief, her fury disappeared in an instant. Colette was suffering enough without feeling her wrath, too. What was done was done.

Allie stayed quiet. She couldn't tell her what she'd learned from Gary Hallam until she was cleared to do so. Only then could she say what had happened.

But she did wonder how much Colette knew about the night Winston Lowe had been murdered. It wasn't the time to ask her now, but she suspected that, just like Michelle, Kevin would have told her that it was down to Jamie.

'I suppose you're going to say that I should stay somewhere else, like you did to Michelle and Lauren?'

'Well, it would be wise until we've apprehended Sanderson and –'

'No.' Colette objected. 'Let him do his worst. My daughter needs to be told, and she'll come home soon. There'll be plenty of police outside, and I won't sleep anyway. Not after... seeing...'

'Okay, for now. I'll arrange for an officer to stay outside your home until the wider team leave.'

As soon as Allie was out of there, there was a ton of things she had to do. First and foremost, they needed to look further afield for Jamie Sanderson. Alert the public to the danger. And then...

The list was endless, but she was out to catch a killer before he struck again.

'He wasn't easy to live with, but I loved him,' Colette said.

Allie gave Colette a faint smile. 'Does he have family?' She had to ask, even though she'd spoken to Kevin's stepfather. They would at least try and locate his father.

'Only his dad, Gary. He lives in Waybridge Street, if he's still there. Kevin hasn't visited him in years, and we haven't seen him since his mum's funeral. He wasn't his real dad. It's number twelve.'

'And is there anyone else you'd like us to contact?'

'No, I'll do that. I want to. I need something to do. And Hannah needs to know so she can come home.'

Colette had told her that already. Allie wondered if she was going into shock. She'd arrange for someone to sit with her until the morning. It was the least she could do.

CHAPTER FORTY-SIX

Jenny was waiting for an update when Allie and Perry got back to the station. With weary feet, Allie made her way upstairs to her office.

'Another one gone, and yet we're no further forward finding Sanderson.' Jenny removed her glasses and pinching the bridge of her nose.

'We're working as hard as we can, ma'am,' Allie responded.

'I'm not doubting that.' She waved a hand in the air. 'I'm airing my concerns that he's still out there.'

'We have officers who've searched everywhere he might be. We thought he may have skipped the city.'

'Well, he clearly hasn't.'

'Colette Ryland says when she saw him this morning, he had a beard but he's clean-shaven now.' Allie got Jenny up to speed with everything she had learned.

Jenny's shoulders drooped. 'I suppose this explains everything after what Gary Hallam did. Where is he right now?'

'In the cells.'

'I don't envy you having to tell him about his son.' Jenny

sat forward. 'Okay, I'll get a press response ready and run with it first thing in the morning.'

'Yes, ma'am.'

Allie couldn't get out of the office quick enough. She jogged downstairs to join her team, thankful that she'd not been torn off a strip. But her DCI knew as well as her that they were doing everything they could. Allie wasn't one not to work to the book either. Everything would be done properly on her watch. She could rely on her team for that, too.

'I've spoken to Mrs Lowe's daughter, boss,' Sam said, stretching up a hand for attention when Allie walked across the floor to them. 'They're going on holiday in the morning, but she's agreed to see us first thing.'

'Thanks, Sam. Frankie, can you do that, on your way in? Pick up on anything she says that contradicts what Hallam's told us. We need to see into this further. And start checking the statements back from the murder trial, please.'

Frankie wiggled the mouse to wake up his computer. 'Anything else, boss?' he said when Allie hadn't moved.

'No.' Allie knew she was putting off the inevitable. 'Now I have to tell Gary Hallam about Kevin Ryland.'

Gary Hallam sat in cell fourteen, his legs covered in a blanket. Despite the mild October day, he couldn't stop shivering.

The noise around him was deafening. One man in another cell was screaming out obscenities at the top of his voice, hammering at the door with his fists.

It had been quite a culture shock to be on the other side of things. Gary had brought in many a prisoner and put them into the very same cell he was in now. He'd stood with them in the custody suite while they were booked in.

Going through it all himself, on the wrong side of the law, was something that had haunted his dreams for years. Yet, now after twenty-five years, he had almost forgotten what had brought him here, thinking it was over.

To find out it wasn't, and that Jamie Sanderson had gone on to commit crimes for most of his life and then started murdering people who he thought had wronged him was beyond his belief. He couldn't be responsible for what another person did, and yet, he realised that it was entirely his fault. He'd started the ball rolling.

The door opened, and Allie popped her head around the door. She closed it to for privacy and then came to sit next to him.

'How are you doing?' she queried.

'Kind of you to ask, but I can guess you know the answer.' He glanced at her. 'It's all my own doing.'

'We're ready to charge you now, and then you'll be bailed.'

He nodded, tears welling in his eyes at the thought.

'But I need to tell you something first. I won't beat about the bush because it's going to be hard to hear.'

He heard her take a breath before speaking again.

'Jamie Sanderson got to Kevin this evening. I'm afraid he died at the scene of the crime.'

What life was left inside Gary died right there, too. Words wouldn't come at first, so he let Allie continue.

'I'm so sorry for your loss, and I'm sorry, too, that we didn't apprehend Sanderson in time. This has been a really difficult case for us. You're not the only one who's been withholding information.'

'How did... how did he die?'

'I don't want to go into detail, not yet, but it was a fatal attack outside his home. Sadly, we don't need anyone to identify his body because his wife was there at the time.'

A sob escaped him.

'Shall I give you a moment before I take you to the custody sergeant?'

Gary wiped at his eyes. 'I'm fine, thanks. I'd rather go home.'

They stood up, and he followed her back to the desk.

'You will be on bail as we don't feel you are a risk to the public,' the custody sergeant explained. 'However, please be vigilant when you do leave here. Jamie Sanderson has not been located yet.'

'Maybe it's best if Jamie does get to me. It's what I deserve.'

'Are you sure you're going to be okay going home alone? I'm concerned about your mental health as well as safety issues. You've had a terrible shock this evening.'

'No, thanks. I'll be fine.' Gary held his head down until it was time to sign out.

'Let me give you a lift,' Allie offered then. 'I'm leaving now, and your house is on my way.'

Gary went to shake his head.

'I won't take no for an answer.'

He followed her again, feeling lost, bereft, and so ashamed. Losing Kevin, even if he hadn't seen him in some years, was a dreadful blow. But most of him felt relieved that it was all over.

CHAPTER FORTY-SEVEN

Allie went back upstairs to her team, every step heavy. It had been a taxing day, to say the least. First she'd found out that Gary Hallam had lied about his son. Then that son had been murdered by the person he'd set up to take the blame.

Having to tell Hallam had been harrowing, and yet, in some ways, she'd wanted to gloat. If it wasn't for him interfering in the first place, none of this would have happened. Instead, they had a man on the loose with an unsettling demeanour. Who knew what he'd do next, who he'd come for.

She had no sympathy for Sanderson, but she did have empathy. The police force should be there to protect the public, not send them down for crimes they hadn't committed. Even so, he had to be stopped.

The next thing they needed to do was put a plan in action as to how to smoke Jamie out. Trying to envisage his next move had proved fatal, literally. It would be a long time before she would sleep that night, if at all.

As she walked across the floor to their desks once more,

Allie saw a deflated team. Shoulders sagged, looks of exhaustion mixed with the stress of it all. They all seemed as dispirited as she felt. It hurt when someone was killed before they'd apprehended a known killer.

'Any updates?' she said, perching on the end of Perry's desk.

'Nothing in yet.' Perry threw down his pen. 'I, for one, wasn't expecting Sanderson to come so quickly after Kevin.'

'I don't think any of us did. He's more unhinged than we thought.'

'We should have found him sooner.'

'Hey, we're doing everything possible! At least Colette is under our protection tonight.' Allie hid a yawn behind her hand. 'I have paperwork to be doing, but you guys can go home if you like. It's late, and it's going to be a long day tomorrow, no doubt.'

Jamie was back at his flat, relaxing on the settee as he caught up with the news, the only light the glow from the gas fire in the living room. He'd changed his clothes, his others being splattered in blood and brain matter from Kevin.

Jamie had taken a knife with him, planning to stab Kevin when he came out of the house. When he saw him with the iron bar, he'd laughed inwardly, especially seeing it put a huge dent in that scrapheap of metal he called a van. He'd made the job easier for him, and actually it had been far better. It had felt good to pound out his life.

He'd always known he'd be the victor because he wasn't scared to die. If Kevin had got the better of him, he wouldn't have cared. Because he wasn't going back to prison. But this way was the best outcome, ready for the finale tomorrow.

Jamie often wondered if he hadn't gone out that night

what his life would have been like. He hadn't a violent bone in his body back then, but the world he'd been wrongly dragged into had changed him.

Maybe he would have married Colette. He certainly would have had a good job even if it had been at average Joe level because he would have gone to college and learned a skill. He'd have been proud to own his own home.

He would have had friends. Holidays he'd spent having fun. Nights out in pubs and clubs. Meals out to celebrate birthdays. Wedding invites. Parties galore.

He would have been able to spend more time with his mum before she died. That had been the worst thing about it.

All the memories of that night when he was sixteen had haunted his dreams all week. The lies and deceit that had put him behind bars. The humiliation that everyone thought he was a killer. The hurt that no one believed he didn't do it, except his mum.

The anger which had built over the years he'd spent in prison. The bursts of fury when he'd been released and found himself locked up again. The spiral out of control, the circling of the drain. And all because of Kevin and his stepfather.

Gary Hallam had managed to escape death. He hadn't been home when Jamie had knocked on his door earlier on. It had been frustrating not being able to wait around in case anyone saw him. But hey, his lad was dead. Revenge had been sweet.

Thoughts of his mum had Jamie's temper rising, and he slung his empty glass at the wall, relishing the sound of the smash and the mess it made as it fell. He picked up the bottle of whisky, a little left in it, and swigged from that instead. He hadn't bought another bottle purposely because he needed a clear head for what he was about to do.

The last day was going to be tricky, but he hoped it all went to plan. It was going to be a doddle to do it because his temper had risen with each day. He was at boiling point now. There would be no stopping him as long as he was vigilant. Everyone would be looking for him, so he'd have to keep a low profile tomorrow.

But he was going to have his say. The truth would come out, one way or another.

CHAPTER FORTY-EIGHT

MONDAY

Allie sat back in her office chair and threw down her pen. She was frustrated as hell about Jamie Sanderson. After murdering Kevin Ryland, he'd gone to ground. Even though they were working flat out on the case, with every available officer drafted in to assist, nothing had been heard from him yesterday at all. She hoped today would bring at least one lead. A further press conference from Jenny had resulted in the same calls as before. Jamie Sanderson appeared to be a ghost.

How could he disappear?

Of course, she knew how easy that was in the short term, having charged several suspects with crimes after hunts when they'd gone to ground. But it was the killing in between that haunted her thoughts. That someone would be murdered, or maimed, before he was apprehended.

At least for now they had things to work on. Sanderson

didn't seem to be a threat to the general public if he was working through a list, but Allie wouldn't take anything for granted. There was nothing more unreliable than a suspect on the run.

The postmortem had revealed Kevin had died from severe damage to his brain. The force he was hit had rendered him unable to live within a matter of seconds. Will had told Allie that he'd never seen such injuries before, even down to a distinctive hole the shape of the top of the bar at the side of Kevin's head.

It had been such a brutal attack that he'd warned against showing relatives in the mortuary. Some injuries they could cover with a cloth, for instance across the forehead, but Kevin had been unrecognisable from the get-go.

Gary Hallam had been informed and wanted to stay away.

Colette had decided she'd seen enough when Kevin had been attacked, so at least a trip to the mortuary hadn't had to happen. Small mercies.

It was shocking to see the crime scene photos. They'd all viewed them once, but then they'd been relegated to a closed file, rather than put up on the board. It was always a painful reminder that someone had died during murder cases, and it served to keep the victim alive in their heads while they carried out their investigations. So they'd added a headshot of Kevin Ryland, with Colette at a recent wedding.

Forensics had come back from Dave, who had worked his socks off to get them in. Sanderson's fingerprints had been all over the iron bar that he'd left behind. Along with a door cam and the witness statements from residents who had run out to help, they had some super CCTV footage from a house directly opposite the attack. Like the stills, it hadn't been good viewing, but with it, there was enough to charge Sanderson with murder.

They needed to find him.

Which was a task in itself. Uniform were out on patrol searching any leads that came in after the many press conferences Jenny was holding. The public were angry, they wanted Sanderson found.

But Jenny couldn't tell them any details other than to say these were isolated incidences, all linked to one man, and that the general public weren't at risk. The police might be working on the assumption that Jamie had a vendetta against a certain group of friends, but they didn't know this for certain. It wasn't information they could give out. So it made them appear weak that they had no suspect in custody.

At least Allie had Simon on her side. He'd done a couple of cracking articles for the paper. He'd always written compassionately. Not like Will Lawrence who was laying it on thick that there was a serial killer on the loose and the police were as inept as usual. The tosser.

Still, she sympathised with them all. They hadn't caught Sanderson yet. Lord knows what his next plan was, and that was frustrating, to say the least.

Jamie woke up with a start. For a moment he wasn't sure where he was, so deep in his recurring nightmare. He pulled back the duvet, sweat pouring out of him as he caught his breath.

He'd been waiting for a knock on the door since he'd killed Kevin on Saturday. Now it was Monday morning. He hadn't been out since, being prepared stocking up on food, but now it was time to get going. The police wouldn't expect him to start again so soon. They might even think he was out of the city by now.

They were pathetic. They didn't even have an address. What were they up to? Although to be fair, he'd given them the runaround purposely. It seemed to be working so far. So one more day, and it would all be over.

He watched the news constantly. His attack on Kevin had made the big TV channels as well as national newspapers. He wasn't proud of what he'd done, but it had felt good, and it was the reason he'd not moved from the house yesterday. With his face splashed everywhere, he didn't want the people around to recognise him. Because if they came to him, he would put up a fight to stop them saying anything.

For now he had to stay calm. He'd wanted to go and see Gary Hallam, tell him how glad he was that Kevin was dead. See his face crumple because it was all his fault. The papers were full of it being Jamie, but no one really knew yet, did they? He'd wanted to tell Hallam what he'd done personally. Then he'd decide whether to let him live or not.

In the end, he'd drunk half a bottle of whisky and passed out on the settee. So Gary Hallam lived to see another day.

Jamie got up now and walked over to the bedroom window. Outside the world went on as usual. No one knew that he was here, a killer among them.

At least, he hoped they didn't.

CHAPTER FORTY-NINE

Colette stood in the bedroom window staring down on the pavement outside. Yesterday, there had been several police vehicles dotted around, crime scene tape across the road either side of her house so that no one could pass. Today it was quiet out there, with only one PC on guard by the front gate. With all the forensics done, and the area searched, the neighbours questioned, it was all back to normal.

Except for her.

She wanted to take something to numb the pain, but even with a body sloshing with alcohol and tablets from last night, nothing seemed to be working. Tonight she'd take a sleeping pill to give her some rest from the thoughts rushing around her head.

At least Hannah had arrived and was here with her now. It was good to have her close. Colette also felt better with a police guard too, knowing she was protected from Jamie. Not that she thought for a minute he would come after her again.

Yet, there was a mystery behind why he'd left her unharmed. He'd had two chances to attack her on Saturday and taken none of them. Even though she was glad, it didn't make sense.

A car door slammed, and she turned to see her neighbours across the road going out. How could people go on with their day-to-day lives when she was breaking? It was only thirty-six hours since Kevin had died, and yet her life had changed, her world fallen apart.

Colette could see every minute of the attack playing over and over in slow motion in her mind. When she went outside after hearing a commotion. Trying to stop Jamie from killing Kevin. Seeing what he'd done to Kevin before he stopped. Cradling her dying husband in her lap, trying desperately to get him to talk to her. Give her a sign he was still with her.

Then moving aside why paramedics worked tirelessly to save his life, knowing that it would be in vain. Screaming at the police because they hadn't caught Jamie in time to stop him killing again. Then everything she'd told them afterwards about the notes and the photographs.

PC Oscar Atwood, who had been there since the early morning, stood guard at her gate. He was old enough to be her son, not swayed by what was happening, and open and honest with information he could share with nosy neighbours.

Rachel Joy was there, too, keeping her up to date. Colette didn't know whether that was ideal or not. She didn't want to know any of the details surrounding Kevin's death. All she wanted them to do was to find Jamie. Get him put away before he could hurt anyone else.

She wanted him in a police cell and then going back to prison for what he'd done. Because she was well aware that he might be teasing her, coming for her last. What she'd kept from him when she was sixteen wasn't very kind, but she'd been young and naive.

At school, they'd called Kevin Crazy Kev – behind his

back obviously. No one would dare say that to his face. Everyone clamoured to be liked by him because woe betide if you got on his wrong side or he didn't like you. He could make you cry as quickly as he could make you laugh. He was top dog, they all did what he said. Colette had loved his bad-boy image.

She didn't have fond memories of school, but she had made a friend in Michelle. There was only a few months in age between them, and they'd become friends straightaway.

She wiped tears from her cheeks. All this stuff with Jamie was bringing up memories she'd chosen to forget. Or, more to the point, she'd blocked out.

She'd quite liked him before Winston Lowe died. But she'd only slept with him to make Kevin jealous. Still, it was made far easier because she and Kevin bonded when Jamie was sent down. Somehow it had held them together.

Until recently, she hadn't thought of Jamie in a long time. He was part of her past, and some things she didn't want to be reminded of. It sounded absurd what he'd done. He wasn't the Jamie she'd known as a teenager. And now he was back, potentially to kill her.

So as much as she minded a family liaison officer here, too, and one who could poke their nose in things they shouldn't, and listen in to whatever she said, she still wanted someone there. She didn't feel safe anymore. Colette had to know what was going on.

Fifteen minutes later, Hannah came into the room. She was wearing her pyjamas, and with no makeup and her hair tied in a ponytail, Colette saw signs of her when she was a little girl. She seemed upset, as if she'd been crying that morning. But she gave her mum a half-smile.

Yesterday, Hannah had been distraught that she'd never got the chance to say goodbye to her dad. At the time, Colette had thought that neither did she. Kevin had been taken so quickly that she was still in shock. But she'd known Hannah didn't need to hear that. It would have been selfish, as if her own grief was more important than her daughter's.

Now, she wiped tears from her own cheeks and applied that brave face everyone raved about.

'Morning, love. Did you get any sleep?' she asked, giving Hannah a hug.

'Not really.'

'Let me make you a cup of tea. And how about some toast? I'm sure you can manage that.'

Hannah gave a faint smile. 'Okay, Mum.'

Colette squeezed her daughter's hand. She was her priority now. With her home, they could help each other through the ordeal. Planning a funeral would be next on the agenda, once the body was released.

She wasn't prepared for that at all.

CHAPTER FIFTY

Frankie turned his car into the gates of Stoneleigh Residential Home. The property itself was set back from the road, an impressive three-storey building with ample well-maintained grounds.

He checked in at reception and was given directions to the community lounge. When he walked in the room, a female in her fifties stood up and waved for his attention. Frankie suspected she was Mrs Lowe's daughter. The older woman she was with smiled up at him from the chair, her blue eyes crinkling at the corners. Both of them had a welcoming demeanour despite the nature of his call.

Frankie introduced himself and sat down across from them.

'I hope you don't mind me visiting you, Mrs Lowe, and thank you for seeing me at such short notice. I believe you're off to Spain today.'

'I am, lad.' She smiled. 'I can't wait for a bit of sun, sea, and... sadly, I'm far too old for anything else I might have got up to when I was in my prime.'

Frankie chuckled. 'Well, I hope I don't bring up too many terrible memories from your past.'

'It's fine. I'm happy to help if I can, we both are. Please call me Vera. This is my daughter, Liz. We were a bit shocked to hear from you, especially after seeing Jamie Sanderson's face on the news. What is it that you want to know?'

'It's quite delicate. Due to recent events, we've been re-examining the case. I have to be honest with you and say we believe Mr Sanderson may not be the person responsible for your husband's murder.'

Both Vera and her daughter gasped. Then the older woman turned to the younger.

'I knew it. Didn't I, Liz?' Vera put a hand to her chest. 'Didn't I say once the trial was over that I thought it might not be him?'

'You did, Mum.' Liz addressed Frankie next. 'Mum was consumed by grief, being there at the murder, seeing my dad die and not being able to do anything to stop it. I thought she must be confused because there was so much evidence.'

Frankie nodded his understanding. It was an easy mistake to make, given the unusual circumstances.

'Vera, you told the police at the time that you were certain it was Jamie Sanderson,' he said. 'Was there ever any doubt in your mind?'

'I did blame him at first, but I remembered voices afterwards, not just his. I told the detective this, but he said only Jamie was there.'

'This was DS Hallam?'

'Yes, that was his surname.'

Frankie bristled, trying not to show his irritation. 'You recognised Sanderson from the identity parade?'

'Well, you see, that was the thing. I did, but only because he was in the shop. I wasn't certain if he was there alone. I told the officer this, too, but he said Jamie had admitted everything and that my evidence would only make the case against him stronger. So I went along with what he said.'

'Did he take a statement from you?'

'Yes.'

'And did you read it and sign it?'

'He said I didn't need to read it as he'd written down what I'd said word for word. So, I signed it.' Vera paused. '*Should* I have read it first?'

'It doesn't matter now.' Frankie smiled to put her at ease. 'Were you called up to court as a witness?'

'Yes, but I was told what to say by the detective. The same one who took my statement. I wasn't really very well. I was still getting over losing Winston.'

'So you only had dealings with DS Hallam?'

'That's right. He told me it was cut and dry, that Jamie had killed my Winston and he would see to it that justice was served.'

'Are you saying the detective was lying to Mum?' Liz asked, leaning forward.

'We're not in a position to disclose anything at the moment, but after some recent developments, the case has been reopened.' Frankie looked at Vera sincerely. 'But whatever the outcome, I will come and let you know what is happening. You have my word.'

'Thank you. And the person who killed my Winston?'

'We'll be checking that again, too. I'm so sorry to bring so many questions to you now after all these years.'

'It's quite all right, son. If you get the person who did kill Winston, I'll still be grateful. But not for the suffering that young boy must have gone through. I suspect he will have been marred with that. What a tragedy to come from a tragedy. I'm sorry.'

'It's not your fault. You were told what to say and do by a detective who should have known better.'

'Do you know why he did that?' Liz asked.

Frankie bowed his head momentarily. 'I can't say for now, but I will when it's been thoroughly investigated.'

He left then, deep in thought until he got to the car. Once inside, he called Sam to update her.

'The heartless bastard.' He banged his fist on the steering wheel. 'He let someone else go to prison for a murder he didn't do to protect his son.'

'And that went well, didn't it?' Sam replied. 'Because we know Kevin was in and out of prison in his twenties, too.'

'I expect corruption was rife back then, but it still doesn't make it any better. I mean, we could have turned a blind eye to many a thing during our time in the force, but we didn't.'

'Maybe it's different when it's your family.'

'Naw, I think it's imperative everything is done by the book in those circumstances. You shouldn't be able to use the uniform to your advantage. It's wrong, especially when you meet a relative who has been hoodwinked. I've –'

'Easy, Tiger,' Sam interrupted. 'I'm on your side, remember.'

Frankie grinned, although she couldn't see him. Her comment eased his tension a little. The case was getting to him, to them all. Having a killer on the loose was one thing, but a corrupt police officer being partially responsible because of his actions was deplorable.

CHAPTER FIFTY-ONE

Allie listened to her DCI while she gave the press conference at midday, standing to one side as she addressed the media. Jenny updated everyone with as many details as she could about the murders of Shaun Green, Nick Farrington, and now of Kevin Ryland.

'We are still continuing to search for Jamie Sanderson,' she said once that was finished. 'As you know, he is forty-one years of age, grey hair, short and receding, but he is now clean-shaven. He's of medium build and was last seen wearing jeans and a navy-blue jacket.

'We are asking the public not to approach him but to call the number displayed on your screen right now. Sanderson needs to be brought into custody as soon as possible.

'We do have a few possible sightings that we are following up on, but if anyone knows of his whereabouts, or if you've noticed anything suspicious in your area over the past few days, again, please contact the number on the screen.'

As soon as Jenny paused for breath, the questions from the journalists and reporters came at her like bullets. Allie was glad she wasn't the one taking them.

'Do you know why he's killing or attacking these people?'

'Are there links to the three victims so far, and if so, are we to expect more?'

'How close are you to catching him, before he does it again?'

Jenny raised a hand. 'I won't be taking questions at this time, but be assured, we are looking into everything we know about Jamie Sanderson, his connections to the city, and his whereabouts.'

'We have an address for Jamie, boss,' Sam said an hour later, raising a piece of paper in the air. 'Seventeen Clay Street, Longton. After the latest press conference, we've had four people ring in with the same one.'

Everyone got to their feet, stab vests pulled over shirts and blouses, and then headed for the doors. A few minutes later, they were out of the car park, sirens and lights blazing, and on their way to join Potteries Way, the ring road around the city.

Fifteen minutes later, they turned into Clay Street to see uniformed officers standing on the pavement.

'Empty, ma'am,' a male officer closest to her said. 'There are signs someone has been here. Food in the fridge is out of date, what there is of it.'

Allie nodded her thanks, put on latex gloves, and stepped inside the property. It was a terraced house with old-fashioned windows.

'This could be his hideout, coming to and fro when he's committed his crimes,' Allie said. 'He'd hardly stand out round here. People keep themselves to themselves purposely. It's a no-go area after dark.'

The hallway was clean but dreary, wallpaper peeling off, bare floorboards underfoot. The kitchen had seen better days – years, in fact – with its old appliances and stained worktops.

A door hung loose on the sink unit. Allie opened a cupboard door to find a tin of tomato soup and a packet of Pasta'n'Sauce.

Officers searched through the rooms while she went into the living room. There was a TV on a stand, a two-seater settee, and a coffee table. The curtains were too small for the window, drawn across haphazardly.

'Check with the neighbours to see if anyone has seen him lately, Frankie,' she said. 'Take a uniform with you – the usual door-to-door. We need all the clues we can get.'

Allie was disheartened seeing the state of everything. No wonder everyone talked about nature versus nurture. Jamie had spent his life in and out of prison, through no fault of his own to start with. Had he not gone out that night, how different his life might have been.

And now Nick and Kevin were dead.

Was this all over that one night, or had something happened since that had made Jamie come for revenge? Was there a catalyst? An event that started the ball rolling? It was one of the first things she'd be asking Jamie once they caught up with him.

Frankie was back a few minutes later. 'No luck with the neighbours either side. A woman further down the street says he's been there for a few months, but she hasn't seen him since the weekend.'

'Does he have a vehicle?'

'A red Vauxhall. She's not sure of the model. That's not been seen since either.'

'Put a call in to Control, get it out to everyone to be on the lookout. We don't have plates, but that will have to do for now.'

Frankie nodded. 'Do you think Jamie and Colette seem to have been an item, or at the least have dated? I wonder if that's why he didn't harm her yesterday.'

'Maybe it was jealousy that started it all,' Sam mused. 'Perhaps he saw Colette out with Kevin and got angry that he'd lost a good many years when he might have been married to her, had kids with her even. There's such a lot that Jamie lost.'

'So where else do we think he might have gone?'

'I can't find anything of interest, boss,' Perry said, coming back into the room. 'There's not much to go through either. I did find this, though.' He held up an evidence bag. 'It was in the bedroom.'

Allie looked at the photo inside the bag. It was of Jamie and Colette. A photograph which would be the equivalent of a selfie back when Jamie was sixteen.

A uniformed officer appeared in the doorway. 'Neighbour down the road says he hasn't seen Sanderson since the weekend. Says he's been here a few months, keeps himself to himself. Didn't realise it was him they were after as he said his name was Jeff. But he did say he wasn't sticking around for long.'

'So he had this planned.' An involuntary shiver ran down Allie's spine.

CHAPTER FIFTY-TWO

The doorbell rang, and Colette went to answer it. Behind her in the hallway, Rachel came through from the kitchen.

'It's my friend, Michelle,' she told her. 'I knew she was coming.'

She nodded, waiting for her to answer the door.

Colette hadn't said anything to her purposely. She wanted to have time alone with Michelle. To Rachel, it would seem they were grieving together. But from her point of view, she wanted to question Michelle to see if she knew anything else. Even after everything that had happened, Colette didn't trust the police, so she was relying on Michelle to fill her in.

They fell into each other's arms, tears flowing freely.

Colette stepped back and ran a finger gently over Michelle's face. 'How are you doing?'

'Never mind about me, I'm fine.' Michelle gave Colette's hand a squeeze. 'I'm so sorry. Where's Hannah?'

'She slipped out to fetch some food. I only found out when I went to her room. I rang her to find out where she was, and she told me then. I said we didn't need anything, and that I'd prefer her to be at home, but she said she was nearly done and wouldn't be long. I think she wanted a little time on her own.'

'Poor mite. She must be so upset. Have you heard anything more about Kevin?'

'No. The police will keep me informed when they have something. For now, they're out searching for Jamie.'

'Well, I know we've spoken about this before.' Michelle paused. 'But now do you wonder if Kevin and Nick were telling the truth about what happened?'

Colette gave a deep sigh. 'I think I've always known they were lying, but I ignored it. Eventually it became the truth rather than a lie.' She flicked away the tears rolling down her face. 'Jamie is blaming us all for it now.'

Michelle agreed. 'I hope they catch him soon. Put all our minds at rest. I couldn't believe it when Nick was killed, so it's a double shock for Kevin as well. I'm so sorry.'

Colette gave her a faint smile. 'I was there when he... he killed Kevin, and he could have done the same to me, but he didn't. It was as if he wanted me to see what happened.'

'Don't say that!' Michelle gave an involuntary shudder. 'Can't you stay somewhere else for the time being? Go to your parents'?'

Colette shook her head. 'He's not pushing me out of my home. And when am I likely to go out on my own at the moment? I'm taken everywhere by a police officer.'

The doorbell went again.

'I'll get it,' Rachel shouted through on her way to the door.

'I can't cope with more visitors,' Colette said. 'So it's good to have Rachel here to let me know who it is first. The neighbours have been great, but I can't help thinking they're being a bit nosy. I know I would be.'

Rachel appeared in the doorway. 'These came for you.' She passed another bouquet of flowers to Colette.

'Thanks.' Tears brimmed in Colette's eyes as she stood up to take them from her.

Kevin had hardly ever sent her any. If she made a fuss, he'd go and buy some, but it wasn't the same. She never got any spontaneously. Now this was the second delivery that morning, and she'd had several yesterday. Already she'd run out of vases. Here she was, receiving so many flowers she could start her own shop, and all *because* of Kevin.

She opened the small white envelope that had been attached to the side. Then she gasped.

No one is thinking about you at this sad time, so I thought I would cheer you up.
I hope you like them. J

'Are you okay?' Rachel asked. 'Come and sit down, you've gone really pale. Is it the flowers?'

'It's just all so overwhelming.'

'Who sent them?'

'Oh, an old friend of ours.' She smiled at Rachel, willing her to believe her. 'It's nothing to do with the flowers, honestly.'

Once Rachel had gone into the kitchen again, Colette told Michelle the truth and let her tears fall.

Michelle comforted her but then blew out a large sigh. 'I need to be straight with you. I had flowers from Jamie, too, at home. They came when Kevin was there, but I told him they were from a friend. I could kick myself now because if I had said something, then he might still be alive.'

'You mustn't think like that. What's happened is because of Jamie.'

'Should we mention it to the police?'

'I don't know, but I can't do it yet.' Colette wiped at her eyes. 'I'm drained. I want to be on my own rather than answer all the stupid questions. It won't bring Kevin back.'

Michelle made to stand up.

'That doesn't include you.' She put a hand on her arm. 'I mean everyone else.'

'But they might be able to trace where he lives from the florist, if he used a card.'

'He's not that stupid. He will have paid cash.'

'They might have CCTV from the shop.'

Colette thought about it, realising it might be a way to find Jamie sooner. 'I'll tell Detective Shenton when she's next here. But right now I can't cope with it. I want nothing to remind me of what's happened.'

She burst into tears then, and Michelle drew her into her arms. When was this nightmare ever going to end? No matter what had gone on in the past, she couldn't live her life without Kevin.

CHAPTER FIFTY-THREE

Hannah Ryland opened her eyes, but all she could see was darkness. She blinked a few times, waiting to get accustomed to the light.

There was something in her mouth. She tried to reach up to it but found she couldn't move her hands from behind her back. She pulled, but they were bound together with something around her wrists.

Confused, she lifted her head. It hit something hard, and she winced.

What was going on? Why was it so dark, and why was she tied up?

She tried to think of where she'd last been. Had she finished work for the day? What time would it be? Then she recalled she'd come home for her dad's funeral. So was she in Stoke rather than Derby?

Hannah listened, trying to figure it out, but all she heard was silence.

'Help,' she screamed, but it came out muffled.

She didn't know how long she'd been there either, wherever there was. Her knees were pulled up, her ankles tied together. She tried to stretch out her legs, but they hit the side of something hard before reaching full length.

She was in the boot of a car.

She banged her feet on the side of the vehicle, but the movement was hard to do. After a few seconds, it exhausted her.

The last thing she did came back to her. She was crossing the car park, walking back to her mum's after buying her favourite chocolates and wine. She'd turned when she'd heard someone say her name.

Her mind was blank after that.

Finally, Hannah's eyes adjusted to the dark. She took small sharp jabs of breath. She hated enclosed spaces, couldn't watch anything on the TV that involved potholing or someone crawling into something they couldn't get out of easily. Her worst fear was being stuck in a lift in the dark.

Stop it, Hannah, she chastised herself. If she went into panic mode, the air wouldn't get to her chest quick enough. But hysteria took over. Hannah screamed repeatedly.

After a couple of minutes, she made herself calm down. She pretended she was lying on a beach, the sun beating down on her, a cocktail and a good book by her side. It was something she did whenever she was afraid. Like when she went to the dentist, she thought of that beach, her happy place.

Tears pricked the corners of her eyes. She didn't want to die here. Her mum would be all alone.

'Please help me,' Hannah said, knowing her voice was no more than a groan. She listened again. Still nothing. No giveaway signs as to where she might be.

It was no use. She'd have to wait it out, praying someone wouldn't kill her, or hurt her, when they did.

Was Jamie Sanderson responsible for her abduction?

She heard her phone beep from inside her bag. Someone

was sending her a message. Although she'd been receiving them constantly as the news about her dad filtered through, she hoped it was from her mum. She'd be worried if she didn't reply quickly.

The tailgate opened, and Hannah froze. A man's face appeared. He grabbed her feet, and she groaned.

'Be quiet.'

He helped her out of the car. Once she was standing up, he came into view, and she groaned again, anxiety coursing through her. It was him. Jamie Sanderson.

'Kick out at me and I will hurt you.' He glared at her. 'Understand?'

She nodded vehemently.

He stooped down and cut the ties around her ankles. Then he grabbed her elbow and walked her round the back of a row of old shops. Most of them were boarded up. She didn't have a clue where she was, though. She realised the best thing she could do was to be quiet.

Halfway along the alley, he pushed a gate open, and they went into a yard. He made her climb through the broken window of an empty property. Why would he bring her here?

All the time she tried not to stare at him but noticed things if she had the opportunity to get away. She counted ten steps to a doorway which led to the stairs.

He shoved her forward. 'Up. Keep your feet to yourself.'

At the top, there was a tiny landing, a door either side. He opened the one on the right, and she went in. It was another empty room.

He guided her to the wall.

'Sit.'

He looped another plastic tie through the one on her wrist and attached it to the radiator. Then he replaced the one he'd removed from her ankles. Fear stopped her from reacting when he glanced at her, her body shaking uncontrollably.

'There's no point in making any noise,' he said. 'The whole row of properties are empty. I'll have to keep the light off, but you'll get a glow from the lamppost out the back.'

Watching him as he left the room, she heard a lock turn in the door. Finally she could give way to her tears. She was alone, no one knew where she was. She had no way of getting out of here. The ties on her wrist were already cutting into her, so she couldn't pull them off. She would have to sit tight and see what happened.

And try not to think bad thoughts.

About why he wanted her.

About why he'd brought her here.

About why there was a strong smell of petrol.

CHAPTER FIFTY-FOUR

An hour had passed, and there was no sign of Hannah. Colette sent her a message asking how long she would be. A message came back about ten minutes later.

I'm okay, Mum. Bumped into an old friend and we're having coffee. I'll be back soon.

Colette frowned. It seemed disrespectful of Hannah not to be with her. But then again, she couldn't blame her. It must have been a shock to see and hear everything when she arrived. She might need space on her own to process things.

'Is that from Hannah?' Michelle asked.

'Yes.' Colette pointed to a photograph album she'd rooted out. 'This is mostly of me and you. Fancy having a nosy through it to take our minds off things?'

The two women sat together, laughing, crying, reminiscing about life when they were younger. There were some terrible hairdos and dress sense at times to match the trends. There were photos from as far back as their schooldays, weddings, birthdays, days away. A trip to Blackpool. A weekend in York.

She turned a page to see a photo of her and Kevin

lounging on a settee. She was lying down with her head in his lap. Michelle was sitting on the floor in front of them.

'I was always gooseberry with you two,' Michelle said. 'You were meant to be together.'

Colette wasn't sure about that, but she nodded. 'I'm going to miss him so much.' She wiped at fresh tears.

She was about to turn to the next page when there was an almighty bang, making them both visibly jump.

'What the hell was that?' Colette got up, putting down her coffee.

Michelle followed as she went into the hallway.

Rachel was coming downstairs after a trip to the bathroom when she'd heard the noise.

Colette and Michelle appeared in the hallway.

'We heard breaking glass,' Colette explained.

'Stay there, please.' Rachel moved Colette aside and went through first.

The large window in the kitchen was broken, and there was a house brick on the floor. It had paper wrapped around it secured with an elastic band.

'What the...' Colette cried.

'Wait here while I check outside.' Rachel went to the door.

'I'm going, too,' Colette said as soon as she was out of sight.

Michelle held her back. 'She said to wait!'

'I can't leave her out there.' Then Colette stopped. 'Wait, that's my phone.' She dashed to retrieve it from the living room.

The outside light came on in the back garden as Michelle stood on the step.

Rachel turned back towards her. 'Get back inside, please.

I can handle this.' She walked a few steps forward. There was movement from her right, a horrendous cracking sound, and she fell to the floor. A clatter of iron followed as it hit the paved area.

PC Oscar Atwood came running from the front of the house. 'What's going on?'

'There's someone in the garden!' Michelle pointed to where she'd heard the noise.

Oscar ran after a figure that had darted across the grass. At the bottom of the garden, he could just about make out someone wearing a balaclava.

'Police. Stop!'

With Oscar hot on his trail, the figure hurled itself at the fence, trying to find a footing to get over it.

'Stop!' Oscar grabbed hold of a leg and pulled but lost his grip as the person kicked out. He reached for it again. The boot connected with his head.

Dazed, he was struck once more, this time full in the face. Blood burst from his nose, and he dropped to the ground.

Michelle ran over to him. 'Oscar!'

Spots floated before his eyes, and he groaned. As his vision returned, he saw the suspect was gone. He pushed himself off the ground, felt faint, and sat down again.

'Are you okay?' Michelle asked.

'Yeah. I'll be fine.' He held his head back and pinched his nose to stem the bleeding. Then, reaching for his radio to call for assistance, he glanced behind her. 'Where's Colette?'

CHAPTER FIFTY-FIVE

In the office, Allie's phone rang. She got to her feet after answering it, running a hand through her hair as she listened to the caller. When she disconnected the call, she swore loudly.

'We think Sanderson has been to Colette's house,' she told Perry, who was with her. 'Rachel and Oscar have been attacked, and now Colette is missing. Her car has gone, too.'

'What?' Perry frowned. 'How the hell did he get to her?'

'Round the back. Oscar was at the front with some neighbours.' She banged her hand on the desk.

'What happened?'

'A brick was thrown through a window, maybe to cause a distraction.'

'Do you think he took her in her own car?'

'We have to assume so, but I need confirmation it was him. There's an ambulance on the way. Oscar took a hit to the face. He got kicked when the attacker cleared the back fence, the bastard. Michelle Price was there, so she might be able to shed some light on what happened.' She walked onto the main floor, shrugging on her jacket. 'Sam, Frankie, come with us. Sanderson's been to Colette's house. He's attacked Oscar and taken Colette with him.'

They scrambled into Allie's car, and she sped off, making her way through the traffic. She banged the steering wheel when she had the opportunity.

'How did this happen? We should have apprehended Sanderson before he had the chance to do anything else.'

'He's been clever,' Sam replied. 'There are only so many places and areas the teams can search without any sightings of him. He's been doubling back on them purposely.'

'We should have caught him earlier. It makes us look incompetent.'

'Jamie is hellbent on getting retribution.' Perry held on to the handle above the door. 'I can't believe he had the audacity to go to Colette's home again.'

'I know it will be Jamie but don't want to assume after what happened with Brian Price earlier.' She papped her horn at the car in front who was slow to pull out of her way. 'Move, you idiot. Move!'

'Allie, we need to get there in one piece.' Perry placed a calming hand on her arm.

Suddenly all Allie's anger dissipated, and she took a breath.

'Why did Sanderson come back, though?' Perry questioned. 'It seems quite risky after what he's already done.'

'He's playing us, isn't he? We thought he wouldn't come after Colette because he left her alone, and all the while his plan was to come for her at a later date. Which means he could come after Michelle, too.'

From the back seat, Frankie held up his phone. 'It's already over the socials. I bet someone will have seen him.'

'Let's hope so.'

There was no time to talk anymore as she parked up in Carter Street. They raced to the house, its front door open wide. A shiver washed over Allie when she saw an ambulance parked in the same spot as two nights ago. Had they missed something that could have stopped this from happening?

But why *had* Jamie come back? To finish what he'd started? Did he know Michelle was there, too? If so, why had he left her behind?

There was no point in thinking about that now. They would reassess everything once they were back in the office.

Allie stopped at the ambulance, the rear doors open. Oscar was sitting on a trolley bed being attended to.

'Perry, get on to finding out about Colette,' she told him. 'I need to check on Rachel and Oscar, and I'll be straight in.'

She beckoned a paramedic and found out that Rachel had been taken to hospital. She stepped aboard the other vehicle.

'Hey, how are you?' She stood by his side, the paramedic moving to give her room.

'Battered and bruised,' he replied. 'And that's my pride.' He pointed to the floor. 'But I got his rucksack.'

Allie put on gloves and picked it up. 'I'll get this in an evidence bag. Can you confirm it was Sanderson? Did you see?'

Oscar shook his head and then winced. 'His face was covered with a bally.'

'Could you see what he was wearing?'

'Dark jacket, jeans, black boots, the usual.'

'Did he say anything?'

'No, I'm sorry.' Oscar groaned in frustration. 'I should have pulled the bastard back over with the bag. And I should have been there earlier to help Rachel.'

'You were lucky to escape with the injuries you have, fella.' She smiled at the paramedic who had given them a few moments. 'Thanks, he's all yours.'

'I'm fine,' Oscar insisted.

'Maybe, but I'd prefer you to be given the all clear. You can keep an eye on Rachel, too.'

'How is she?'

'She's in the best hands right now.'

Allie went into the house next to see how Michelle was doing. She spotted Perry in the kitchen doorway.

'How's Oscar and Rachel?' he wanted to know.

'Rachel has gone to hospital. Oscar's on his way now, but doing okay, considering. He managed to pull this bag from the intruder's shoulder in a brave moment.' She quickly scanned the kitchen, seeing the damage for the first time. 'What a mess.' She popped the holdall on the worktop and opened it. Rummaging around inside, she found a notebook.

She flicked through the pages, coming to a list:

Nick lied
Michelle lied?
Kevin lied
Colette lied?
Hallam lied.

'It's the same thinking as the notes that were left with Nick Farrington and Kevin Ryland, isn't it?' Perry remarked as he stood beside her.

Allie nodded gravely. 'I'll get this sent off to test for prints ASAP. Can you send someone to check on Gary Hallam while I speak to Michelle? His name is on the list, too, and we've had enough mishaps for one day.'

CHAPTER FIFTY-SIX

Allie went into the living room to talk to Michelle. She found her sitting on the sofa, being comforted by a woman in her fifties.

'Are you okay, Michelle?'

'Yes, but your officer isn't.' Michelle burst into tears. 'She was unconscious for ages.'

'She's on her way to the hospital. She'll get the best care.' Even to Allie, her words sounded uncaring, prerecorded even, but she had to stay focused on the here and now.

'And Oscar?' Michelle went on.

'He's a bit bruised, that's all. The emergency services are seeing to him now.'

'You don't seem very bothered.'

'Believe me, I am, but I like to keep my emotions at bay.' And my thoughts, Allie mused. It was none of her business how she was, even though inside she was apprehensive about what had happened. It wasn't nice when officers got injured in the line of duty. Sadly it was becoming more of the norm.

She eyed the woman with Michelle, wondering who she was.

'I live across the street,' the woman explained. 'Number twenty-seven. I was getting the shopping out of the boot and heard the commotion.'

'Did you see Colette?'

'She came out, and there was a man waiting by her car. He took the keys from her and got in the driver's side. I saw her face as they passed. She was scared. I couldn't do anything to stop him from leaving, though. I'm sorry.'

'You did right not to approach him. He's extremely dangerous.'

'He's going to come after me again, isn't he?' Michelle was visibly shaking.

Allie knew this would come, seeing as it was the first thing she'd thought about when she'd heard what had happened.

'You have to protect me,' Michelle went on. 'I'm not going home.'

'It's imperative at the moment that you stay here anyway, while we put into motion things we need to do. There are a lot of officers around who can protect you.'

'Like you protected Oscar and Colette?'

Allie was about to say something else, but the neighbour beat her to it.

'You can come across to my house, if you like.' She waited for Allie to approve.

Allie nodded. It was going to be horrific staying there, plus they needed to seal the crime scene, again.

'That's very kind of you, Mrs...'

'Bailey. Tricia Bailey.' She turned to Michelle. 'Come on, duck. Let's get you out of here for now.'

'I really appreciate your help,' Allie reiterated. 'Someone will be across to you soon to take a statement, Michelle.'

'You will let me know if you hear anything?'

'Of course.'

Allie rejoined her team in the kitchen. 'Michelle has gone across the road to a neighbour's house, Oscar is on his way to the hospital, and Angie is already there. He didn't have to do that to her.'

'He's a coward,' Perry said.

Allie took a deep breath. 'Right, enough emotion. Let's crack on with what we need to do here.' It was then she noticed the house brick on the table. 'I forgot about this for a moment. What did the note say?'

'"Tell the Truth."' Frankie held it up for her.

'Ah.'

'He *is* telling us a story, boss. He's saying Nick Farrington and Kevin Ryland lied, and he's killed them both. In the notebook, there are question marks next to Colette and Michelle. Gary Hallam's doesn't have one. And with all the evidence in the past linking everything to him, Jamie wanted us to open the case again.'

'Still doesn't mean he can get away with taking Colette. Do we know where he might go with her? She's obviously gone of her own accord.'

'Are there any clues in the bag?'

'That's all there is, the notepad.' Allie gave the rucksack a shake. 'He doesn't think we're that stupid, surely?' She tutted. 'No, this is definitely a setup. It's bound to lead up to something else.'

'But what?' Perry turned his attention to Allie then.

'I don't know but I'm not leaving here until I've had a word with Michelle again. She must know something. Like why he didn't take her, too.' She frowned. 'Unless they're in it together.'

'Boss?' Perry frowned, clearly not following her line of thinking.

'Four adults, two dead. One woman attacked and left for

dead, and one kidnapped. What has Jamie now got to gain by killing Colette and leaving Michelle behind?'

'I'm not with you –'

They all turned to the door as Michelle rushed in. 'I've had a message from Colette. Well, it's a forward of another. Jamie has Hannah, too.'

Oh, no.

Allie took the phone from her.

I have Hannah. Come with me and she won't get hurt. Meet me by your car. DO NOT tell the police. Slip out during the commotion I'm going to cause.

She showed it to Perry.

'I didn't hear it come in, and I haven't checked my phone until now.' Michelle pointed to it. 'But it has a tracker on it. We put one on each other's phones yesterday. There's one on Hannah's phone, too.'

Allie could have kissed the woman. 'I need to keep this.'

Michelle nodded. 'Find them, please.'

Once Michelle had gone, Allie closed her eyes briefly to take a breather. One minute she was complaining about everything being slow and the next it was all fast and furious.

'Right, we need to concentrate on working out where Sanderson has taken the women. And pray this isn't the time he takes revenge on Colette.'

CHAPTER FIFTY-SEVEN

Colette sat in the passenger seat of her car. Her seat belt was fastened but, even so, there was no way she could try to escape because her hands were tied together. Sure, she felt scared and was fearful of what he was going to do, but she wanted to know why he'd killed Kevin and Nick and attacked Michelle. And he shouldn't have involved Hannah.

The thoughts she'd blanked out must be right. Kevin had got away with murder, and he'd lied to her since that night. Not once had he confessed to her what really went on.

And yet, she'd known. She'd always known, no matter how much she'd denied it to herself.

How could Kevin and Nick have been so horrible to lay the blame at Jamie's feet? And now, was she about to suffer the consequences?

She should have taken the police's advice and moved out of her home, but no, stupid Colette thought Jamie wouldn't come after her again. He'd lured her into a false sense of security, and she'd fallen for it.

'Where's Hannah?' she asked, when they stopped at a set of traffic lights on the main road. 'Please tell me she's all right.' When he didn't speak, she tried again. 'Where are you taking me?'

Jamie smiled. 'To the place that was the stuff of my nightmares for years.'

Colette's heart rate ratcheted up. She wanted to hate Jamie for what he'd done to Kevin, and yet, if he'd been in prison wrongly accused of stabbing Winston, then she could understand to some extent why he wanted revenge. But why now, after all this time?

A few minutes later, Jamie turned into a street of boarded-up terraced houses, leading on to a row of disused shops. He went left into a side alley that led to the back of the properties and parked up.

'Don't make any noise and follow me,' he told her.

'I want to know where Hannah is first. Please, I need to know she's okay!'

'Relax, I'm taking you to her.'

Relax? Was he mad? Yet Colette had no choice but to believe him.

He came round to her side and opened the door so she could slide her legs out and stand up. Then he led her through the alley and into the back of a middle property.

Jamie pulled a board away from the windowsill and pointed. 'You need to get through there.'

'What? No.'

'If you don't do as I say –'

'Okay, okay! But you'll have to help me.'

Getting through the window was an ordeal. She flinched when Jamie touched her but suddenly she found herself in a kitchen.

Jamie marched off, and she followed behind him.

'This is where it happened,' he said, leading her through a door.

'Is Hannah here?' she wanted to know. It was all she was interested in.

Jamie ignored her comment and pointed to the floor. 'This is where Winston Lowe died. Where I tried to save his life after Kevin had stabbed him.'

'He told us it was you.'

'And you believed him?'

'Yes, no. I don't know! But he threatened me and Michelle if we said we weren't together all night.'

'And yet you never said anything to anyone. I bet you thought I'd forgotten everything you'd done once the years went rolling by.'

She shook her head, but then curiosity got the better of her. 'Why did you wait so long?'

'I wanted you all to be settled. To have families, homes, good lives, so I could take it all from you in the blink of an eye. I never had the chance to have a wife, or children, a home even, because I was in prison for so long.'

'You came out for that fifteen years ago.'

'It wasn't my only rodeo. The first time I was released, I was so angry, went for a drink and ended up in a fight that got me straight back inside. Being on parole, I couldn't get in any type of a fracas. I couldn't believe I'd been so stupid.'

He was pacing the room as he spoke.

'After a while, it became the norm. I went in, I came out. I went in, I came out. The system is set up so people like me fail. We get shoved in a shitty room in a shitty hostel, sometimes with a shitty job, but always with little money. It isn't hard to think we'd be better off inside. Warmth, food, shelter all provided. Okay, there'd be the odd dickhead, but I soon learned to facilitate them. Beating them up, making my mark before they could do the same to me.

'But every time I went back inside, heard that door clanging shut behind me, it was another time I wasn't out on the streets looking for you lot. Following you, watching you, seeing if you were doing well in your life. Turns out, you made nothing of yourself, too.'

Colette paled at the thought of someone stalking her. It gave her the creeps, even now when she knew this was more than a voyeuristic pastime. How long had he been watching her? All of them?

'I saw you with Hannah a couple of months ago. That's her name, isn't it?'

Colette nodded, tears pouring down her face at the thought of what he might do to her daughter.

'I'd been following you and hadn't spotted her with you until then.'

'She lives in Derby.'

'I know now.'

Colette gasped. Had he been following Hannah, too?

'Please don't hurt her,' she begged. 'None of this is her fault.'

'I worked out the only way I could be certain to get Hannah home was to kill Kevin.' He was talking but not listening to her. 'Which was my plan anyway. He took away everything I had.'

Colette was crying openly now, still unable to move. She dreaded what he was going to say next. Because he knew, didn't he?

She had to listen to him, but equally she was scared of what he might say.

'Hannah is my daughter, isn't she?'

CHAPTER FIFTY-EIGHT

Hannah sat up straight. She'd heard Jamie leave the building about an hour ago, but now someone was downstairs again. She waited for the door to open, but it stayed locked.

There were no footsteps on the stairs. Yet she could hear him. She froze, trying desperately to hear.

Voices, but they were muffled. There were definitely two people, and one was a woman. Was it her mum? Or a police officer?

As best as she could with her ankles tied together, she banged her feet on the floor. She had to let whoever it was know that she was there.

As she stood in front of Jamie, Colette realised her worst fear had come true. When she'd found out she was pregnant shortly after Jamie had gone on remand, her world had fallen apart. At sixteen, she'd done the only thing she thought to save herself. She'd started dating Kevin, fudged her due date, and said the baby was his. Both Kevin and Jamie had blond hair, and with Jamie in prison, there was no way anyone would see a resemblance if they even suspected anything.

Jamie was agitated, but she knew she had to look him in the eye.

'I didn't want anyone to find out,' she told him.

'Because everyone would know you're a lying whore?'

Colette gasped at the ferocity of his tone. 'I am not a whore,' she hissed. 'And it takes two to do what we did.'

'I'm not the one who's denying anything.' In two steps, Jamie was in front of her. He took her hands in his. 'Don't you feel anything for me?'

'We were kids, it was a long time ago. And you've killed people! Why, Jamie, why did you do that?'

'It's a list I was working through.'

'A list?'

'I started with a bloke who I was in prison with. Shaun Green. You might have seen his name in *Stoke News*?'

She nodded, unable to speak.

'I stabbed him first, to make sure I could go through with it all. He made my life hell when I was doing time, for a crime I never committed. I swore I'd get him back one day.' He huffed. 'I admit I messed up with Michelle because her fella came home, but I staged Nick's death as I had woken up one morning. I'd taken pills and drank loads of booze, but I was so drunk, I must have fallen asleep before taking enough to have an effect. That's how low my life got.'

'But you're still here! You can start over and –'

'After what I've done? There's no going back for me. You should have stood by me when it happened. But worse than that, you then *married* Kevin. After what he'd done.'

'I told you, if I'd have known the truth for certain, I would have said something to the police.'

'You lied for him.'

'We were sixteen!'

'You traded him in for me! You took away everything I had and then gave it to Kevin. How could you do that?'

'I did what was best for Hannah.'

'No, you didn't. You wanted your dirty secret keeping. You could have told me about her when I left prison.'

'I didn't know where you were and –'

He pointed in her face. 'Do you realise how different my life could have been? I would have had a purpose!'

'She was only eleven then. What would I tell her? That the man she thought was her father wasn't?'

'Yes! Because it's the truth.' Jamie laughed unkindly. 'Unless you were fucking us both at the same time?'

'That's not fair. I slept with you because I liked you. And then when you'd gone and I found out I was pregnant, I started dating Kevin and it went from there. I had Hannah, and me and Kevin got married when we were eighteen.'

'So you lied to him all his life, too.'

'I did it to protect Hannah!'

'You did it for you!' He pointed a finger in her face. 'No one else.'

There was a noise. Both of them turned to their right.

Then Colette frowned. 'Was that Hannah? Jamie, is she here?'

Allie had parked in the next street to where Hannah's and Collette's phones were showing markers and waited for another unit to arrive. She knew the properties had been searched and that they were at the location of Winston Lowe's murder. But the element of surprise wouldn't be with them as they couldn't break the front door down and rush in. It was boarded up.

'I think it's best we all go in together,' Allie said. 'I'll call for an enforcer to get us access while we check out the rear of the property. There's no saying what Jamie's mental state is like, and the safety of Colette and Hannah is paramount. They are our top priority right now.'

They walked around the back.

Frankie pointed ahead. 'Colette's car?'

Allie peered inside a window. 'There's no one in there, nothing that might tell us if the women are with him. Let's leave this for now and search it once we've been inside the building.'

In the back yard of the shop, Perry pointed to the large window, now broken and uncovered. 'Looks like someone has definitely been in since it was last checked.'

'We might be better getting in this way.' Allie spoke in a loud whisper. 'Let's keep our distance but see if we can see signs of life. Can you and Frankie go back round to the front? Me and Sam will stay here until uniform arrive. You know how the lofts in these properties are open, creating a rat run. We don't want him sneaking out of another house and legging it.'

'Yes, boss.' The two men walked away.

'And let me know when the other team gets here. Tell them to come round the back, too.'

Allie and Sam moved out into the entry at the back of the shop.

'Enforcer's here, boss.' Perry's voice came over the waves. 'Any signs?'

'Negative.'

'Stand by.'

Perry and Frankie returned with two officers left at the front. They had to ensure Jamie didn't escape.

The third officer held the enforcer to the door. 'Ready?' he enquired.

'Ready,' Allie told him.
Three bangs on the door, and they were in.
None of them knew what might be waiting for them.

CHAPTER FIFTY-NINE

In the front room, they found their target. Jamie Sanderson was standing in the corner, his back against a door, his arm firmly around Colette's neck. He held a knife to her side.

Allie put a hand in the air. 'We just want to talk, Jamie. There's no need to be alarmed.'

'You don't know the full story,' he cried.

'Why don't you tell me about it?' Allie encouraged. 'Because we now don't believe that you killed Winston Lowe.'

Behind her, Allie could feel her colleagues waiting to rush forward at her command. At the moment, her other hand was behind her back, palm down to give reassurance. She wanted time to stabilise the situation.

'What's the point?' Jamie said. 'You won't believe me.'

Allie tried to weigh up how Colette was. Her hands were tied, but there were no physical signs of injuries, and although she'd only been here for an hour, she was in good form. She gave her a tiny nod of reassurance, enough of a sign to say, "We've got this." Something to give her hope.

'Do you love Colette?' she asked Jamie next.

It stalled him for a moment. It was almost as if the question was too painful for him to think about. Allie knew there and then that he did. He must have carried a torch for her for all those years.

How would he have felt when he found out she had married Kevin? That they'd had a child together when all Jamie's hopes of a family had gone for good?

'At one time I'm sure I did,' Jamie said quietly. 'But even so, I know she doesn't love me.'

Allie took a step further, but he held the knife out in front.

'Come any closer and it's game over.' Jamie seethed. 'I'm tired of other people telling me what to do.'

'I want to help you this time, Jamie.' Despite his warning, Allie inched forward again.

'I've told you, no one can help. Not after what I've done. I'm not going back inside. Which is why I set all this up. This is the end for me.'

'No, Jamie. Please,' Colette said, her hand pressed on top of his around her neck. 'We can make this work. I'm sorry for what happened. I let you down, too.'

Allie stepped forward again. It was time to bring this to a halt. She was always one for conversation, but she'd rather do that at the station, with Colette safe and out of harm's way.

Perry and Frankie were moving forward, too. Jamie was surrounded. It was a dangerous move, and they would step back if necessary, but they wanted Colette to feel safe and Jamie to know there was no way to go but to put down the knife.

She noticed tears on his face.

'I tried so hard to get on with my life, but everything got on top of me,' he said. 'I had no one, nothing. I was already dead.'

'You wanted justice.' Allie held up her hands. 'I get that, I really do. But you have to let Colette go, and then we can sort things out rationally.'

'Did you know that Hannah is my daughter?'

Even though that was new information, Allie remained calm. She still didn't understand the relevance of it right now, and her main focus was to get Colette away from Jamie.

'I didn't, no,' she replied.

'Me and her were an item before Kevin fucked it all up. And then she went and married him. Said the baby was his. How could she have done that to me?'

He was speaking as if Colette wasn't with him. Dangerous talk. Had his plan been to take all three of them at the same time?

'I'm sorry, Jamie,' Colette said.

'No, you're not.'

'Jamie.' Allie stepped closer. 'Put the knife down and step away from Colette.'

'If you hadn't interfered, it would all be over now! Us, this place, would have gone up in flames.' Jamie held the knife out first at Allie, then to Perry and Frankie.

Before they could think of rushing him, he pushed Colette into the middle of the room and dashed through the door behind him and upstairs.

With them hot on his tail, he shot into the front bedroom, closing the door behind him.

Allie raced upstairs, the rest of the team hurtling up behind her. She flung the door open, half expecting Jamie to have a window open ready to climb out. He'd come a cropper from that height, the odds against falling unhurt extremely low, but she had seen it done before.

What she hadn't expected to see was a pile of rubbish in the middle of the room, on fire. He must have planned this, too. The flames had taken hold in seconds. Were they able to get to him now?

He was standing with his back to the window.

'Stay back!' He held a house brick up in the air. 'Come any closer and I'll sling this through the window. The backdraft isn't going to be pretty for any of us.'

'Put it down, Jamie!' Allie spoke to him as if he were a toddler, but she knew the fire wasn't big enough to cause that kind of damage. The flames were getting higher, but it would sizzle out after a couple of minutes. There was nothing for it to cling onto, ensuring its growth. Again, Jamie hadn't thought through his plan.

Allie glanced at Perry, and in one swift movement, she went round one side of the fire and Perry the other. Frankie followed Perry, the uniformed officer with Allie, and they all hurled themselves at Jamie. They wrestled him down to the floor, Perry straddling his back as Allie cuffed him. In seconds, he was dragged upright.

She read him his rights, while Frankie stamped out the final few embers. Afterwards, he wiped his hands in theatrical style, as if that was a good job done. Then he helped Perry take Jamie downstairs, calling for backup to escort a prisoner to the station.

Hearing the commotion, Hannah yelled. She knew it was only a muffle, but she banged her feet, too. A few seconds later, the door opened, and a woman came into the room.

'Hannah, my name is Sam, and I'm a police officer. You're safe now.'

Hannah began to sob.

Sam removed the scarf from around Hannah's mouth and repeated what she'd said. 'It's over.'

While Sam cut the ties free, Hannah heard her mum shouting up to her.

'She's okay,' Sam shouted back. 'I need you to stay there. I'll bring her down when it's safe, but she is okay.'

CHAPTER SIXTY

Allie went to find Sam, who she knew had disappeared into the other room. She found her there with Hannah.

'Hi, Hannah.' Allie stooped to her level. 'I'm pleased to see you! Are you okay?'

'Yes, I want to see my mum.'

She checked the young girl over quickly. 'You weren't hurt in any way?'

'No. Why did he take me, though?'

'Let's talk about that later. We can get you to your mum now.'

'Is it safe to go downstairs?' Sam asked.

'Yes, he's in our custody.' Allie went to the top of the stairs and shouted down to Colette, 'You can come up now.'

Heavy footsteps rushed up. Colette appeared in the doorway, bursting into tears at the sight of her daughter. 'Hannah!'

'Mum!' Hannah rushed into her arms.

Allie smiled at Sam, leaving the two women to embrace. There were photographs to be taken, statements to put together, and clothing to be bagged up and removed. There would be questions that needed to be answered. But for now, it was a mother-and-daughter moment.

Colette and Hannah were safe.

And they had got their man.

An hour later, Colette sat with Hannah in a soft interview room. It had a settee and two armchairs, a coffee table, and a few prints of the city on the wall. It was made to looking inviting, homely, she assumed, so that people felt they could talk in safe surroundings.

They'd been there nearly an hour, and were offered tea twice, as well as something to eat. Now, Hannah was sitting next to her, with her head on Colette's shoulder. She'd been really quiet since their arrival, and Colette was worried by it. Of course, Hannah had been through a frightening ordeal, but there were things that were unsaid, and Colette knew she needed to unburden them so that she could see how her daughter would react. After what had happened, Hannah had a right to know everything.

So she was glad, even though nervous, when Hannah started the conversation.

'Why did he come after us, Mum?'

Colette stalled. Those final words were still hard to speak.

'He's your father, love,' she said. 'Jamie Sanderson.'

'What?' Hannah's eyes widened, and she pulled away from her mum. 'Why didn't you tell me?'

'I didn't want you to find out your dad wasn't your father.'

'So Dad was aware?'

'No, I never told him.'

'Well, at least there's that.'

The room dipped into silence. Colette knew it had to be filled. So she told Hannah everything. About her and Jamie. The murder of Winston Lowe. Finding herself pregnant after

Jamie had gone. Loving Kevin like no other, despite his ways. Never really knowing what he'd done and yet suspecting it. Protecting Hannah from knowing the truth.

Hannah said nothing at all until she'd finished. Even then, she sat quietly before speaking.

'I can't believe that you wouldn't share anything like that with me. I'm your daughter. I thought we were close.'

'We are! But I made a promise with myself not to tell anyone so that it would never get out to your dad. It would have broken his heart to know he wasn't your father. So I couldn't tell you either, that the man you called Dad for twenty-five years isn't your real dad. I'm sorry.'

Hannah couldn't speak so Colette went on.

'He always wanted a family, so he was over the moon, even though we were so young. Everyone thought we were mad to get married so soon. When you came along, he worshipped you. I've never stopped loving him for that, despite everything. Because try as I might, I couldn't get pregnant again.'

'So Dad couldn't have children?'

'Perhaps, or maybe *we* couldn't.'

'So that monster came back to see you?'

Colette shook her head.

It took a few seconds, but then Hannah's features creased. 'He came back to see me?'

'Yes. And I think you saved my life because of it.'

As her daughter broke down in her arms, Colette vowed to keep another secret. She would never tell Hannah what Jamie had planned to do to all three of them.

There was a knock on the door, and Allie came into the room.

'Hey,' Allie said. 'I'm just checking how you are.'

'We're okay,' Colette told her. 'Well, not fine, but we will be.'

Allie smiled. 'Can I get you a drink? Anything to eat? I'm sorry that we haven't been able to speak to you yet, but we won't be long.'

'Tea would be great, thanks. Although I'd rather be making it in my own home.'

Allie was about to sit down across from them but stopped. 'I think you're right. We can take your statements in the morning. I'll arrange for someone to give you a ride.'

Colette's shoulders dropped, relief clear on her face.

Despite procedures, Allie realised it must be equally hard for the two women to know that Jamie Sanderson was in the same building, albeit in a cell. Their evidence would be included in the forthcoming court case, but for now, they needed to rest. Recuperate. Talk things through between themselves. Figure out how to rebuild their lives, without Kevin, too.

And she and her team could then concentrate on getting Sanderson charged.

CHAPTER SIXTY-ONE

TUESDAY

Allie was waiting impatiently, her stomach rumbling. It was half past nine, and she'd had nothing to eat before coming to work in preparation for what was to come. It was her shout for an oatcake breakfast.

'My stomach thinks my throat has been cut,' Perry moaned, rubbing a hand over it. 'I haven't eaten a thing since... an hour ago.'

'Lucky you. I've had nothing since last night,' Sam joined in.

'Well, if you can count half a bowl of Coco Pops as Alfie didn't want to finish his breakfast, that is...'

'It's more than I've had and –'

'Breakfast!' a voice roared. Frankie walked across the office, holding up a white bag. Inside were several orders wrapped in silver foil.

'About time,' Perry moaned again. 'I'm –'

'Stop your whining, old man.' Frankie passed a parcel to Perry first. 'There you go.'

'Have I ever told you how great you are?' Perry murmured as he opened the package with delight.

'Only when I'm dishing out an oatcake breakfast.' Frankie gave a parcel to Sam who eagerly took it from him.

Allie, who had come rushing out the minute she'd heard him arrive, stood by his side, her hands held out in anticipation of her parcel. He dropped it in them and removed the final order that was his own.

In seconds, there was silence apart from the odd sigh of delight. Allie had wheeled over a vacant chair and sat at the end of Perry's desk. She grinned after devouring her first oatcake.

'It's so funny how quiet we can be. We should have more oatcake breakfasts, so I can get some peace from you lot teasing each other all the time.'

'Where's the fun in that?' Frankie replied. 'Besides, if you have too many, it doesn't become a treat.'

Perry disagreed. 'I'd have oatcakes every day if I could.'

'There's nothing stopping you.'

He tapped a hand to his stomach. 'This would grow much more than it has. I wouldn't be able to sit near my desk.'

'You can't do that now anyway,' Sam teased.

Perry feigned angst. 'I'll have you know I work hard to keep my stomach this size.'

Allie chuckled, enjoying the banter between her team. She knew she was lucky to have a good crew. No one corrupt – well, not now anyway. No in-house backstabbing.

And it wasn't down to her because she was the boss. It was due to them all, always watching out for others. No need to be told what to do, simply getting on with things to the best of their ability.

She knew the people of Stoke were safe with her team overseeing things.

'Right, enough of that.' She wiped her hands and cleared up her mess. 'Let's recap where we're up to and see if we can cross anymore t's and dot the i's to make sure this case is watertight for prosecution.'

'Any more news on Rachel?' Frankie asked.

'Broken nose, stitches across her cheekbone which will leave a scar. Not life-threatening though, thankfully.'

Allie had been appalled at the mess Sanderson had made of Rachel. She'd had to stop from crying out when she'd seen the damage. But at least she was on the mend, on the outside at least.

What Jamie had done to everyone would hang over them for a long time. It had been a shock to hear from Colette as to why Jamie had set out with a plan, and who else he was going to kill until he went underground. Allie hadn't been certain everyone was on the list they'd found. She also wondered if Jamie would have stopped if they hadn't found out where he was.

Like she had with Lauren, Allie had offered to go inside the house with her, and Hannah, but Colette had refused. She said she'd have to get used to it. But after what had happened, she was thinking of moving to something smaller now there was only her, perhaps out of Stoke and closer to Hannah.

Allie's phone rang, and it was Mark. He was getting in some shopping while Poppy was at school. Allie had asked Pops what she'd like for tea, seeing as she was going to be home at a reasonable time to join them. Her choice was the same as always. Pizza, and chocolate cake for afters.

'Gone are the days when we had to put up with The Jam,' Perry teased, hearing a Taylor Swift ringtone.

'Poppy and I both like this one!'

They spoke on the phone as if they hadn't seen each other only an hour ago when Allie had left for work, leaving Mark to take Poppy to school. It still gave her a buzz, the whole fostering thing, having been certain their life wouldn't involve children.

When she disconnected the call, her team were in the incident room, ready to dissect the case and what evidence they needed to collect for the pending court case. Catching Jamie Sanderson was only the half of it.

Let the fun begin.

CHAPTER SIXTY-TWO

At five o'clock, Allie stretched her arms above her head and gave out a huge sigh. She'd been in her office for the past couple of hours, getting through paperwork. Her back was stiff from sitting for so long, and she cursed herself for not getting up to move around. But she was determined to finish work when she said she would that evening. It would be a nightmare sitting in rush-hour traffic, but it would be worth it.

She had one more check of her emails, thankfully seeing nothing new to deal with. Then a quick skim through her calendar for tomorrow's work. There was a Safer Estates follow-up meeting booked in for eleven. Grace must have found some intel she wanted to share with them all. That might be interesting, and at least she'd get to see her friend, even it if was at work again. She made a mental note to lock down their curry evening while she was there, and to call her babysitter to watch over Poppy.

When she was content that enough was enough, she switched off her computer and shrugged on her jacket. The weather was still mild, but if the ten-day weather forecast was right, she'd need her big coat in a couple of weeks. Slipping her bag over her shoulder, she turned off her office light and went out onto the main floor.

Perry, Frankie, and Sam were at their desks.

'I'm off, you horrible lot,' she said. 'Anyone coming?'

'I'll be gone soon,' Perry replied. 'Just finishing off some actions with Frankie.'

Sam yawned. 'Me, too, but not quite yet. What are you in a rush for?' she teased.

'A night doing nothing. I could chill out at the thought of it. Don't stay too long, guys.' Allie waved and made her way outside. It had started to rain, so she hurried across the road to the overflow car park.

A message came in on her phone. It was from Poppy, asking how long she'd be. Allie replied to say she was on her way. She smiled at the thought. Boy, was she in need of a night sitting on the sofa.

'Detective.'

Allie glanced up to see an elderly woman a few feet in front of her. She was wearing a long black mac and a woollen hat covering most of her grey curls. Her eyes were giving her a hard stare, and there was a scowl on her face to go with it.

'Yes, are you okay?' Allie asked, putting her phone in her bag.

'You don't remember me?'

She sounded disappointed, so Allie took a closer look. But she was none the wiser.

She shook her head. 'I'm sorry, I don't. Do you need my help?'

The woman released a hand from her pocket and stepped nearer.

Before Allie could react, *before* she realised what the glint of metal was, the woman lunged at her. She buried a knife in Allie's stomach so hard that Allie took a step back.

'A life for a life,' the woman said. Then she pulled the knife out and walked away.

Allie gasped as blood poured out of the wound, covering her fingers. A metallic tang was in the air, white-hot searing pain making her drop to her knees.

'Help,' she said.

She glanced around, but there was no one there. The woman had walked away.

Despite being brightly lit by streetlights, the road was a dead end. The only thing it led to was their car parks.

'Help!' she said a little louder.

With all her might, she crawled to the pavement and lodged herself against the wall. Her heart was beating rapidly, and she had flashes before her eyes. Maybe someone would be out to their car soon.

Pain gripped her again, and she grimaced. She knew she couldn't wait. She had to get her phone. Groaning, she opened the stud on the side of her bag and got it out of the pocket.

Her hands were covered in so much blood that the fingerprint recognition wasn't able to know it was her. She put the phone down on the ground and stabbed in her code. Then she located her contact list, all the time whimpering in pain.

It must have been a matter of seconds, but it felt like a lifetime. She pressed a number, knocked it onto speaker, and prayed it would connect quickly.

'Have you forgotten something?' Perry asked, laughing. 'What are you like?'

'Help me,' she stuttered.

'Allie, what's wrong?'

'Stabbed, rear car park. Help me.'

'I'm on my way.'

Allie burst into tears then, relieved to know someone was coming to her. It would only be a matter of minutes, but the knife wound was deep, the pain excruciating. She wondered if she'd have enough time to survive, if any of her vital organs had been punctured.

Who was that woman? Why had she done that to her?

Allie prided herself on being good at her job. People threatened to get her back all the time, but she'd always thought it was talk in the heat of the moment.

'Allie!'

Heavy footsteps, and lots of them, were heading her way, thundering at her like a herd of elephants. Perry came into view, Frankie and Sam behind him with a multitude of officers.

'Perry,' she said as another wave of pain washed over her. She didn't even have the strength to cry.

'I'm here. There's an ambulance on its way.' He crouched down beside her on the wet pavement and took her hand. 'What happened? Can you tell me?'

'I...' Allie saw tears in his eyes, but she couldn't speak. It hurt too much. But she did have to say one thing.

'What is it? Allie, talk to me!'

'Don't let me die, Perry,' she sobbed.

Seconds later, she lost consciousness.

CHAPTER SIXTY-THREE

'Allie!' Perry cried. 'Allie, stay with me.'

Her eyes remained closed, and he checked her neck for a pulse. It was weak but it was there.

'Is she...' Sam asked and then gave out a wail.

'No! She's not. Not on my watch.'

'Did anyone see what happened?'

'There's no one out here but us. Whoever it was has legged it. Fuck!' Perry gulped down his emotion. No one would blame him for crying. This was Allie after all. But he kept himself steady, at least for now.

The welcome sounds of an ambulance grew louder as the vehicle turned in at the far end of the street. Frankie stood up and waved his arms in the air to get them to drive right to the end.

'Hang on in there, my friend,' Perry said softly.

Next to him, Sam held Allie's hand. 'Allie, we're here,' she whispered.

They moved away to let the paramedics do their job, standing in a huddle of shock while they watched them work on their boss.

'Did she say what happened?' Sam asked, wiping at the smears of blood on her shirt, as if wishing them to magically disappear.

'I couldn't get anything out of her,' Perry said. 'When she called, all she could say is where she was and that she'd been stabbed.'

They stood dazed in disbelief while Allie fought for her life.

Ten minutes later, as the area was being cordoned off with crime scene tape, the DCI ran over to them.

'I've just heard,' Jenny said. 'Is she okay?'

'We don't know, ma'am,' Perry said, his attention not leaving Allie as he told her what had happened.

'You stay with her, and I'll put the wheels in motion here. I'll get CCTV first and see if we can make out her attacker.'

'Why would anyone do that to her?' Sam cried openly. 'They had no right.'

'Do you think it was whoever has been sending us messages?' Frankie asked, his face deathly pale.

All of them were looking at Allie, urging her to pull through. No one wanted her to die in front of them.

'Let's check the area first and we'll know more,' Jenny reiterated.

A female paramedic rushed over to them.

'How is she?' Perry wanted to know.

'We've managed to stabilise her enough to move her to the Royal Stoke. The trauma team are on standby, and we're ready to go. Is anyone coming with her?'

'I am.' He raised his hand, and the woman went back to aid her colleague. 'I'll need to ring home first. Oh, Christ. What about Mark and Poppy? They're expecting her home early.'

'I'll do that,' Jenny said.

'No!' Perry raised his voice. 'I have to ring him. He needs to hear it from me.'

'He just needs to hear it.' Jenny placed a hand on his arm. 'Your job is to be with her until he gets there.'

Perry was about to argue, but then he nodded. 'Tell Mark to ring me if he needs to.'

'I will. And I'll get things up and running here.' Jenny shooed him away. 'Go.'

'We'll be behind you,' Frankie said. 'Do you want to come with me, Sam?'

'Yeah, I don't think I can drive at the moment.' She burst into tears again. 'Oh, God, I hope she'll survive.'

Before boarding the ambulance, Perry rang his wife to update her. It would have to be a short call as he didn't want to get too emotional. But hearing Lisa's voice had him in tears again. He wanted to hold her close, to know that she was safe.

'It's Allie,' he said. 'She's been stabbed.'

'Ohmigod. Is she okay?'

'She's being taken to the hospital now. I'm going with her.'

'Are you all right?'

'Yeah.' Of course she was going to be concerned for him, but all he could think of was Allie. Lying there, covered in blood. 'She was on her own, at the back of the building. It could have been any of us, Lise.'

'She's in safe hands now, love. I can't believe it, though. Not Allie. How is Mark?'

'I don't know. Jenny said she wanted to call him.'

'Well, let her know to tell him that he can bring Poppy here if he needs to. I can take care of her.'

'I will. I have to go but... I love you, Lise.'

'I love you, too. Let me know how she goes on.'

Perry disconnected his phone and took a moment. The night was going to be hell, but he had a good friend to support. He made his way to the ambulance and climbed inside.

Allie was on a stretcher, her eyes still closed. The door shut behind him, the engine kicked in, and they rode off, blue-lighted as they flew down the street.

All the way there, he wondered who could have attacked her. They'd both made their fair share of enemies over the years they'd been in the force together. Something like this was always a possibility. And yet you never expected it to happen. Especially not outside the back of the station.

Someone would know who it was. They had to flush their culprit out.

And pray that Allie survived. No one wanted to lose her. Not like this.

They approached the ambulance station, and Perry got out first. He waited until Allie had come off and was wheeled away. He followed close behind, the bright lights contrasting against the blue-black sky. Evenings were closing in. It would soon be Christmas at this rate.

He prayed his friend would still be with them then. He couldn't face work without her.

CHAPTER SIXTY-FOUR

Mark tried not to put his foot down as he made his way to the Royal Stoke. Poppy was in the seat beside him, her quiet muffles catching his ear every now and again. He'd told her that Allie had been hurt in an accident, but nothing else. Because he didn't really know much about what happened.

He assumed everyone must dread getting that call, about a loved one at work who'd had an accident, or worse, died away from the home. Allie's DCI, Jenny Brindley, had been kind and straight to the point when she'd called. A rush of nausea had floored him, and he'd had to sit down.

All he'd wanted to know was how it happened, and yet Jenny couldn't tell him anything other than someone had attacked his wife. But they were looking into it. He knew they'd do everything they could to catch the attacker, and quickly.

At the hospital, he parked up a tad erratically, but at least he was only taking up one space. Then he grabbed Poppy's hand and ran as fast as she was able to across to the Accident and Emergency entrance. He waited impatiently while someone was in front of him, all kind of thoughts going through his mind as to whether to push them out of the way. But then it was his turn.

'My wife.' His voice broke with emotion. 'She's been brought in by ambulance after being attacked.'

'What's her name please?'

'Allie Shenton.'

It was the longest few seconds while the receptionist checked the computer. She pointed to a door at the side. 'I'll buzz you through, and someone will come to you.'

'Is she okay? I was told –'

'They'll let you know as soon as –'

'Mr Shenton?'

Mark turned to see a man holding the door open for him. Taking hold of Poppy's hand again, he followed him.

'Come and sit in here. What's your first name?'

'Mark.'

Before either of them could speak again, a man in a pale-blue uniform came across to Poppy.

'Hi, my name is Baz.' He held up his hand and waved. 'There's a vending machine down the corridor. Why don't we get your dad a cup of tea? I think he could do with one.'

Poppy shook her head. 'I want to stay here.'

Mark's heart almost broke at the sight of Poppy's lower lip trembling. 'I know you do, sweetheart, but I need to speak to the doctor alone first.' He rummaged around in his pocket and pulled out a bunch of change. He handed it to Poppy.

'The vending machine is only down there.' Baz pointed ahead. 'What's your name?'

Poppy told him, reluctantly following him.

'I won't be long, I promise,' Mark told her.

They went into the relative's room. His heart was hammering, and he hoped he didn't pass out with the stress. He sat down quickly so the conversation could begin, mentally crossing his fingers.

'I'm Mr Amison, Louis. I'm in the trauma team that is taking care of your wife. How many details have you been given before your arrival?'

'She's still alive?' Mark gasped, choking back his emotion. 'I got a call to say she'd been stabbed, and I rushed straight here. I don't know why but I thought she'd be... by now.'

'She's still with us, but Allie is in a critical position. We've done a CT scan, and it's shown that the knife wound has caused a lot of internal bleeding. We need to operate to see what's going on, and we have to do that with great urgency. With your permission, we'd like to take her down for emergency surgery straightaway.'

'Yes, of course.'

'I'll get the paperwork for you to sign.'

'Can I see her?'

'She's unable to respond, but yes, for a few minutes. I wouldn't like your daughter to see her, though. I'll keep her with the nurse. Baz works in paediatrics, and he's a great asset to us. He'll keep her occupied.'

Mark nodded.

'I'll take you there now.'

They left the side room, walked along a corridor full of patients lying on beds waiting to be seen, and into a wider area. Mark could see a hospital trolley, with a mass of people around it, and an array of machines. The noise was palpable, but necessary and orderly. All around him was the smell of... well, he didn't want to think about what it was. He curled his fingers into a fist and crammed it into his mouth to stop from shouting out.

'This is Mark, Allie's husband,' Louis told everyone.

Mark couldn't speak. He couldn't take his eyes off Allie, her pale face, the blood on her hands and under her fingernails. Her eyes were closed, a monitor beeping nearby.

'You can talk to her if you like,' Louis encouraged. 'But we can only give you a few seconds. I need to move her quickly.'

Mark wanted to see Allie up close and yet he didn't. It might be the last image he had of his wife.

Pushing all morbid thoughts away, he stepped forward, tears welling. He could almost think Allie was asleep, a sheet pulled up to her chest covering the damage done underneath it.

He ran a hand over her forehead and then kissed her.

'Hey, you. Bad day at the office?' he joked. Then with a loud sob, he took hold of her hand.

Allie seemed so blank, so... lifeless.

He didn't want to live without her.

'I love you, Allie. Pops is here, too. We'll be waiting for you.'

'Mark, I have the paperwork for you to sign right here.'

Mark turned back to Louis. 'She will survive, won't she?'

'I can't guarantee that right now, but she's in the safest hands and the best place.' He held out a pen.

Mark took it from him and signed the forms. Allie was wheeled off immediately.

In seconds, he was left staring at the space she'd vacated, wondering what the hell he was going to say to Poppy.

CHAPTER SIXTY-FIVE

Perry sat in the waiting room, Frankie and Sam opposite. The room was large, with three groups of anxious relatives dotted around. There was a hushed silence, people talking quietly, trying not to impose on anyone else as they readied themselves for what was to come.

The door opened, and he spotted Mark coming towards them holding Poppy's hand. Mark had messaged him to say that Allie was going to theatre and that all he'd told Poppy was there had been an accident, and he would tell her more when Allie had been operated on. At least none of them would slip up and upset the poor child even further.

He stood up as Mark drew level and gave him a hug. Sam and Frankie did the same.

'I have everything crossed, Poppy,' she said to the little girl, holding up two fingers. 'I know Allie is a strong woman.'

Poppy burst into tears. 'I'm scared.'

'Oh, love.' Sam held her in her arms, Mark giving her a half-smile.

'Is there anything we can do?' Frankie asked. 'The DCI said she'd keep us informed, but there's nothing from her yet.'

'No, thanks. Apart from to keep her in your thoughts.'

'She'll never leave them,' Perry said defiantly.

Mark sat down, deflated, exhausted. They all followed suit. Poppy spied a bookcase in amongst a children's corner and went to grab a book. For a few minutes no one spoke.

All Perry could think of was Allie and how he didn't want to lose his best friend.

It was an hour later when Jenny arrived. No one was expecting her, so it was a nice gesture, Perry thought.

'Mark, I'm so sorry.' As she reached them, she offered her hand to him. 'I want you to know that we are doing everything we can to find out who did this.' She glanced at Poppy and smiled. 'You must be Poppy. I've heard so much about you. Allie never stops talking about you.'

Poppy smiled shyly.

She turned her attention back to Mark. 'How is Allie doing?'

'She's in surgery at the moment. We'll know more once she's out.'

She nodded. 'Could I have a word, Perry?'

They moved away from the group.

'I didn't want to say anything in front of Poppy and Mark, but I'm sure you can tell him what you feel is necessary when I leave.'

'Did you see what happened on CCTV?'

'Yes, we got it all. But it was quite a shock.'

'Why?'

'It was an elderly woman. We reckon in her seventies.'

'Her what?' Perry frowned. 'Were you able to follow her, see if she got in a car or a taxi? She couldn't have gone far quickly. Maybe she took a bus? The station is only a few minutes away.'

He was telling her things she knew already, but she didn't comment on that.

'We followed her on the council's CCTV. She walked across to Tesco and went inside. She came out minutes later with a small bag of groceries. Then she got in a taxi, so we're locating the driver. I have a couple of stills.' She got out her phone and showed them to him. 'Do you recognise her?'

Perry scrolled through them, staring at the image. 'She looks like any woman going about her shopping. I have no idea who she is. Can you send them to me, and I'll show Sam and Frankie discreetly?'

'I'll do that now and then I'm going back to the station. I wanted to come in person to see Mark first.'

'I'll be back shortly.'

'No, come in fresh in the morning. You've all had an emotional day. Get some sleep, and we can reconvene first thing. We'll probably have more details then and we can decide a plan of action.'

'If you're sure.'

'I'll leave quietly. Tell Mark I'm thinking of him and give him my number. He can contact me anytime.'

Mark sat in a daze, not really taking in anything around him apart from Poppy. She had her head in a book, which was a great relief. She'd sat quietly reading while visions of him and Allie flashed before his eyes.

Happy memories. The first time he saw her. Their wedding day. The night Poppy came to stay with them. Allie's joy about rescuing Dexter from the dog's home.

Silly things. The way she'd belt out songs in the kitchen, dancing as if no one was watching. Her little snort when she laughed.

Her kind nature that made her who she was. Her empathy towards others. Her resilience, her strength.

Her love.

'Mark, we're going to head off home now,' Perry said. 'If that's okay with you. We want to get a bit of sleep before starting the investigation in full tomorrow.'

'Yes, of course.' Mark stood up and shook his hand. 'Thanks for everything. I know she means a lot to you.' He glanced at Sam and Frankie. 'To you all. She's strong. She'll pull through.'

'She will.' It was nearing half past nine. Perry glanced at Poppy and then back at Mark. 'Are you staying here until the operation is over?'

'I have to. I can't leave.'

'Then let me take Poppy home for the night. I can bring her back first thing.'

'Well... I, yes. I think that would be best.' Mark gnawed at his bottom lip. 'That way, if I can't deal with... things, she'll be away from it.'

'Okay. Sam is giving me a lift as my car is at work. We'll see you in the morning, but please, message me the minute you hear anything. And call, you know, if you need me to come back.'

On the drive home, Frankie kept Poppy entertained in the back seat telling her really awful jokes. In no time, they arrived outside his house. It had never felt so welcoming.

'Thanks for the lift, Sam,' he said, removing his seat belt.

'No worries. I'll pick you up in the morning if I don't hear from you before that. Is eight okay? I'd say earlier, but we're all drained.'

He gave a faint smile. 'Eight is fine. Come on, Pops. Let's get you inside.'

They said their goodbyes and went in. Lisa was sensitive with Poppy, getting her set up in the spare room. It meant that Perry could have a bit of downtime alone.

The day had been harrowing, and it hadn't ended yet for Mark. Perry didn't know who to think about first. Allie meant so much to them all.

Lisa joined him on the settee. She kissed him, and he drew her into his arms.

'What if she dies, Lise?' he whispered.

'Oh, Perry. I pray she won't, but we all know how strong Allie is.' Then she chastised herself. 'Hark at me. Allie *is* strong but, well, you know. I'm trying to keep your spirits up.'

Perry noticed the tears welling in her eyes.

Then he let his own fall while she held him.

CHAPTER SIXTY-SIX

WEDNESDAY

Allie opened her eyes and closed them again quickly. Bright lights over her head startled her. She waited a moment before trying again. This time she let her eyes adjust.

Where was she?

'There she is.'

Allie saw a woman beside her, a face she didn't recognise. The light above her was a strip light, and from her position lying down she could see lines of white cupboards around the edge of a room. Lots of people in blue milling around confused her. Beeps from something next to her.

'Allie, my name is Kelly.' The woman beamed at her and gave her hand a quick squeeze. 'You're in the hospital, in the recovery room after having emergency surgery. But everything went fine.'

Wait, where did she say she was? In her confusion, Allie tried to sit up but winced as pain grabbed her lower stomach.

Kelly gently pushed her down. 'Relax. You're in safe hands, but I need you to stay still.'

'What happened to me?' Allie's voice was croaky, her throat sore.

'I'll let the consultant give you more details.'

Allie lay back, looking at the ceiling. She tried to remember what she'd been doing last. Had she left for home? Yes, she recalled replying to Poppy's message.

After that she had no recollection, not even why she was in hospital.

'I...' She cleared her throat. 'I don't understand.'

'Someone attacked you.' Kelly leaned in closer. 'I'm not supposed to tell you any more than that. I'll call for Mr Amison and see if he's free to talk to you.'

Allie's lids went heavy, and she closed them. What felt like a minute before she opened them again was actually twenty. There was a man by her side this time, and no sign of Kelly.

'Hi, Allie.' He smiled. 'I'm Louis Amison, the consultant who performed your operation. Can you remember anything about yesterday?'

'Some of it, but not why I'm here.'

'You were brought into us around six p.m. with a stab wound to your stomach.'

'I was stabbed?' Allie recoiled. That was the pain she was feeling?

'You were. You came by ambulance.'

'What time is it now?'

'It's nearly half past two.'

'In the morning?'

'Yes. You've been in surgery for several hours. There was a lot to sort out, but we finally got the bleeding under control.'

'Do you know who it was? Who stabbed me?'

'I'm afraid I don't have those details. I'm sure your colleagues will be able to shed some light on that. All I know is that you're very lucky to survive, and you're not quite out of the woods yet.' He smiled. 'We're moving you to the emergency surgery recovery ward soon. Your husband is here, waiting for you. I'm going to chat to him now, and I'll get him to the ward so that you can be reunited.'

Allie wanted to say so much more.

She needed to know if someone was in custody or not.

She wanted to know if her team were okay.

She had to...

Her eyes closed again, the affects of the anaesthetic washing over her once more.

The next time Allie opened them, Mark's face was the first thing she saw. He was sitting beside her, holding her hand. He looked worse than she feared she did. His hair was sticking up in random spikes where he must have been running his fingers through it, and his face had no colour. His eyes were puffy, too.

He must have been worried sick about her.

The ward was quiet except for a little noise around the nurses' station.

'Hey,' Mark whispered, sitting forward when he realised she was awake.

'Hey,' she replied.

'They said I could be with you for a few minutes before I'd have to leave. How are you feeling? Daft question, I know.'

'Confused more than anything. The consultant said I'd been stabbed.'

He nodded. 'It's been a rough few hours.'

'Where's Poppy?'

'She's staying with Perry and Lisa. I thought it was best in case...' Mark paused. 'Well, never mind. I'm just glad to see you awake.'

'I can't remember anything, Mark.' Her voice started to crack. 'I don't know what's going on.'

He moved forward and wiped the hair from her forehead. 'Someone attacked you when you left the station. You managed to contact Perry, and he called for an ambulance. They rushed you straight into surgery as you had internal bleeding. Hasn't the consultant explained things to you?'

'About what's happened, but not who did this to me.'

'No one really knows yet. Jenny came to see how you were. She told Perry she'd be in touch in the morning. Once you've had some rest.'

'What if it gets worse, Mark?' Tears fell from Allie's eyes as it suddenly hit her that she might not have pulled through. 'Mr Amison said it took ages to sort me out, and I'm not out of danger yet. What happens if –'

'Hey,' Mark soothed, leaning forward to kiss her gently on her lips this time. 'The fact that you're here at all makes me know you're made of strong stuff. Not that I've ever doubted that.'

'But what if –'

'You're not going anywhere. I need you. Poppy needs you. Dexter needs you. And your team definitely do.'

He was trying to make her smile, but she couldn't. All the fear from the past few hours came flooding out. She had been lucky. And she was here.

The drowsiness attacked her again as she spoke. 'I need to get back to work soon.' Her eyes began to close. 'I have to sort this out.'

Mark sat back in his chair. 'You *need* time to recover.'

'I have to find out who... did this... to me.'

'And you have to rest, Allie.'

CHAPTER SIXTY-SEVEN

Perry woke with a jolt. It was half past five. He'd been awake most of the night, lying on the settee waiting for Mark's call. It came just after three, so he must have dozed off after he knew Allie's surgery had been successful.

What a night. What a day. He hadn't been through so many emotions since Alfie was born.

Half an hour passed, and he was wondering whether to go in early, call a taxi, when he heard footsteps padding down the stairs.

Lisa opened the living room door, coming in with bed hair and a yawn.

'Hey. Have you heard anything?' She plonked herself down next to him on the settee.

'She's out of surgery and on a ward being monitored,' he said. 'Mark rang a couple of hours ago. I didn't want to wake you to tell you.'

'I haven't slept much, to be fair. I couldn't stop thinking about everything that happened earlier in the year. Was it linked to the attacks on the team?'

'We don't know yet. I was about to get myself showered and go in. Grab a taxi.'

'I think you should wait a while. Sam is picking you up at eight.'

'I can't rest.'

'Yes, you can if I say so. You're going to have a long day working on this, so I want to see you have a good breakfast and a couple of mugs of tea.'

'You mean you want to mother me.' He pulled her close and kissed her.

'Always. I worry about you every time you leave the house until I see you again. Now you know why.' Lisa yawned. 'Go and get a shower and try to be quiet. I bet Poppy was exhausted. I can take her to Mark this morning if you like, after I've dropped Alfie off at school?'

'That would be great, thanks. One less thing to worry about.'

Sam arrived at eight as planned. She wanted to know everything as she drove them to the station. Not that there was much to tell, apart from his conversation with Mark.

Neither of them could believe what had happened. Both were glad Allie made it through the night.

'It took me ages to get to sleep,' Sam admitted. 'I was wound up like a wooden top. I kept seeing her, lying on the pavement.'

'So did I. We should go and see her as soon as we can, stop those images from rolling.'

'Do you think she'll be okay? It's a massive trauma, even if the physical side of things goes to plan. She might heal well on the outside, but I wouldn't blame her if she was a wreck mentally.'

'Knowing Allie, she'll want to get back to work as soon as possible.'

'Really?' Sam shook her head. 'I think she might struggle. She's been wondering whether to quit for a while now.'

'She told you that?'

'Now and again. I thought it was an age thing. None of us are getting any younger.'

'Well, we'll have to get her through whatever we can. She might talk more to us than Mark. We're her family, too.'

Once in the station, Perry found a message on his desk to go and see Jenny. He held up the note to show Sam and saw she was holding one, too.

'From Jenny?' he checked.

'Yes.' Sam glanced at Frankie's desk. 'And there's one there for Frankie.'

'One what for me?' Frankie walked across to join them. 'Morning.' He sighed. 'I feel like the living dead.'

'At least we can joke about it today.' Perry ran a hand over his head while Frankie read his note. 'I really did think we might lose her. But we didn't, and now we need to crack on finding out who it was.'

'Have you heard anything?' Frankie placed his jacket on the back of his chair.

'Not yet.' Perry stood up. 'Come on, let's go upstairs and see.'

Once assembled in the DCI's office, Jenny sat with them and discussed what had happened overnight.

'We had several staff working on it. The woman, as you know, was in Tesco, bizarrely coming out with a bag of groceries as if she hadn't attacked someone with a knife half an hour earlier. She left via a taxi, so we have an address for her now, and there's an unmarked car sitting nearby in case she tries to leave. You might not agree, but I felt it only right to give a little consideration to the woman's age, and her obvious mental state to do what she did, so I decided to arrest her this morning unless she made to leave.'

'Have you not been home, ma'am?' Perry queried.

Jenny shook her head.

'But we could have helped.'

'Allie is a great asset to the team, but she is also a special colleague, too, as well as a good friend to you all. I wanted to do all I could to help during the night, so that you could get a result today.' Jenny glanced at each one of them in turn. 'However, I'm afraid I wasn't expecting the woman to be known to us.'

They all sat up a little straighter.

'The car is registered to Maureen Stott.'

'Jesus Christ, no!' Perry stood up, his chair screeching across the floor. 'What the fuck.'

'That's exactly what I said.' Jenny nodded. 'The exact same words, so please don't think you have to apologise.'

'So she meant to kill Allie?' Sam queried.

Frankie looked on, a little bewildered. 'Who is Maureen Stott?'

Realising that Frankie wasn't with their team when Allie had been kidnapped in 2015, Perry sat down and told him.

'She's Graham Stott's mother. He was the guy who attacked Allie's sister, Karen, leaving her for dead. He came after Allie days before Karen died, but we managed to apprehend him. He was sentenced to life.'

'Ah, yes, I remember Allie telling me what he'd done. So why is his mother coming after Allie now, rather than ten years ago? Has something happened that we don't know about?'

'Yes,' Jenny said. 'Graham Stott was found dead in his cell a month ago. He took his own life.'

A silence dropped on the room. Perry finally broke it.

'So she came after Allie because of that? The man was a lunatic.' Perry slammed his hand on the desk. 'We need to go and bring her in.' He remembered his manners. 'Ma'am.'

CHAPTER SIXTY-EIGHT

Allie started to feel a little more awake around half past nine. Mark had gone home a few minutes after she'd arrived on the ward, and she'd slept through until eight. The first thing she'd done on waking was to ring him, have a reassuring chat, and ask if he would bring Poppy up to see her. Then she'd spoken to Perry, wanting to know if there were any leads yet. Perry said they were still going through CCTV and would keep her up to date when there were developments.

She was pleased her team were okay. It was one of the things she'd been worried about when her memory failed her last night. She still couldn't remember anything and was depending on them to find out information for her.

For once, she couldn't be boss, she had to leave it to them. She was in no fit state to help them anyway. She couldn't even sit up at the moment. Thank goodness for morphine.

Due to the ward being for emergency admission, patients were recovering around her, so it was mostly quiet. There were six beds to a bay, and two side rooms. Visitors were kept to a minimum of two. Allie wondered how long she would be here for. She didn't feel ill, merely a little tender.

She cursed herself inwardly. She was here for a reason. Maybe her mind couldn't cope with how close to death she'd been.

Perhaps that was because she couldn't yet recall what had happened.

Maybe it was because she was blanking it all out. It was too much for her to bear.

The whole thing was bound to hit her soon, she was certain. The fact that she could have died. That someone had wanted to kill her. The list of suspects could have been endless, but if anyone was to take her out, Allie assumed it would be someone linked to Terry Ryder and his crew. She'd put so many of them in prison over the years.

She closed her eyes, hoping to rest before Mark and Poppy could come at two o'clock.

Perry headed the team that would go and arrest Maureen Stott. He still couldn't get his head around what she'd done. How could she put a knife into someone? Maybe she had motive and opportunity, but it was beyond his comprehension. The woman must be in her late seventies.

Mrs Stott lived on the edge of the city in the south, a neighbourhood called Lightwood. With Sam and Frankie in the car, and a police transport van following behind, he pulled onto a small estate of council-owned houses. They were after number eleven, Seddon Road.

Sam pointed as they drew level with it. 'I don't know whether I'm dreading this or not. It's all so wrong.'

Perry blew out a breath. 'It's not going to be pleasant. I really hope she comes without a fight. Imagine the hoo-ha if we're seen dragging her out.'

'There'll be no dragging anyone!'

'I was joking.' Perry smirked. 'Maybe.'

They walked up the path.

The front door opened before they reached it. The woman in the photo stills stood with her arms folded. Up close, she seemed to be older than late seventies. More into her early eighties. Her blonde-grey hair was short, messy. She was dressed in black slacks, red slippers, and a white jumper.

'Did she die?' she wanted to know.

Although seething at her harsh tone and matter-of-fact manner, Perry kept his face void of emotion.

'No, she didn't. Can you step outside, please?'

'You can come in to do your dirty work. I don't want all the neighbours gawping at me.'

Perry caught the look that passed between Sam and Frankie and shook his head. The woman had disappeared into the house. They followed her in.

She was standing in the middle of the room, in a defiant manner as if she had already accepted her fate.

'Maureen Stott,' Perry began, taking out his cuffs.

Before he said anything else, she held out her hands. He read the rest of her rights, flabbergasted at her manner. She was so nonchalant and yet she'd set out to kill someone yesterday. Someone they all loved dearly.

'That was my son.' She glanced at a photo on the wall. 'Graham was in his late teens then, a wonderful boy, kind and sensitive. And then he changed. I found out years later when he came after that inspector of yours what he'd done before. Was I shocked? You bet, I was. But my boy had served his time, and I was waiting for him to come home. I'd lived on my own for ten years, waiting for him to come back to me. I would have loved him as before. He'd paid his penance.

'But then last month, before he was eligible for parole, he took his life.' She glared at Perry. 'Do you have children?'

Perry didn't reply.

'It doesn't matter now anyway,' she went on. 'And at least

I'll get food and lodgings for the rest of my life while I'm inside. I'm broke and I'm dying, so let someone else take care of me. I have nothing left to live for.'

Sam's face was like thunder, and Perry wasn't sure he'd stop her if she lunged for Mrs Stott. Unless it was anything to do with her son, the woman was an emotional brick. She had devoted her life to him, but he had maimed and killed. Graham Stott wasn't a son to be proud of.

Frankie and a uniformed officer led Mrs Stott out to the transport that would take her back to the station, where she would be booked into custody. Perry and Sam stood, dazed, shocked, in disbelief.

'At least she didn't get any further than her son,' Sam muttered.

'Sorry?'

'Well, like Graham, she didn't do the job properly because Allie is still alive.'

'Yeah,' Perry noted. 'And like him, she'll never get another opportunity to go after her again.'

By the time Mark arrived with Poppy at visiting time, Allie was feeling much more like herself, albeit with a knife wound and a three-inch scar where they had operated on her.

Mark was holding a large bouquet of roses, Poppy a brown paper bag. Allie burst into tears as they approached her.

'Mum, don't cry,' Poppy said while she raced to the side of the bed.

Allie kissed her on the cheek when she bent closer to her, but her tears increased.

Poppy had called her Mum.

'I'm going to be fine, Pops.' She ran a hand over the little girl's face.

'Are you coming home soon?'

'I'm not sure.'

Mark kissed her then, and she smiled at him.

'You bought me roses!'

'Naw, they're for the woman in the next bed.'

'I'd slap you if I could reach you. I can't sit up yet.'

'Has anyone been in touch with you from work? I mean about what happened to you?'

'Perry messaged me to say they were still going over stuff and that he'd keep me in the loop.' She pointed to the bag Poppy was still holding. 'What have you got in there? I hope it's an oatcake filled with bacon and cheese and smothered with brown sauce. I'm starving.'

'She's getting better if she's not off her food.' Mark raised his eyebrows.

Allie giggled. But the pain that rushed through her when her stomach moved had her grimacing. It was obviously being hidden well by painkillers while she lay still.

CHAPTER SIXTY-NINE

It was after Mark and Poppy left after visiting hours at two p.m. when Allie received news that her stats and vital signs were all going in the right direction, although she wasn't going to be allowed home for a couple more days.

She had sat up then and would be able to get out of bed in the morning. Right now, all she wanted was a shower and to wash her hair, but she was glad of small mercies. With the help of a nurse, she could wash in her bed. Her hair would have to do until the morning. She wasn't going to be seeing anyone.

Famous last words.

In between messages from her team and other work colleagues who had her number, asking how she was, there were lots of people stopping by.

Dave Barnett arrived around half past four. He'd been to visit his daughter and had sneaked in unofficially as he knew one of the nurses on the ward. His grandson had finally arrived. Felix Arthur had been born that morning at 07.32 and weighed in at seven pounds eight ounces. He and his mum were doing well.

When he'd first got there, Dave had taken one look at her and wept. Then he'd given her a gentle hug before sitting by her side and opening a box of chocolates he'd brought for her. He'd shared photos of Felix on his phone, like the doting granddad she knew he'd always be.

Mark and Poppy came back for an hour at six. Grace and Simon came at seven. Grace brought flowers, a pile of magazines, and Allie's favourite chocolates. It was a whirlwind of more tears among smiles. Allie would be glad when she'd seen everyone she needed to, so they were out of the way. But she was grateful to see anyone at all after her ordeal.

Even so, she was waiting for a phone call from Perry. He'd kept her informed via messages throughout the day, but she could tell they were written strategically, without actually saying anything specifically. He'd told her they were still investigating when she'd messaged him.

It was as the ward was settling down for the night that she spotted him walking towards her.

'You must have sweet talked someone,' she teased. 'Visiting hours were over an hour ago.'

'I used my charms. But I didn't push my luck, so Sam and Frankie will be in to see you tomorrow. They send their love. How are you?'

'I'm on pain management, but I'm good. I have to stay for a couple more days, though. At least I can use my phone and iPad.' She pointed to two crime novels on her bedside cabinet. 'Poppy thought I might like those.' She grinned. 'Can't get away from the job.'

Perry didn't laugh. There wasn't even a smile, so she sensed there was more to his visit than a social call.

'Did you get him?' she asked, her voice hushed.

Perry drew round the privacy curtain and sat down in the chair beside her. 'We arrested someone this morning, but I wanted to tell you face to face. They've since been charged with attempted murder.'

'Good work. Was it anyone we know?'

Perry didn't speak.

'Perry?' she urged. 'Who was it?'

'It was Maureen Stott, Graham's mum.'

'A woman?' Allie felt light-headed. Of all the names that had run through her mind, that wasn't one of them.

'Graham took his own life last month, and she holds you responsible.'

'But that's ridiculous.'

Perry took out his phone and showed Allie the photo stills. While she viewed them, he explained what had happened from arresting her to then subsequently charging her late that afternoon after she'd finally admitted everything. She was due in court in the morning.

While Perry spoke, Allie stared at the images, and it all came back to her in a rush.

The woman approaching her.

Feeling like she'd been punched as the knife went into her stomach.

The phone call she made to Perry.

The fear that she would die.

The terror that her life was over.

How close she'd come to losing everything.

How cruel it would have been to leave Mark and Poppy without her.

How selfish Maureen Stott had been after what Graham put Allie and her family through. What he did to her sister. What he'd been sent to prison for.

'I'm sorry, Allie,' Perry said. 'We've known each other long enough that I had to tell you everything face-to-face, no matter how much it pains either of us.'

'I wouldn't want it any other way.' She smiled, her eyes

watering. 'It's a shock, though. I thought it might be one of Terry Ryder's minions. And it can't have been her who came at our team earlier in the year. If it was only notes being delivered, I might say it was. But the business with Frankie when that car ploughed into his house? We've still got to figure out who that was, and why.'

Perry smirked. 'Do you ever switch off, boss?'

'Believe me, I've tried. But I feel responsible for you all. And if it is Ryder, then I started it all those years ago.'

'No, you didn't! He's a grown man, able to make his own stupid mistakes.'

'He'll be after revenge one day.' She gnawed at her bottom lip. 'I think he'll wait until he's out. He'll want to come after me in person.'

'Don't say that.' Perry shook his head.

'Well, who would have expected Maureen Stott to try and kill me?'

'Allie.'

She stopped mid rant, realising that no matter how angry she was, now was not the time or the place.

'I'm scared, Perry,' she admitted. 'This talk is me hiding behind my fears. I can't take it in that someone would want to harm me like this.' She pointed at her stomach. 'I have a child, too. I have Mark, and I have a life.'

'And that's the way it will stay. *I* have your back, Allie. The whole team does. The station does! We're right behind you, no matter what.'

It should have eased Allie's mind, but instead it made her teary. Perry was right, but she couldn't help being worried about the future. It was one thing to keep her team safe. But how the hell did she keep her family protected?

CHAPTER SEVENTY

Friday

Allie sat in a chair beside her hospital bed. She had a new patient beside her, come in during the night. Her bed had been made up in readiness for the next one. Her overnight bag was packed in anticipation. She had been discharged and was going home!

Having had a shower and put on a bit of makeup, and now out of her pyjamas and into some loungewear, she almost felt human again. Her pain was easing, and it was all a matter of recuperation now, both physically and mentally.

Because she had been discharged, Mark was able to collect her out of visiting hours. She was staring at the entrance, willing him to appear. Desperate to get out of the ward and back home, with her feet up on the settee while her family pampered her and cared for her every need.

She was going to milk it for the next few days, for sure. She had to be careful until her stitches were removed next week. Her scar was minor considering what had happened, a couple of inches at the most, and in a place that only Mark would see.

An image of Maureen Stott flashed before her eyes. She still couldn't recall everything about the attack, but Simon had written a report for *Stoke News*, which included a photograph so now Allie could torment herself with images of her as well as Graham.

It had been a shock to find out that Graham had taken his own life. But equally she didn't feel sorry that he had. If that made her callous, so be it. He had caused her family irreparable damage. Her father had gone to an early grave, she was sure, after the stress had brought on a heart attack. She would never forgive Graham for that. And now she had Maureen on her mind as well.

She gave a huge sigh. There was no use moping about it. It had happened, and she had survived. Then she sniggered under her breath. As if it was going to be that easy to get over.

She smiled when she saw someone come in. It was Mark. Time to get out of there.

'Your chariot awaits,' Mark said as he crossed the ward to her.

'I can't bloody wait.' She stood up slowly. 'Where's Poppy?' she asked, not seeing her with him.

'She's gone to school. She has a maths test that she wants to do, but she was upset because she thought you might be angry with her. That you might think she didn't care.'

'Oh, bless.' Allie smiled. 'A maths test, though! That girl will go far.'

'She's been an angel while you've been in here. I'm glad I had her with me.'

'She called me Mum when she first saw me after my operation. It was so nice to hear.'

'She called me Dad last night. I felt this ball of love hit me in the chest.' He took her hand in his own. 'Shall we take the next step, see if we can adopt her?'

'I think we have to. Although we'll need to have a chat about my job. I've had a *lot* of time to think over the past couple of days and I'm not sure I should do it anymore.'

Mark balked. 'That's not Allie talk. Being a detective is in your blood.'

'Being a wife and mother is more important.'

'You need to be both, Allie.'

'Hark at you,' she teased. 'Years ago, you always wanted me to leave the force.'

'I've matured since then.' He pointed at his hair. 'Grey hair, poor eyesight, middle-aged spread.' He smiled. 'Joking aside, every day when you leave the house, I pray it won't be the last time I see you. Every phone call, like the one I got from Jenny, I always assume the worst.' His voice broke. 'I don't know what I'd do if someone took you away from me.'

'Then I'm done.' She saw the distress on his face. She couldn't keep putting him through so much angst.

'Let me finish.' Mark held up a hand. 'But I know that you work with a fantastic team who will always be there for you. Look at their response to what happened. They already have the suspect charged. I feel better knowing you're with them.'

'I could do something less dangerous.'

'Even if you went back into social work – because I know you'd have to do something like that as helping people is your forte – it's not a safe profession. Most of the time you'd be doing visits on your own. People have been murdered on single-person calls. It's not as safe as it was when you first did it.'

'What are you saying exactly?' She'd thought he'd be pleased that she was quitting.

'You need your job, you're good at it, and I think you

should continue. Besides, you'd be hell to live with if you were doing anything else.'

Allie smirked and hit out at his arm. Then she reached for his hand.

'Come on you, let's go home.'

As he chaperoned her out of the building, Allie felt a warm feeling enveloping her. Weighing up everything that was important to her was all she'd done since being admitted to hospital. The attempt on her life had knocked the stuffing out of her. But she was resilient as much as she was cautious, empathetic as much as she was wary. She *was* good at her job and had a certain way to draw information out of people.

And, despite the dangers around every corner, she hoped that would never change.

***

First of all, I'd like to say a huge thank you for choosing to read Past Mistakes. I hope you enjoyed my eighth outing with Allie Shenton and the team.

If you did enjoy Past Mistakes, I would be grateful if you would leave a small review or a star rating on your Kindle. I'd love to know what you thought. It's always good to hear from you.

Why not join my reader group? I love to keep in touch with my readers, and send a newsletter every few weeks. I also reveal covers, titles and blurbs exclusively to you first.

Join Team Sherratt

ALL BOOKS BY MEL SHERRATT

These books are continually added to so please
Click here for details about all my books on one page

DS Allie Shenton Series

Taunting the Dead

Follow the Leader

Only the Brave

Broken Promises

Hidden Secrets

Twisted Lives

Family Matters

Past Mistakes

The Estate Series (4 book series)

Somewhere to Hide

Behind a Closed Door

Fighting for Survival

Written in the Scars

Eden Berrisford Crime Dramas (2 book series)

The Girls Next Door

Don't Look Behind You

DS Grace Allendale Series (4 book series)

Hush Hush

Tick Tock

Liar Liar

Good Girl

Standalone Psychological Thrillers

Watching over You

The Lies You Tell

Ten Days

The Life She Wants

Missing Girls

ACKNOWLEDGMENTS

To all my fellow Stokies, my apologies if you don't gel with any of the Stoke references that I've changed throughout the book. Obviously writing about local things such as *The Sentinel* and Hanley Police Station would make it seem a little too close to home, and I wasn't comfortable leaving everything authentic. So, I took a leaf out of Arnold Bennett's 'book' and changed some things slightly. However, there were no oatcakes harmed in the process.

Thanks to my amazing fella, Chris, who looks out for me so that I can do the writing. I wish I could take credit for all the twists in my books but he's actually more devious than I am when it comes down to it – in the nicest possible way. We're a great team – a perfect combination.

Thanks to Alison Niebieszczanski, Caroline Mitchell, Talli Roland, Ed James, Louise Ross and Sharon Sant, who give me far more friendship, support and encouragement than I deserve.

Thanks to my amazing early reader team - you know who you are! I'm so blessed to have you on board.

Finally, thanks to all my readers who keep in touch with me via Twitter and Facebook. Your kind words always make me smile – and get out my laptop. Long may it continue.

ABOUT THE AUTHOR

Ever since I can remember, I've been a meddler of words. Born and raised in Stoke-on-Trent, Staffordshire, I used the city as a backdrop for my first novel, TAUNTING THE DEAD, and it went on to be a Kindle #1 bestseller. I couldn't believe my eyes when it became the number 8 UK Kindle KDP bestselling books of 2012.

Since then, I've sold over 2 million books. My writing has come under a few different headings - grit-lit, thriller, whydunnit, police procedural, emotional thriller to name a few. I like writing about fear and emotion – the cause and effect of crime – what makes a character do something. I also like to add a mixture of topics to each book. Working as a housing officer for eight years gave me the background to create a fictional estate with good and bad characters, and they are all perfect for murder and mayhem.

But I'm a romantic at heart and have always wanted to write about characters that are not necessarily involved in the darker side of life. Coffee, cakes and friends are three of my favourite things, hence I write women's fiction under the pen name of Marcie Steele.

All characters and events featured in this publication, other than those clearly in the public domain, are entirely fictitious and any resemblance to any person, organisation, place or thing living or dead, or event or place, is purely coincidental and completely unintentional.

All rights reserved in all media. No part of this book may be reproduced in any form other than that which it was purchased and without the written permission of the author. This e-book is licensed for your personal enjoyment only. No part of this text may be reproduced, transmitted, downloaded, decompiled, reverse engineered, or stored in or introduced into any information storage and retrieval system, in any form or by any means, whether electronic or mechanical, now known or hereinafter invented, without the express written permission of the author.

Past Mistakes © Mel Sherratt
E-edition published worldwide 2025
Kindle edition Copyright 2022 © Mel Sherratt

Printed in Dunstable, United Kingdom